SWEET LIPS

MEL SMITH

SWEET LIPS

A NOVEL

alyson books
NEW YORK

Manufactured in the United States of America.
This trade paperback original is published by
Alyson Books, P.O. Box 1253, Old Chelsea Station,
New York, New York 10113-1251.

Distribution in the United Kingdom by
Turnaround Publisher Services Ltd., Unit 3,
Olympia Trading Estate, Coburg Road,
Wood Green, London N22 6TZ England.

First edition: September 2006

06 07 08 09 10 **a** 10 9 8 7 6 5 4 3 2 1

ISBN-10: 155583984-3
ISBN-13: 978-155583984-0

An application for Library of Congress
Cataloging-in-Publication Data
has been filed.

cover photograph courtesy Getty Images

To Mother. I miss you.

CHAPTER 1

SOMETIMES A MAN'S DESTINY is determined by the smallest of things; things like which fork in the road he chooses to travel, or what time he happens to enter a certain saloon or, in my case, where he chooses to masturbate.

I was born in the Dakota Territories in 1823. My pa ran a livery stable and my ma was a ma. She cooked and cleaned and did whatever needed doing for five men. She was the only woman among us—me, my pa, and my three older brothers. I honestly don't remember much about her beyond that. She was always there, a part of the house as much as the wood stoves and the furniture, but I can't say as I really knew her. I got my looks from her, though. We had the same muddy brown, straight hair and the same bay-colored eyes, with skin that tanned quick and dimples that showed on those rare times when we smiled big.

I remember my pa much better. He was big and impatient. Not cruel but not close to gentle, either. He expected us all to do our share of the work, from birth on. I have memories of handling horses before I could walk. Least ways it seemed like that.

Our life, like the lives of all folks living in the Dakotas, was one of survival. We knew of the wars ending and brewing all about us. We knew of slavery and statehood and fights for independence. But those things didn't concern us. Making it to the next day was all we worked for; the most we could hope for. Looking back on it now it's hard for me to figure what was so all-fired great about the next day since it generally wasn't any different than the one before it, but that's what drove folks. Plain old survival.

I was the youngest of the four McAllister boys, which is what most folks called us. I don't think many people even knew our given names. We never attended school because there was too much work to do and teachers never lasted long in the territory. I had no friends and, other than my family, I only talked to shopkeepers or my father's customers. It made having a first name kinda pointless. Even my pa tended to call us all just "boy".

I knew I was different from my brothers, though, from the time I could put together thoughts. I couldn't put my finger on the difference but I felt it; I felt it in my bones or inside my head. I'm not sure what told me I wasn't the same, but it gave life this odd sort of haze, like I was forgetting something and just needed my memory jogged. I kept feeling the answer was around the next corner, the next happening, the next day. But it stayed just out of reach, leaving me frustrated and a little confused.

I was about ten when the answer started coming to me. That's when I began to notice that I admired men in the same way my brothers admired women. They appreciated the softness of a woman's body and the gentleness of her nature, while it was the hard power of a man's body, his smell of sweat and dirt, and his rough nature that stirred something inside of me. There was nothing in my life to tell me that what I was feeling was wrong. Nobody ever said to me, "Men love women. They don't love each other," but my instincts told me it was something I was safest keeping to myself. So I went from living in a haze to living in secrecy, becoming more and more certain of what I felt and less and less happy about it.

Two nights before my twelfth birthday a stranger rode into the livery stable just before bedtime. Something in his eyes caught me and held me and I realized, like a mule kicking me in the stomach, that we shared the same secret. It scared the shit out of me, but it excited me in a way nothing ever had before. Everything told me to steer as far clear of the stranger as I could, but the draw of knowing there was someone else feeling my feelings was just too great. I think the need not to be alone must be one of the most powerful needs a body has, so no matter how loud my head was screaming at me to leave him be, the rest of me knew I'd be taking a much closer look.

Like most of the flat-broke drifters that we got at the livery, this one was paying the little extra to bed down with his horse rather than paying the high cost of a hotel room. I took care of his mount while he paid up with my pa. We exchanged a couple more knowing looks and with every one a tingle of excited fear ran through my body. I felt my dick, which only recently had been giving me trouble, tingling the most.

I finished with the horse and went into the house. I knew I'd be sneaking back out to the stable once everyone else was in bed. I wasn't sure what I was expecting or what I was hoping for but I had to talk to him. I needed to see the look up close without the chance of someone else seeing. I had to know I wasn't the only one.

Once I was sure everyone else was asleep, I snuck back out to the stable. The stranger was awake and waiting for me. He'd known I'd be coming back. Face to face with him alone, none of the words I'd been putting together would come out. He seemed different up close and the excited fear I'd been feeling became just plain old fear.

"What do you want, boy?" His voice was ugly, his words more of a curse than a question.

"I . . . I'm sorry. I thought . . . " I turned to leave, the hairs standing up on the back of my neck, but he had me down on the stable floor before I realized what was happening. I struggled hard but he was too strong for me. By the time my pa came out of the house to see what the commotion was, the stranger had me face down in the straw, my pants around my ankles and my legs forced wide.

Pa shot him in the head. The bullet passed clean through his skull and grazed my right cheek. Blood poured over me and the full weight of the dead stranger crushed me. Before I could clear my head, my pa yanked the body off me and started beating me with his fist and rifle butt. The sheriff came running at the sound of the gunshot and pulled my pa away. Through my haze I could see my brothers standing 'round us, their faces twisted with disgust.

After hearing my pa's story the sheriff agreed the shooting was justified. He had nothing to say about my beating. He and his deputy dragged the stranger away while my pa brought me my horse. He said, "Get out as soon as you're saddled," then he went in the house, with my brothers following. I never saw any of them again. My ma brought me a sack of food and wished me luck. I think she was happy to have one less man to take care of.

I led my horse out of the stable and looked around. I was eleven years old and on my own, with nothing but the horse, some bloody clothes, and an ugly secret to my name. It never occurred to me to try to explain that the stranger had forced me. I never thought of claiming innocence or denying that I was the same kinda man as the stranger. The truth was, I didn't know myself if I'd really been forced. Maybe I could have struggled harder. Maybe it's what I'd gone into the stable looking for. Maybe the stranger and I were more alike than different. Those were maybes that haunted me for many years to come.

The first couple of years on my own were the hardest. I still looked like a boy, which meant I got treated like a boy. But as my body grew and my skills improved, I started earning respect. I made my way to full-fledged cowpoke and started earning decent wages. Decent wages, that is, for a cowboy. I drifted across the states and territories; across both borders, north and south. I moved on whenever I got even an inkling of an idea that I might be found out, and I got good at being friendly without making friends. That was the best way I knew to keep folks from asking any questions. To everyone I met, I was just a harmless, good-natured cowboy.

There were a few times when I saw that look again in another man's eyes, but I didn't do nothing about it until I was round about eighteen. I was near to six foot two then, with muscles worn hard by all my years of horse-handling, and I knew it were unlikely any man'd be able to force me to do anything. After the rough lesson I'd learned as a boy, I wanted to make sure I would always be on the giving end of anything that happened, not the receiving end.

That first time happened in Missouri in a hotel room during some local celebration. Seems the whole town was drunk and the sounds of gunfire and whooping drowned out all other noises. An older gent I'd spotted earlier outside the saloon and had exchanged looks with stumbled into my room. He pretended to be drunk, although I knew he wasn't. Most times a man's gotta find excuses to do what we done. I guess being drunk was his.

What we did together was violent and it was messy, and the whole time I was riding him I could see the disgusted faces of my brothers circled around me. But the truth be told, I ain't never felt anything like that first fuck with another man. It was an explosion that set loose my body; freed it, I guess you could say. I knew while I was fucking him that right or wrong, normal or not, it's what I was. The feelings afterward were a lot more jumbled and not so pleasant, but I never forgot that feeling of understanding when I was doing it. I was a man lover. It was what I was supposed to be and nothing was going to change that. It's hard to explain because it didn't make me happier, but it made me accept, and that made my life easier from then on. Living's a mighty hard thing to do when you're fighting yourself every step of the way.

It also made the craving for something more than just jacking off more powerful than ever. But the chances to fuck other men were still few and far between, so fisting my dick to keep from going crazy became something of a necessity. I was a cowpoke, working side by side every day with lean, sweaty men, and sleeping side by side with them every night. If that ain't torture I don't know what is. Most times it was just the physical aching that kept me up at night but there were times when I lay in my bunk, surrounded by the sounds of sleeping men who were close enough to touch but who were untouchable, and I ached with this odd sort of wondering. What would it feel like to have another man's body pressed up to mine through the whole night? What would it be like to fuck him and not walk away? To actually look into the face of the man beneath me and see him? Really see who he was and to like him.

Those nights I'd picture myself standing on the porch of my own ranch house, looking out over my spread, and I could feel somebody nearby. I could never really see a face or a body but I could feel him right behind me, and I would feel like a full man, warm with satisfaction.

I'm ashamed to say that those nights I fell asleep hating myself for being so foolish, my eyes burning and my heart aching like some silly little school girl.

In the early summer of 1855 I hired on to a spread called the Crooked J. It was in California down near the Mexican border. I'd heard about the Crooked J as far back as Texas and not much I heard about it was good. Harlan Jennings, the owner, was supposed to be a mighty powerful and right ornery man who kept a hired gun named Ray Saunders as his foreman. Jennings took what he wanted, giving Saunders free reign to get it for him in any way necessary. If rumors were true, that included maiming or killing anyone who stood in the way. Working the Crooked J meant a wrangler took the chance of getting caught up in their dirty shit, but my hankering to have my own spread had gotten impossible to ignore and Harlan Jennings paid over top dollar. I was thirty-two years old and running out of time. If I was ever going to be able to buy my own ranch I needed to earn the kind of wages Jennings paid. Besides, I figured it was more 'n likely that most of the hands working on a spread like the Crooked J would have their own secrets to protect, so a man's past weren't going to be a big topic of conversation 'round the bunkhouse table. That idea was most appealing to me.

I'd been working the J for about three weeks when the need to relieve some pressure was getting to be about all I could concentrate on. Whenever I started work on a new spread, I was extra cautious about taking care of my needs because I didn't want to get caught with my dick in hand. Most cowboys did it with fair regularity, but considering my circumstances I didn't like any other men around when I was riled up and humping. Things could get complicated. So I was edgier than shit and anxious to get some time alone.

My chance finally came when I was told to quit the herd early and do some saddle mending back in the tack room. Barely able to hobble through the door with my dick being so hard, I had my pants undone before the latch closed behind me. With all the other hands still back working the herd, it never occurred to me to lock the door.

I settled back against a saddle, already racked and ready to mend, and I slid my jeans down my legs. I watched my dick bounce up to greet me and I couldn't help but smile. There's just times when it feels good to be a man and this was one of them. Can't really explain it but there's something very satisfying about the way a hard cock behaves.

I closed my eyes and brought up the vision of a soft-mouthed boy I once had down in Mexico. The kid would never let me fuck his ass but he sucked me dry two nights running. He was one of the few in my life I went back to for seconds.

My hand started working my cock in slow, tight, steady strokes. I pinched the back of my balls and felt precome ooze out of my slit. I got the Mexican kid's face solidly in my mind and I went to work in earnest. It didn't take long to feel the stirring in my sac and the stretch inside my belly that told me I was ready. I pounded my cock, my fist flying up and down the shaft. A growl built in my throat and that boy from Mexico was about to take my load when I heard the tack room door click open. I opened my eyes, unable to stop the flying of my hands, and there stood the most beautiful fucking boy I have ever laid eyes on. My cock bucked and surged and I watched as three loads of cream shot across the tack room and landed on the boy's boots.

Time stood still as we stared down at the mess I'd made. When I finally looked up, our eyes met and his were so blue it startled me.

Startled my dick apparently, too, because it shot another huge spurt without being touched, hitting him this time in the knee.

"Shit."

I'm not sure which one of us said it, but I was suddenly yanking my pants up and he was rubbing at his boots and I pushed past him and ran out the door and I didn't look back.

I couldn't eat my grub that night. I couldn't hardly think. I had no idea who the kid was or who he might tell, but the worst part was the feeling he'd left in my gut. It was twisted and I felt confused and it all made me edgier than ever. What if he was a new hire and I had to work around him every day? What if he was going to be sleeping in the bunkhouse with me night after night? There's just no way I could handle having that kid's face near me around the clock.

I didn't sleep a wink. I kept expecting him to walk through the bunkhouse door. My dick pounded the whole night through but I was afraid to touch it. By morning, I was ready to blow in more ways than one.

Luckily, there was a shitload of branding to do so I volunteered for fire duty. It would be a hundred degrees before noon and a cowboy usually has to be forced to stand by the fire all day manning the iron in that kind of weather, but I didn't cotton to the idea of sitting in a hard saddle for hours with an equally hard cock. Fire duty seemed the lesser of two evils.

By noon I was soaked to the skin with sweat. I was getting steam burns from being so close to the fire, so I peeled off my shirt and tried to ignore my half-nakedness. I confess to being a tad attracted to my own body, and under the circumstances I didn't need any more stimulation. My cock hadn't softened since it revived itself right after unloading on that damn boy's boots, and I was definitely hurting.

I bent over to stoke the fire, lost in my thoughts of him, and when I straightened up he was there, sitting a few yards away from me on a palomino horse with hair as honey-golden as his own. It didn't seem possible but he was even more beautiful than I remembered. His hat was pushed back on his head and his palomino hair stuck out in front, thick and silky. His eyes reflected the sky, and his nose and cheeks were dappled with faint freckles. And his mouth—damn. I'd been too surprised the night before to notice, but his lips were like sweet slices of fruit, berry pink and good enough to eat. No woman could be prettier and yet there was nothing feminine about the boy.

He stayed on his mount and watched me, fiddling nervously with his saddle horn. I wanted to look away, but I couldn't stop staring into those sky blue eyes of his. I recognized the look in them; the questions. There was no doubting that we shared the same secret, and I was guessing this was his first time seeing it in another man's eyes. It took me back to that night in my father's stable, when everything changed for me. With a jolt, I realized I didn't want it to be like that for him. I didn't want it to be ugly like it had been for me. I felt the need to make it all different for him and that scared the shit out of me. The only way I'd made it this long was by not caring about anything, and I didn't need some golden-haired boy changing all that.

He stared back at me and I couldn't get my head clear. My gut was twisting and I was feeling things I'd never felt before. I was trying to sort it all out when a tiny sigh escaped from his sweet lips and I realized it wasn't his saddle horn he was fiddling with. The boy was masturbating. I about shot a load right then. Maybe he wasn't the innocent virgin I'd thought he was. Maybe he was just some angel-faced whore. I didn't know any more and my confusion doubled.

I looked around, scared shitless someone else was watching, but all the other hands were in the middle of the herd. I looked back at him and he sighed a couple more times then he reached back with his free hand and laid it on the palomino's rump. He rubbed his crotch harder and harder through his jeans until his ass rose out of the saddle and he made a sound like the bawling of a newborn calf. My head suddenly cleared and I could picture his dick unloading in his jeans. I watched his beautiful lips quivering and imagined them helping my pole deliver a similar load.

His hips kinda jerked a couple of times then he settled back down in his saddle. He looked me in the eye and I expected him to flash me some teasing, whore-look, but instead his lips plumped up with a shy, embarrassed half-smile. The smile of an angel.

He turned his horse and rode off, leaving me dizzy and feeling sick.

Before my body or brain had time to settle, a cowboy named Shorty rode up with a bawling calf in tow. As he wrestled the calf into position, I pulled the brand out of the fire and asked, praying that my voice gave away no secrets, "Who's the kid on the palomino?"

Shorty pinned the calf down with two legs in each hand and a knee on the shoulder. "The boss's kid. Been back east at school."

"Oh."I took a deep, jagged breath. "Nice horse."

I burned a crooked J into the calf's flank and Shorty set him free.

"Coming into town tonight, Deke? There's plenty of saloon girls to go around and from the looks of the bulge poking out from our chaps, I'd say you could use a saloon girl right about now."

I looked down at my crotch and saw the denim-covered bulge Shorty was referring to. Life would be so much easier if all that bulge needed was a saloon girl.

"Naw. There's no point, Shorty. You'll take all the pretty ones and I'll be left with some heifer."I waved the brand toward the herd. "I can get plenty of them here for free."

Shorty cackled a laugh, flashing a tobacco-stained mouth half full of teeth, and spit a brown glob of chewing juice into the fire. "I'd go for the pretty bald-face yearling. She's had her eye on you."

"Thanks, Shorty. I'll let you know if she's any good."

Shorty walked away, still cackling. As he swung onto his horse and returned to the herd, I looked back down at my crotch. Harlan Jennings's son. The most powerful, most dangerous rancher in all the West had a son who hankered for dick. My boss, who had a hired killer for a foreman, had a kid who not only shared my secret but obviously wanted me to do something about it for him. Now what do you suppose, I asked myself, a man like Jennings would have a man like Saunders do to a man like me if he got caught poking more than just Jennings's cows? The things I supposed weren't pretty which meant, from here on out, I'd be steering as far clear of that boy as I could. It didn't matter if he was an innocent angel looking for help. I didn't care if he was the most beautiful thing I'd ever seen with an ass that was probably so tight I'd blow my load just looking at it. I couldn't think about how much I wanted to be looking down into his baby blues while plowing his virgin hole. No fuck was worth my life, not even a tight-assed, blue-eyed, beautiful angel fuck. So it was my fist I'd be making love to again tonight, not him.

Fuck, I wanted him.

Back at the bunkhouse after the day's branding was done, we got our month's wages and the only topic of conversation during chow was cheap saloon girls, cold beer, and warm holes. The beer and the holes sounded real good to me but I kept my mouth shut. Payday had become my best chance for spending time alone and taking care of my needs. At every ranch I'd ever hired on to, it was the only night I generally had the place to myself. This night would be no different and I was looking forward to it.

I stayed inside the bunkhouse while the other hands stripped down naked out back, washing themselves in the troughs. The last thing I needed to see in my state was a bunch of naked, half-hard cowboys. But, naturally, the last thing I needed was exactly the thing I got when about fifteen bare-naked cowpokes came whooping and hollering into the bunkhouse and pulled me off my bed. They pinned me to the floor and started stripping me of my boots and clothes.

"You'll thank us for this later, Deke."

I struggled at first but half-hard cocks kept bumping and rubbing against my bared flesh, and grappling hands kept accidentally getting a hold of my fully hard dick so I stopped struggling and put my full concentration on not blowing a load all over my pussy-loving coworkers. It weren't easy.

Once they got me stripped clean, they carried me out the back door and dumped me in the nearest horse trough.

"Just wanted to make sure you looked your best for the bald-face heifer."

Shorty and the others walked away, howling with laughter and slapping each other on the shoulders. I watched their lean asses and dangling balls and shot a load into the murky water. Why couldn't I have been born normal?

When my dick was soft I climbed out of the trough and rinsed myself clean with fresh pump water. By the time I got dried off and back in the bunkhouse, the rest of the hands were dressed in their best go-to-town clothes.

"This is your last chance, Deke."

"Thanks, Simon, but you know I'm trying to save up for my own spread. I'll never get it if I keep wasting my pay on pussy."

Leo, a tall, dark cowboy who had even fewer teeth than Shorty, slapped me on my still bare ass. "Pussy is never a waste of money, son."

"See you in the morning, Deke."

"Yeah, Deke. Don't wait up for us."

"The heifers have all been wormed so you shouldn't have anything to worry about."

They piled out the door and got on their mounts, laughing and singing and making me hard again.

When the dust had settled and I finally had the place to myself, I stretched out bare on my bunk. The first light from the moon shone on my body and I ran my hand down my chest and stomach, closing my eyes and enjoying the feel of tight skin over hard muscle. I wrapped my fingers slowly around the base of my cock and started stroking to the memory of the boss's son jacking off on horseback.

I was just getting to the part where he had leaned back in the saddle, when I heard the bunkhouse door creak open. My hand froze and I swore under my breath. I could see the shape of a man in the backlit doorway and I wondered which idiot cowboy forgot something and was interrupting my lovemaking.

The door closed and I listened to my heart beating as the sound of boots on the floorboards got closer. Getting caught fucking my own fist when I could have been fucking a woman with the rest of the hands was going to earn me a lot of sidelong glances, no matter what excuse I came up with.

The figure was getting close and I wondered why he didn't light the lamp or say something. Then he walked into the patch of moonlight and his honey hair glowed in a halo of yellow light. He looked at the stiff cock in my hand and his tongue slowly circled his sweet lips, like a starving man gazing at a banquet. I knew exactly how he felt.

I tried to remind myself that if I ate at this banquet it would most likely be my last supper, and I tried to convince myself to pull on my jeans and ride into town with the rest of the cowboys. But Harlan Jennings's son was smiling that shy, lip-plumping half-smile of his,—and those sweet, sweet lips were moving closer and closer to my hole-hungry pole,—and I never heard a word I said to myself.

The boy was definitely not experienced—I could tell that by the teeth scraping and the throat gagging—but damn was he eager. I did everything to that boy that I'd ever done to another man, and tried a few things I'd been wanting to try, and he was still begging for more. His begging spurred me on, too, and I found myself wanting to show off for him.

It gave me this odd kind of happy hearing him grunt my name and knowing I was giving him something no other man would ever be able to give him—his first fuck. I wanted it to be unforgettable; a night that would be damn near impossible for anybody to top. And I wanted it to be . . . Shit. The only word I could think of was pretty. I wanted his first time to be pretty for him.

I had him bent over the chow table with my cock deep inside his ass for the third time when the bunkhouse door crashed open and I was blinded by lantern light.

"Wyatt. Get your clothes on and go up to the house."

Wyatt. So that was his name.

"Pa . . ."

"Shut the fuck up, Wyatt, and do as I say."

Saunders lit the wall lamps on either side of the door. My eyes adjusted to the brightness and I saw Harlan and Saunders, both with rifles pointing at me. I was standing there with the boy's insides all over my cock and I guess I should have been scared, but Iwas feeling too stupid to feel much else.

Wyatt looked at me, then back at his father.

"Pa, I wanted him . . ."

"You say another word, Wyatt, and I'm shooting him right now."

Wyatt looked back at me. He was scared, no doubt about that, but there was something else in his eyes as we looked at each other. It was a sort of desperate gratitude, like I saw in the eyes of a horse once when I'd had to shoot it 'cause its leg was broken clean in two. Wyatt's eyes got my gut to twisting again.

I jerked my head toward the door and whispered, "Go."

He didn't move until he heard the sound of a rifle being cocked, then he scooted around me and grabbed his clothes from the floor by my bunk. On his way to the door he stopped and looked me in the eye again, the gratefulness making me hurt, and he said in a loud, clear voice so's his pa could hear, too, "Thank you."

I cleared my throat, afraid of what my voice might sound like, and said, "Don't mention it." His virginity was most likely going to cost me my life but, what the hell? I figured there were worse ways of dying.

Wyatt turned and walked out the door, the disgusted look his father gave him bringing back memories of my own father.

"Tie him up, Ray."

Saunders leaned his rifle against the wall by Jennings and took a lariat off a nearby bunk.

"I'm going to tie you to a fence post, tie your cock to a horse, and then have Ray ride that horse off at a gallop. And while you're bleeding from the hole where your torn off cock used to be, I'm going to shove this rifle as far up your ass as I can and pull the trigger, and I'm going to keep pulling the trigger until there's nothing left of you but a pile of guts."

See? Now that right there was a fine example of a worse way to die.

Escape didn't seem possible. There was no way I could make it out a door or even to cover before Jennings would get off a shot. Although I didn't much like my chances with the whole castrating-and-turning-into-guts plan, at least it would give me a little more time.

Saunders slipped the lariat over my head and shoulders, cinched it too tight for me to breathe or wriggle, and pushed me toward the door. Jennings slammed his rifle butt into my stomach as I went by. My knees hit the floor hard but I used my shoulder against the door frame to keep from landing on my face. Saunders stepped in front of me and yanked hard on the rope. I hit the boardwalk outside of the bunkhouse face first and Saunders dragged me along the wood. From the burning of my dick, I didn't think a horse was going to be needed to rip it clean from my body.

I went over the edge of the boardwalk and landed in the dirt. I managed to twist onto my back, which was a lot less painful, but now that I was face up Jennings had a clear shot at my head. I saw the rifle butt just before it connected with the underside of my jaw. I tasted blood in my mouth and watched the world spin out of control.

They pulled me to the nearest corral and Jennings hauled me to my feet. I struggled, but it wasn't much of an effort as dizzy as I was, and it earned me a knee in the balls. My struggle ended and they tied me to one of the posts. Jennings grabbed my dick and started winding a rope around it.

"I'm going to make sure you never rape another man's son again."

There was no point in me arguing that it wasn't rape. Jennings's son was a man-lover, and he needed to punish someone for it. I just happened to be the one stupid enough to get caught with his dick in the cookie jar.

Jennings handed the other end of the rope to Saunders. "Get on your mount, Ray, and ride as fast as you can. I want to stand here and watch this."

Saunders smiled and gave the rope a good tug. Pain shot through my body, forcing my head back against the post. I'd never been a believin' man but I prayed to God that He strike me down dead before Ray got on that horse and rode away with my dick dragging behind it.

God, however, had a better plan. Ray turned and took two steps toward his horse. A shot rang out and Saunders dropped like a rock. Jennings crouched next to me for cover, rifle raised. Mustering every ounce of strength I had left, I mule kicked Jennings in the face. His rifle hit the ground and he fell back against the fence rail. Spurred on by my success, I kicked again and Jennings slumped to the dirt.

Naked, bleeding, and aching in places I didn't know I had, I twisted against my ropes. There was no way of knowing if the person who had just saved my life had done it to rescue me or was just out to kill Jennings and Saunders. If Jennings and Saunders were being targeted then I was nothing more than an unwanted witness. I needed to get free.

I heard hoof beats coming and I twisted harder. This was not turning out to be a good night.

The hoof beats got closer, then silence. Whoever it was planned on approaching on foot. I stretched my leg and tried to reach Jennings's rifle.

"What are you going to do? Pull the trigger with your toe?"

The boy appeared from behind me. His rifle was in one hand, my clothes were in his other, and a shit-eating grin was plastered on his face.

"Untie me, quick. Your pa's going to be coming to soon and he's going to be more'n a little peeved at the both of us."

Wyatt threw my clothes at my feet and propped his rifle against the fence post. "I don't even get a 'thank you' for saving your life?"

"You ain't saved it yet, boy. Right now all's I can tell is you're just delaying the inevitable."

The ropes fell away and my legs gave out. I dropped to my knees, the dizziness returning full force.

Wyatt kneeled next to me. "You OK?"

"Not really."

"Your dick's bleeding."

I gave it a little tug and sighed. "Yup, but it's still attached."

That's when we heard the whooping and the hollering.

"Oh, shit."

"The men are back from town. We have to get out of here." Wyatt grabbed my clothes and his rifle. "I've got horses over here. Come on."

I looked down at my naked self. I'd never ridden bare-balled before and I must admit slamming my nuts up and down on a galloping horse wasn't real high on my list of things to try, but then that was the way this night was turning out to be.

I grabbed Jennings's rifle out of the dirt and struggled to my feet. As I stumbled after Wyatt, I made myself a promise. If I managed to get out of this alive, from now on I would only work for ranchers who had daughters.

I caught up with Wyatt at the far end of the corral and stopped dead in my tracks.

"You brought the palomino?"

"She's the best damn horse on the ranch. I've had her since I was ten. Trained her myself."

"She's also the most goddamned recognizable horse this side of Texas, and with the two of you looking like fucking twins we're going to stand out like pigs in a sheep herd everywhere we go."

Wyatt swung onto the golden mare's back. "Well, excuse me for not being familiar with proper fugitive etiquette. Next time I save your life I'll be sure and plan ahead a little better." He threw the reins of the other horse in my face, lightning bolts shooting from his clear blue eyes.

" 'Proper fugitive etiquette.' What the hell kind of talk is that? Just give me my fucking clothes."

Wyatt spun his horse and rode east, taking my clothes with him.

I shouted at his disappearing back. "Asshole! I shoulda fucked the bald-face heifer instead."

I gingerly mounted the bay Wyatt left for me and tried to ease myself into the saddle, but the sounds of liquored-up, just-fucked cowboys were getting too close and I had no choice. I kicked the bay hard, gritted my teeth, and rode off after the biggest mistake of my life.

CHAPTER 2

I CAUGHT UP WITH WYATT in a grove of oaks well out of sight of the ranch yard. He tossed my clothes toward me and they landed in the dirt. I slid stiffly to the ground and began dressing in silence. The only sounds were from the winded horses and the yipping coyotes in the nearby hills.

"Where are my boots?"

"I couldn't get them. I could hide the fact that I was carrying two sets of clothes but not two pair of boots."

"What the hell am I supposed to do without boots?"

Wyatt jumped from his horse and squared off in front of me. His eyes boiled and stormed.

"I don't know," he shouted. "Why don't you go on back? I'm sure my father will be more than happy to help you find them."

"You know something, boy? Those lips of yours are a whole lot sweeter when there's nothing coming out of them."

"I didn't notice you complaining too much when I was begging, 'Harder, Deke, harder.'"

I hit him square in the chest and he fell back on his ass. I jumped on him, my shirt and jeans on but still unbuttoned. I wrestled him to his back but he got a solid fist against my chin. I lost my grip, and in my already damaged condition he was able to flip me onto my back. He pinned my arms to the ground and I saw that he was crying.

We stared at each other, chests heaving and dicks hardening. He gulped air and sort of sobbed, and I tried not to notice how incredibly beautiful he was or how my gut was starting to twist again.

"I'm sorry." He shouted it but his voice dropped down as he repeated, "I'm sorry. I just wanted to know what it would feel like." He let go of my wrists and sat back on his heels. "I was afraid you'd be my only chance."

I wanted to sound angry but it didn't come out as mad as I'd been aiming for. "Was all this worth it? Was getting another man's dick in your ass worth it?"

For a flash his eyes stormed again, then he sighed in defeat and got off of me.

"No. I just wanted to know what it would feel like to be normal."

I stayed in the dirt, too stunned to get up. "What we did, Wyatt . . . that was not normal."

Wyatt leaned against the palomino's body and stroked her neck. I could barely hear his words. "It felt normal to me."

I watched him pressed against his horse, trying to control his tears. It had been a long, long time since I'd gone through the kind of achin' he was going through. I remembered those days, a whole lifetime ago, of hoping the world wouldn't care that I was different. Wyatt was learning fast that that was never going to happen. There was no place for men like us, and he was having a hard time choking that down.

"I thought if I found . . . someone else. Someone like me . . . " Wyatt kissed the palomino on her nose and she chortled a horse's purr, lipping at his golden hair as if she were trying to comfort him. He cleared his throat, wiped at his eyes, and said, "You better finish dressing. We've got to get out of here."

I stood up, his last words busting through the muddle of things I was feeling. "We? What do you mean 'we'? I'm on my own now. Your father will be able to forget your part in all of this but he'll never be able to forget mine." I buttoned up my shirt and tucked it in past my still hard cock, not completely sure that what I said was true. Forgiveness had not come to my father. Jennings might not be any different. Still, going with me was not a choice I was willing to give him. "Go back home, boy."

"I can't, remember? I shot my father's right hand man to save your life."

"He'll get over it."

Wyatt pulled himself up into his saddle and stared down at me. "I'm going with you whether you like it or not."

We heard gunshots and distant shouting and we both looked back toward the ranch.

"They'll be organized and on our trail in a few minutes. You're wasting time, Deke."

He was right. He was going to get his way for now but I was dumping him as soon as possible. The kid was trouble, pure and simple, and no matter how sweet his lips or how tight his ass or how bad the aching in his heart, I wanted no part of him. So I adjusted the stubborn bulge in my jeans, got on my horse, and rode toward the rising sun with Wyatt following behind.

We stuck to the hardest ground we could find, crossed or traveled in water whenever possible, and looked back frequently. We didn't know where we were heading but we knew we wanted to get out of California as soon as possible. Harlan Jennings's money would get him what he wanted just about anywhere, but his reputation was not going to help him much outside of his home state.

We rode until dusk, stopping only to rest the horses and drink some water. Wyatt had surprisingly good instincts for an eastern-taught boy, but the bigger surprise was the way we never had to say a word to each other. I could feel it when Wyatt spotted a better trail or saw a good resting spot ahead, just as I could feel my horse beneath me telegraphing his moves through his muscles. It was downright unsettling, like having someone inside my head with me. I also didn't like the way my dick stayed hard just having him around. He was creeping slowly into me somehow and I admit it scared me. I had no words for what he made me feel—no name to give it or knowledge of how to fight it—but I didn't like it. It threatened my survival and that's all I needed to know.

When night started to fall we pulled the horses up in a small meadow bordered by trees and a stream. Still without a word we dismounted, silently agreeing it would be a good spot to bed down for the night. We unsaddled our horses and tied them in the grass to graze.

While Wyatt gathered the choicest tidbits to hand feed his mare, I went through the saddlebags. He had managed to stuff some supplies in them before rescuing me and I had to admire him for that. Still, when Wyatt joined me all I did was let loose on him.

"You coddle that horse too much. You should be spending your time figuring out how to fix this mess, not picking daisies for your goddamned pretty pony. We're getting rid of her as soon as we can anyway, so you need to get used to not having her around."

"We are not getting rid of her."

There was a steeliness to Wyatt's voice that I didn't expect and that just made me madder.

"I told you, boy, she's too recognizable. Both of you are."

"Then I'll cut off my hair or grow a moustache. I'll paint her black. I don't care but I am not getting rid of her."

"Grow up, Wyatt. You're not a rich rancher's son any more. You're a dick-loving fugitive and you can't keep your pet. We ain't got the time for such foolishness."

Wyatt fixed me with a stare that told me he wasn't backing down. His words came out slow and steady, his fists balled at his sides. "That horse is the only thing that has ever loved me. I shipped her back east with me and I shipped her back home. I will take a knife to my face and scar it up if that will make you happy but I am not getting rid of my horse."

I was stumped. Truth be told I think I felt a might jealous, but I'm not sure of what. Maybe because I'd never cared for anything like that before, or maybe because it wasn't me that Wyatt was caring about. Whatever the reason, it knocked the wind right out of my sails. "I guess it doesn't matter much anyway. We're not going to make it on the run for long the way things are. We got no handguns, enough jerky maybe for two days, no money, and one pair of boots." I pulled off my bandana and squatted by the stream, soaking the rag in the cool water. When it was good and wet I laid it on the stirrup cuts covering the tops of my feet. "Since we're in this mess 'cause you couldn't wait to get a taste of dick, I'd like to know what the next step is in your brilliant plan."

Wyatt was suddenly next to me, catching me off guard. Heat spread through my body and I felt myself leaning toward him without wanting to. He reached for the bandana.

"Take off your clothes."

His baby blues were pulling me in and I had to pry myself away from them. I yanked the bandana back and looked down at the stream. "Didn't I just mention that's what got us in this mess in the first place?"

He took the bandana from my hands again and dipped it in the water.

"We need to clean your wounds. It probably won't do much good now, but it's better than nothing."

"I'm fine."

"I've been watching you. I know you're in pain. Just take off your clothes and let's get this over with."

I didn't want to admit to him that if I took my pants off my freed dick would head straight for him. I didn't need him figuring out just how much of an effect he had on me. The thought of that cool, soothing rag on my burning dick was just too tempting, though, so I stood up and began to strip. Wyatt pretended to concentrate on getting the bandana good and soaked, but I saw the sideways flicker of his eyes.

I looked down at my body to see what he was seeing. My skin was taut and brown and muscles rippled up my stomach. My dick pointed up, long and fat, with the dark head peeking out of its hood and juice glistening at the slit. With him watching I couldn't keep myself from standing taller or squeezing my ass tight, and that made my pole twitch like a snake about to strike. I smiled inside. I'd seen a lot of cocks in my life, and most were nice enough to look at and served the usual functions, but some cocks just looked like they were made for nothing but fucking. Mine was one of those, mean and impatient and wanting to be set loose, like a dog on the scent of prey. And with Wyatt and the memory of his hungry, tight holes so close by, my dick started to slobber.

Wyatt's eyes weren't flickering any more. They were fixed in my direction. He licked his lips and shifted his feet. I knew it was getting tight in his jeans. I felt like I was getting back in control and that made me happy.

"All right, Sweetlips, I'm ready. Start cleaning."

Wyatt shifted to face me, still squatting. He held the balled up bandana over my cock and squeezed. Ice-cold water dribbled onto it. I sucked in my breath and grabbed his head in both my hands to steady myself. He looked up at me, his blue eyes so pretty and full of need that I wanted to drop to my knees and kiss him. But instead I pushed his head down and said, "Concentrate on your work, boy, and stop looking at me like some silly schoolgirl."

He jerked his head away from my hands then shook out the rag and wrapped it around my cock like a bandage. He squeezed, hard enough to force the cold water deeper into my scrapes but not hard enough to be painful. Wyatt tried to sound uninterested but the quiver in his voice gave him away.

"Not that I care, but being this hard is probably making it worse. You should jack off or something. Take some of the pressure off."

"You're probably right. The thing's throbbing like a motherfucker, but I don't exactly relish the idea of dragging my fist up and down those cuts."

Without a word and before I could stop him, his mouth opened wide and he swallowed my pole, rag and all. The warmth of his throat seeped into the coolness of the wet rag and a strange mix of temperatures spread through my cock and into my balls. I held his head again and closed my eyes. He sucked me gently until he had drained my dick soft. The throbbing pain was almost completely gone when he finally pulled his mouth away. He unwrapped my cock, rewet the bandana, and went to work on my other wounds.

I wanted to thank him but I knew something pissy would come out so I kept my mouth shut. When he was done I put my clothes back on and volunteered for the first watch.

"And no fires," I added as he started to gather wood. "My guess is your father's already got a posse of more than just his ranch hands after me. Most likely he's had the sheriff telegraph every other lawman in California that I've raped and kidnapped you and murdered Ray Saunders."

"I'll just tell them the truth."

I snorted out a laugh. "I know you ain't that stupid, Sweetlips. There ain't a man in this country who wants to believe his son can grow up begging for other men's cocks in his ass. Even the ones who've done some dick-loving themselves don't want that kind of life for their sons." I took my bedroll to wrap around me while I stood guard and picked up one of the rifles. "We need to face facts, boy. I'm a wanted man now and for whatever reason you're along for the ride. You need to start thinking like an outlaw. Now get some rest. I'm going to be waking you around one."

I went to the edge of the woods where I had a clear view of the way we'd come and sat down with my back against a rock. I was dying for a smoke, something I only did when I was particularly edgy. I was hungry. And I was getting hard again. I told myself once more that I should lose the kid—saddle up after he fell asleep and ride out on my own. I'd been in nearly every corner of the West and I knew a lot of the ranches I'd worked on in the past would be more than willing to hire me back on. But cowboying would be what Jennings would expect me to be doing and word would get around quick that I was a wanted man. No. It'd be best if I steered clear of ranches altogether. The kid might come in handy with his book-learning and such. So, for now, it would be best to keep him around.

That's what I told myself, anyway, but what I was remembering was the twist in my gut every time I looked in his eyes and the feeling of his nearness while we rode together in silence. Those things right there shoulda been warning enough that I needed to get rid of the boy, but something inside of me just wasn't ready to let go yet. As scary as it was to be feeling those things, it was exciting, too, and I was curious to see where it all might lead.

I couldn't have been sitting there for more than an hour when I heard bootsteps coming my way. I raised my rifle but it was only Wyatt, yawning and scratching and looking just-fucked. I lowered the rifle and looked back down the trail, knowing my dick would be on the rise again soon.

"You better get some sleep, boy. There's no telling when you'll get another chance."

Wyatt stretched and yawned some more then settled down in the dirt across from me.

"I can't. There's too much going on in my head."

I shrugged. "Don't suppose you got a smoke on you."

"Sorry."

Nothing more was said for a bit. An owl silently flew by. Crickets and coyotes took turns singing to each other. I could hear the horses shifting back in the meadow. I felt Wyatt's body close by and for a moment, just a moment, I was standing on the porch of my own ranch, looking out and admiring everything that was mine. I sucked in my breath, like suddenly waking from a dream, and looked over at Wyatt. He was lying back, propped up on one elbow. His eyes were closed and a tiny breeze moved a curl of hair that fell across his forehead. The corners of his mouth turned up, like the beginnings of a smile. A shiver ran up my back and I looked away from him.

"Where are you from, Deke? Originally."

I cleared my throat, trying to chase away anything in my voice that might give away what I was feeling. "The Dakotas."

"I've never been that far north. What's it like?"

"Like hell, only emptier."

"Sounds nice."

I looked back at him and he still had his eyes closed, that same peaceful half-smile teasing at his mouth. Warm satisfaction. I felt it like a knife to the chest. That late-night longing while lying in my bunk. It was hitting me now like a knife to the chest.

"When was the last time you were there? In the Dakotas, I mean. Not hell."

I couldn't stop looking at him. I felt a terrible need to look inside of him, to see if I could see what he was feeling; to see if it matched what I was feeling. I cleared my throat again before answering. "When I was eleven."

"Where'd your family move after that?"

His conversation was heading to places I didn't want it to go, so I changed direction. "Where'd your pa get the palomino? You don't see too many like her around."

"He bought her for me in Mexico for my tenth birthday. She came decked out in hand-tooled leather and so much silver I could hardly look at her in the sun." His eyes were open now but he was looking down at the dirt, fiddling with a stick and making patterns. "I know it sounds silly, but there was something between us from the first time I touched her. She just seemed to know me." He looked up at me and his eyes caught me off guard. "You ever have that with a horse?"

"No." I looked away and shifted against the rock, trying to ease the growing tightness in my jeans and the twisting urges in my gut. "No. I never had that with a horse before."

He was quiet for a bit and I could feel him watching me. As much as I didn't want to, I looked back at him. His eyes were on me but it wasn't like he was studying me or trying to figure me out. It was more like he was memorizing me. Or remembering me. I shivered again. That was it. He was looking at me like he was remembering me.

"You ever have that with anybody, Deke? Meet someone and feel like you already knew them somehow?"

We stared at each other for a while, both of us knowing the answer and both of us wondering if I was going to tell the truth. Before we could find out, though, something drew my attention to the trail below us.

"Shit."

A thin wisp of smoke rose up from about five miles back. Wyatt saw it, too, and we were heading back to the horses before either of us could say a word. Gathering our few things together, I did some figuring out loud.

"They've made camp so they're done tracking for the night. If we leave now and change direction, chances are we can put some real distance between us and them."

"Which way we heading?"

"North." We got on our mounts and aimed them at Canada. "We'll head east again when we're sure we've lost 'em."

There wasn't much of a moon so we let the horses find their own way. We kept the pace at a steady lope, feeling comfortable that the posse wouldn't be up and tracking again for several hours. We wanted to give the mounts as much rest now as we could. No telling when we would have to be running them long and hard again.

Just before daybreak we stopped to rest. Wyatt handed me a chunk of jerky then took to doctoring my feet. I didn't fight him any more. The attention felt good. My feet were starting to toughen up a bit, but they still burned a good portion of the time and his touch seemed to ease it.

"Want to start heading east again?"

He was looking down at my feet while he talked. His golden hair was picking up the beginnings of the day. I wanted to lay my hand on his head. I could remember the softness of it. I'd held fistfuls of his curls while I fucked him back at the ranch, and I'd steadied myself while he sucked my cock, burying my fingers in his hair.

He looked up at me and I realized that he'd asked me a question.

"What?"

"You all right?"

"Yeah. Just got my mind on other things."

"Are we going to head east again?"

I looked back where we'd been then ahead to where we might be going. "I guess. Doesn't much matter."

He finished with my feet and stood up. "Sure you're all right?"

"I'm just peachy, boy. What could be wrong?"

I was feeling edgy again. Not just the usual needed-to-blow-a-load edgy. It was that different kind of edgy I'd felt since seeing Wyatt for the first time. It had a familiar feel to it, a long ago feel to it, but I couldn't put my finger on it. It seemed to dangle just out of reach.

Wyatt didn't answer. He got himself some jerky and we chewed in silence until it was time to head out again.

We'd ridden about fifteen minutes when Wyatt suddenly announced, "I used to dream about you when I was a kid."

I reined in my horse. "What?"

"I used to ride around on the ranch, as far from the house as I could, and me and my horse would have all kinds of adventures. Indian attacks and pirate raids and tornadoes and in every single adventure I would get rescued by some handsome stranger, bigger than life and sort of magical."

"You're just a little bit tetched, boy. Anybody ever tell you that before?"

He laughed and turned his horse so they were both facing me.

"It was fun, Deke. It helped make me feel less alone. Don't tell me you never played make believe when you were a kid."

"I didn't have time for such foolishness."

"So even as a kid you were disagreeable and serious?"

I kicked my horse and started moving again. "I ain't disagreeable. Most folks think I'm downright amusing."

Wyatt sputtered out a laugh and turned his horse right-ways to follow me.

I looked over at him. "What does that mean?"

"What does what mean?"

"That laugh."

"Nothing. You said you were amusing and I was just agreeing with you."

Wyatt started whistling a tune I couldn't recognize, riding just ahead of me. I watched his ass swaying in the saddle, matching the rhythm of his horse. I tried to keep quiet but I had to know.

"Who was I?"

Wyatt stopped and turned to look at me. "What?"

"You said you used to dream about me. Who was I? Pirate, Indian, who?"

Wyatt's smile about split his face. "You were the handsome stranger, of course."

I was hoping he would say that.

"Handsome, huh? Sure it was me?"

"No doubt about it. Same big, powerful man with brown hair and reddish eyes. Muscles so big he could whup any other man or animal."

It was getting right hard not to smile along with him. He was using his hands while he talked and his eyes were smiling, too. I liked the way he made me sound like a hero, even if he was just making it up.

"Only difference was my stranger had a great big smile with dimples."

I stopped. "What did you say?"

"The man who used to rescue me had a great big smile with dimples. And no scar on his face. How did you get that scar on your cheek?"

I touched the scar, the one I'd mostly forgotten about. The burning of the bullet came back to me now. I could suddenly feel the weight of the body lying on me in my father's stable and the wetness of the blood flowing down on me.

"I don't remember." I didn't feel like smiling any more.

Wyatt's smile was gone now, too. "I'm sorry. I didn't mean to . . ."

"Forget it. Let's pick up the pace a bit." I kicked the bay and passed Wyatt, not wanting to see his swaying ass or his golden hair or his remembering eyes any more.

At some point we started drifting south again, sticking with our plan of frequent changes in direction. At nightfall we found a spot much like the one we'd camped in the night before and decided to bed down 'til morning.

I soaked my feet in the stream and packed them with mud. We finished the jerky and filled the rest of our bellies with water. Without a word about keeping watch, we rolled out our bedrolls and fell into them. I think Wyatt said something to me but I was asleep before his words reached my ears.

I woke up to a pitch-black night and I forgot for a moment where I was. A strange feeling of panic got a hold of me until Wyatt's breathing made me remember. I stayed in my bedroll, looking straight up, until my eyes adjusted to the little bit of starlight. I slowly turned my head toward him. He was rolled so that he was facing me. I could see the curve of his body and the way the blanket folded into the space between his legs. I could smell his breath; that hint of honey that seemed to come from him, lightly mixed with jerky and earth. I had a hankering so powerful to touch him that I grabbed my rifle and went to keep watch.

I found a spot outside of the ring of trees and began to pace. I knew one of two things would happen if I sat down: I'd either fall asleep or start pulling on my dick. Both of those were bad things to do while keeping watch. I had some figuring to do anyway and I did that best on my feet.

The boy was going to get me killed. That much I was pretty sure of. He'd come damn close to it already. It wasn't so much him but the effect he had on me that was to blame. I couldn't quite nail down what it was that made me act such a fool when I was with him, but it was certain that I didn't think clearly. I let my guard down. I thought of things I had no business thinking of; things like warm bodies nearby on a ranch of my own. I thought of things that weren't real and things that could never be real and he made me believe, for brief moments, that just maybe . . . And that's how he was going to get me killed. By making me believe.

I shook my head and paced harder. We had to split up. It was the only thing that made sense. Not only because of the posse but also because of those tiny moments. It's what was best for both of us.

I was trying to decide if I should do the right thing and talk to him in the morning, or if I should just hightail it while he slept, when I heard the horses start to shuffle nervously. I stood still and listened. I heard nothing, but the horses' heavy breathing and their shuffling feet told me there was something else out there. A light breeze blew my way and I raised my nose to the air, but couldn't catch the scent of anything out of the ordinary.

The horses' hooves began stomping in place and their puffing turned to high-pitched, frantic whinnies—the kind of sound a horse makes only when something that might eat it is close by.

Carrying my rifle at the ready, I ran back toward camp in a half crouch. At the edge of the meadow I stopped and let my eyes adjust. I looked toward the horses first, hoping they'd give me a hint of where the danger was. They were still squealing and doing their dance, their heads facing toward camp.

My eyes moved slowly toward the boy as I tried to see into the shadows for anything that might be spooking the horses. Then I saw it. About forty yards from Wyatt's sleeping form was the dark shape of a huge boulder—a boulder that hadn't been there when we'd made camp. From the size of it, I figured it was a grizzly. He was probably going to check out the camp for easy pickings before putting any effort into killing the horses. A sleeping man might be just what he was looking for.

Shooting the bear from where I stood was useless. Even at close range a rifle shot wouldn't do much to a grizzly that size except piss it off. He might end up charging for the nearest thing to take out his anger on and that would be Wyatt. Firing into the air might scare him off but it might not, and it would give away our location to anyone following us. If I called out a warning, Wyatt would move and become an instant target for the bear. About my only option left was hand-to-hand combat, and taking on a grizzly with my bare hands was about as smart as fucking my boss's son.

I decided the only thing I could do was to distract the bear and get him away from Wyatt. I crept along the edge of the woods, careful to stay down wind from the grizzly, and I prayed that Wyatt wouldn't move or wake up. I circled round 'til I was on the other side of Wyatt. The bear, taking his time and exploring the camp, was now about twenty yards from the boy. I found a good-sized rock and, with everything I had, I heaved it into the stream. The bear stopped and turned his head toward the sound of the splash. He snuffled the air, trying to decide if it was worth investigating. He took a step toward the water—away from Wyatt—and I breathed a sigh of relief.

Then Wyatt coughed and rolled over.

The bear growled and rose up on his hind legs. He was a good nine feet tall and nervous now. I ran across the camp, shouting and waving the rifle. The bear roared and Wyatt sat up.

"What the . . . ?"

"Bear! Get the fuck out of there."

Wyatt twisted toward the bear and the grizzly dropped back to all fours, ready to charge. Wyatt grabbed his rifle and scrambled to his feet. The bear took two galloping steps in Wyatt's direction and covered more than half the distance between them. Wyatt took quick aim and shot. The bear stopped long enough to swat at his face, like he would at an annoying bee, then continued after Wyatt. I had almost reached the woods when I saw Wyatt coming my way.

"Split up!"

Wyatt swerved and headed toward the horses instead. The bear, hearing my voice, paused. I picked up another rock and landed a hard blow to the bear's head. Letting loose with another bellow, the bear made me his new target. I surprised the hell out of myself when I thought, "Good. Wyatt's safe."

I turned and ran, surprising myself again when I fell headlong over a dog-sized rock. I hit the ground hard, knocking the wind clean out of me. I heard the bear thudding closer but I couldn't breathe or move. I closed my eyes tight, waiting for the tear of his claws. I heard a scream and it shocked the air back into my lungs. The scream hadn't come from me.

I waited for something to happen: for the bear to eat me or Wyatt to call for help. When nothing did happen, I rolled cautiously onto my back. The bear was stopped about fifteen feet from me, his head swung back toward the meadow. I heard a soft cry and recognized it as the whinny of a dying horse. The bear looked at me, undecided about what to do, then the smell of fresh blood was so strong that even I could smell it. The bear snarled at me but turned and galloped toward the horses.

Relieved but confused, I sat up and felt around for my rifle.

"Deke."

I nearly jumped out of my skin as Wyatt came out of the woods to my left, wiping his knife on his thigh.

"Come on, Deke. Let's get out of here."

I got up and followed him, the pieces starting to come together as my brain cleared. Wyatt must have slit the bay's throat to bait the bear away from me, and I had to admit I was impressed.

We came to the edge of the woods and I pulled up short in surprise. The bay was there, tethered to a tree. I looked toward the meadow and saw in the moonlight the golden carcass of Wyatt's beloved palomino being torn to shreds by the grizzly. I looked back at Wyatt, who had pulled himself up onto the bare back of the only horse we had left.

"Wyatt . . . "

"She trusted me. I knew she wouldn't fight me like the bay would. Besides, you said yourself she was too recognizable."

He held out his left arm to me. I stared at him, everything inside of me twisting and burning, and then I grabbed his hand and swung on behind him.

Wyatt wiped his arm across his eyes and said, "Better hang on. I'm pretty sure I heard gunshots from the west. That rifle shot of mine probably gave us away."

I slipped my arms around his waist and, without thinking, kissed the back of his neck. His body gave a little shudder, which did nothing to stop the stiffening of my cock, then he kicked the bay's sides and we took off across the stream, heading east once again.

CHAPTER 3

"ALL RIGHT. LET'S REVIEW." It was around noon. We'd spent all night and morning trying to cover our tracks and confuse the posse. We were on the edge of a deep ravine that ran in both directions, north and south, for as far as the eye could see, leaving us at a dead end with few choices. "We got one horse, one pair of boots, no more food or water, no saddle or bedrolls, and no money. We got this fucking crack in the ground that makes it near impossible to hide our trail from anybody following us, and my feet are throbbing like a motherfucker."

The horse was exhausted, and neither Wyatt nor I had had any real food or rest since before the fateful fucking in the bunkhouse. I felt like I had no skin left on my ass or my feet, and my cock, no matter how much I cursed it, would not stop being hard. I was pissed and I wanted to stay that way. The fact that Wyatt had sacrificed his beloved horse to save me had lost most of its importance about four hours back. In fact, thinking about it now only made me angrier. What gave him the right? Who was he to make gut-wrenching sacrifices to save my life? What right did he have making me feel things I had no hankering to feel? I never asked him to save my life. Twice.

I felt more pent up than I could ever remember feeling and there he was staring at me, his clenched jaw throbbing as hard as my dick and his golden beauty making me feel sick in my belly.

"Did I miss anything, Wyatt? Is there something about this fucking nightmare that I forgot to mention? Oh, yeah. Despite the fact that I am now a wanted man with a posse after me, I got no handgun and very little ammunition."

Wyatt's blue eyes shimmered and his fists clenched, but he said nothing.

"'Bout all I see that I have is your pair of sweet lips." I grabbed a handful of his hair in my left hand. He tried to slap it away but I yanked his hair harder. I pulled my cock out of my jeans and forced Wyatt to his knees. "I need my cock sucked again. I say it's time you put those sweet lips to some use, since it's about the only thing you're good for." I forced his face closer to my cock. "Suck it."

Wyatt looked up at me and his eyes still shimmered but I saw his face changing slowly from defiant boy to smitten schoolgirl. My gut and my brain twisted in that now familiar confusion he caused and I pulled his hair harder. His mouth opened and he moved closer to my cock, his eyes still turned up to me staring straight into mine, drinking me in like he couldn't get enough of me; like no matter what I did to him, it would only leave him wanting more.

I wanted to fuck his throat so hard it would make him puke. I wanted to make that face of his disappear.

His eyelashes fluttered and his lips spread to take me in. They were nearly touching my cock and I loosened my grip on his hair. I fought it, but my eyes started to close in anticipation of that first melting touch of his soft, hot lips and then, without warning, Wyatt slapped the shit out of my cock. He hit it so hard I screamed and it bounced off my belly, splattering precome onto my face.

"Suck your own fucking cock, asshole." Wyatt stood and stormed down into the ravine.

I held my crotch with both hands as I watched Wyatt's back disappear into the earth. I wanted to kill him. I wanted to fuck him. I wanted to kill him while I fucked him.

"You suck like a goddamned woman, anyway!" I hated the way my voice broke when I screamed at him.

Wyatt made a gesture. I didn't catch all of it but I got the general idea. I hobbled to a rock and sat down. Lord, how I wished I'd gone into town that night.

Sitting on the rock watching my cock deflate for the first time in days, my weariness overtook me. I knew it was too dangerous to sleep in broad daylight with no one standing guard, but I found I couldn't muster enough energy to care any more. I needed to escape, and sleep seemed the only possible way.

I lay back on the rock and a jumble of pictures spun in my head in that dizzying, scary way that they do when a body is beyond exhausted. Just before I dropped off, though, the pictures settled down to one— Wyatt, all golden and sweet, slapping the shit out of my cock before he stormed off. I heard myself chuckle right before I fell into darkness.

"Deke."

I shot awake, my heart pounding so hard I couldn't breathe.

"Deke." Wyatt was standing over me, looking excited.

"Don't fucking do that, boy. Damn." I tried to slow my breathing down and get my bearings straight.

"I checked out the ravine, Deke. It splits into three forks a ways up. The ground is hard and rocky and I think we can really throw them off our trail if we go into the ravine."

I sat up and rubbed the sleeping memory of Wyatt from my eyes. There was no escaping the boy. He was even in my dreams.

"We can lead the horse down to the bottom, pick one of the forks, and just follow it for as long as we can."

"What if we get stuck in a dead end? I don't think that posse is too far behind. We could get trapped down in there."

"We haven't seen a sign of them since the grizzly. I think it's worth a try. If we hit a dead end we can either get up and out the side or we can go back and try another fork."

I went to the edge of the ravine and looked down. The sides were way too steep to get the horse down.

As if he were reading my mind, Wyatt said, "I found a slope about a hundred yards from here that we could walk the horse down."

I looked at his eager face. I thought about him pulling that schoolgirl fast one on me just before he backhanded my cock and I fought back a smile.

"All right. We'll give it a try."

The slope Wyatt found was still mighty steep, and leading the horse down the dirt into the ravine was slow and more than a little dangerous. The bay was a steady, hardworking horse, but I imagine he'd had just about his fill of us. Once at the bottom, we let him rest a bit. The only feed we could find him was some scrub grass and cactus apples. That's about all we could find for ourselves, too. The apples and cactus leaves gave us enough wet to soften our thirst a bit, but I knew it wasn't going to be much longer before we all needed some real water.

When we got back up on the bay, I figured it was close to two o'clock. I sat behind Wyatt, half relieved and half disappointed to find that my cock didn't even attempt to stir when it slid up against the boy's ass.

We rode in silence until we reached the three way split. Wyatt reined in the bay, did some considering, and then headed down the right fork without saying a word to me. I think he could already tell I agreed with his choice. I found myself studying the back of his head, wondering if I could actually hear his thoughts if I concentrated a bit. His body shivered, as if he sensed some kind of intrusion, which made me shiver back.

We'd been riding again for a few minutes when Wyatt cleared his throat.

"How is your . . . cock?"

"Not hard any more."

Five more minutes of silence then, "I'm sorry. I shouldn't have done that."

I didn't answer him 'cause I was afraid he'd hear the smile in my voice. I wasn't ready for him to know that I admired him for it. The boy was one big surprise piled on top of another, and whatever it was he'd done to my life, making it boring was not it.

"Deke?"

"Yeah?"

"Do I really suck like a woman?"

"Don't know," I mumbled. "Never been sucked by one."

I felt his whole body smile as he kicked the horse into a canter. I slipped my arms around his waist and noticed for the first time how pretty and red the sun made the clay of the ravine walls, and how the birdcalls sounded more like singing than just background noise.

We rode until darkness. The going had been slow; parts of the ravine were so narrow we had to dismount and lead the horse, single file. At one point, at a particularly tight passage, the bay refused to go any further and we thought we might have to head all the way back to the main part of the canyon. But after a short rest and some more cactus apples, we were able to coax him through.

Whenever we walked we foraged for whatever food we could find, and when we were riding, the one in back tried to get a little sleep. I'll tell you right now, trying to sleep while riding double on a barebacked horse in a rocky ravine ain't the easiest thing to do.

Just as the last of the daylight disappeared and before the moonlight could do us any good, the ravine suddenly yawned open and before us stretched an endless expanse of scrubland. It wasn't true desert. It was that dry brush particular to the southern portion of California, but it could be just as harsh. The ravine had taken quite a few twists and turns but best as we could figure, we'd come out a good distance east and south of where we'd started.

"We might not be far from Mexico. I say we head south."

"Southwest. They'll never be expecting that."

I considered what Wyatt said. "Maybe tomorrow in the light we can double back a bit. Tonight let's stick with south."

"Can't we make camp here? We haven't seen them for a full day. I'm sure we lost them."

"Rather not take a chance. Besides, we need to find some real water or we're going to lose the only horse we have; and unless you're willing to carry me on your back, I don't relish that possibility."

"But I'm so tired and hungry."

"It's been less than an hour since we ate. We can't keep stopping for food."

"Sorry, Deke, but it's not like two handfuls of dry grass and a fucking lizard are going to fill me up for long."

"I told you to take some of those beetles to have as snacks."

"There's no fucking way I'm eating those things. There's a reason they call them stink bugs, you know."

"That's called seasoning. I swear they taste just like chicken."

I handed a large, shiny, black beetle back to Wyatt. The truth was they tasted like shit but anything was better than starving. I urged the bay south while I listened to Wyatt crunch and moan his way through the beetle.

Wyatt gagged. "Remind me never to let you cook a chicken for me."

About five hours later we still hadn't found a source of water. The bay was struggling and Wyatt's whining had picked up pace with every hour. Between my raw ass, grumbling stomach, and Wyatt's non-stop complaining I was close, once again, to killing him.

"Can't we stop for a nap? Just a short one? One of us can stand watch."

"For the hundredth time, Wyatt, please shut up."

"But the horse needs to rest, too."

"The horse needs water more. In fact, I think we may need to start walking if this animal is going to make it."

"Walk? I can barely sit up straight any more."

"Wyatt. Please."

He was quiet for less than ten seconds.

"I gotta take a piss."

"Oh, for Christ's sake, Wyatt, why didn't you do that the last time we stopped?"

His voice drilled into my brain like water dripping on a tin roof. "What do you want me to do? Piss in my pants?"

I reined the bay in hard and Wyatt's head bounced off of mine. "Ow."

"Go on. Go piss."

His whine churned into a pout. I hadn't decided yet which one I hated more.

"Never mind. I'll hold it."

I squeezed my eyes tight and spoke very slowly. "Get off the fucking horse now and take a goddamned piss."

"Geez, Deke. You act like I'm doing it just to piss you off." He slid off the horse. "Hey. That's funny. I'm pissing just to piss you off."

I clenched my fists. I was already wanted for a murder I didn't commit. Maybe I should just make it worth my while and actually kill Wyatt. I looked down at him, ready to let loose with both barrels, but he was looking up at me through feather-soft lashes and I could see the moon reflected in his sky blue eyes and no words came out of my mouth.

Air stuck in my lungs like a chunk of meat and my chest burned. It muddled me something fierce how every time I looked at him it was like seeing him for the first time.

I finally got my air back and I said, "Don't do that."

"Don't do what?"

"Don't look so goddamned fucking beautiful. It makes it near impossible for me to kill you."

He smiled his shy smile but it was a pleased smile, too; a smile that was beginning to realize it had the advantage over me. Wyatt slid his hand across my thigh toward my crotch.

"C'mon. Let's stop and eat. I can think of something big and meaty I could have."

I looked down at my crotch. There was no way in hell.

"Sorry, Sweetlips. I'm afraid right now one of them beetles would be more filling."

Wyatt laughed, and with that sound I heard the breeze rustling the leaves and the night songs of birds I had heard a million times before but had never really listened to. I felt this warning stab that told me to leave and never look back, but my hand reached for him instead and I brushed back the golden hair on his head and said,

"Go piss, Wyatt. We need to get moving."

He watched me for several seconds, kinda puzzled, then he turned his back to me and undid his fly. I thought about his pretty pink cock and realized that for the first time in my life I wanted to suck another man's cock. I had sucked a few in the past, but it had always been a return favor, sort of an obligation for getting some ass. But with Wyatt, I wanted to do it. I wanted to hold his cock in my mouth and taste him, to feel every ridge and every vein before I felt my throat burn with his come.

Leave now, I told myself, before it's too late. But I couldn't yet. Not yet.

"Rabbit!"

Wyatt's excited shout brought me back. He went sprinting after a huge jackrabbit, his fly still open and piss spraying in every direction. I kicked the bay and tried to circle around, but the rabbit was so fast at changing directions that my horse couldn't keep up. Wyatt ended up face down in the dirt more than once but unfazed, he would pop back up, his cock still dangling free, and get back in the chase.

Wyatt finally had the rabbit headed in my direction, with a boulder blocking its escape to my left. I angled the bay to the right, hoping to cut off our dinner, but without warning my mount decided he'd had enough. He dug in his front legs and ducked his head, sending me sailing over his neck. I did a flip in the air and hit the ground hard, landing on my back. I heard a loud *snap* when I landed and felt warm moisture soak my shirt. I closed my eyes to block out the spinning stars in front of me and had visions of my backbone sticking out of my skin, blood, and bone splattered everywhere.

Wyatt's voice cut through my daze. I felt his hands on my sides.

"Are you all right?"

He pushed me onto my side to check my wounds. The fact that I wasn't feeling any real pain made me sure I'd injured my back or neck.

"How does it look, Wyatt?"

"Completely mangled." I took a deep breath to steady myself as Wyatt poked around beneath me, ready to hear the worst. "Still edible, though."

What?

I opened my eyes and tried to look behind me. "What?"

"You smashed the shit out of the poor thing, but it's still edible."

I sat up and felt my back. Blood and flesh stuck to my shirt. Wyatt reached behind me then proudly held up the mutilated body of the jackrabbit.

"Nice shot, Deke. I never would have thought of doing that." He stood up and held his hand out to help me up. "Let's eat."

Wyatt gathered cactus leaves as I skinned the rabbit with my buck knife, feeling more than a little foolish. All of that was soon forgotten, though, as we feasted on our first fresh meat in days. I'd never had rabbit raw before and didn't plan on doing it again if I could avoid it, but I had to admit, that was the best damn meal I'd ever had. Not even Wyatt's much-exaggerated reenactment of my hunting style could dampen my good mood.

We leaned back against a boulder and watched the sun come up, feeling satisfied and rested. The endless sky changed from purple to pink to blue and I noticed that Wyatt's eyes reflected the sky no matter what color it was. The color of his hair changed, too, from copper to amber to golden, as the sunrise painted him along with the day. The fading sounds of crickets was like a song and I pondered on how everyday sights, like dust devils and the glint of sunlight off of quartz, were suddenly wonders to behold. I felt a peace I'd never known before in my thirty-two years, and it made me smile to think that the most dangerous time in my life was turning out to be the best.

Wyatt started to stand, volunteering for the first watch. I put my hand on his leg and stopped him.

"I think your idea of traveling in the ravine might have done the trick. At least for now. I think we're safe skipping guard duty this morning."

Wyatt watched me; not puzzled, just waiting.

"I been sitting here thinking. We've done fucked every which way and sucked in all four directions, but I ain't never kissed you before." I ran my thumb softly along his lips. "Did you ever notice that, boy?"

Wyatt smiled and I felt his sweet lips plump under my thumb. His shy smile was gone, most likely for good along with that schoolgirl look of his, but in its place was a growing self-confidence and an understanding that made him even more beautiful. It made me a little proud to think that maybe I had a part in that.

He leaned in close to me and said, "I noticed. I figured if you didn't kill me first, you'd get around to kissing me sometime."

I laughed as I tangled my fingers in a mess of his golden hair and pulled him even closer. I whispered, "Sweetlips", and I put my mouth to his. My tongue slid between his lips and I was pleased, but not real surprised, to find that they tasted as sweet as they looked.

I pushed Wyatt back with my body, my mouth still loving his, and I laid him down in the dirt. I covered his body with mine and lost myself in a kiss the likes of which I'd never known. When it was over though—minutes, hours, or maybe days later—I realized I'd done just the opposite with that kiss. I'd found myself instead.

Wyatt fell asleep beneath me, our legs tangled as one and a smile that said everything I felt spread across his face. I kissed both his eyes, the tip of his nose, and his honey-sweet lips then I fell asleep, too, my head on his chest and his heart beating in my ear.

CHAPTER 4

THE BLAZING HEAT of the noonday sun woke me up. We had changed places in our sleep and Wyatt was now on top, stuck to me like a sweaty shirt. I felt smothered and damp but I didn't want to let him go. Sweat dripped from his face onto mine and flies buzzed around us.

I surveyed our surroundings as best as I could. I knew things were bound to look different with the excitement of a good meal gone and some decent rest behind me. It was time to do some serious planning.

The landscape was as harsh and as endless as I remembered it, only now it was lit by the glare of a straight up summer sun. No romantic sunrise softened the reality. And something else seemed different, too. I had a strange feeling of something being changed or missing.

I poked Wyatt.

"Hey, Sweetlips. Wake up."

Wyatt stirred and moaned. He wiped drool from his mouth with the back of his hand and tried to focus his eyes.

"Hmm?"

"Where did you tie the horse?"

"What?"

I gently pushed him off me as I tried to hold down my rising panic.

"The horse, Wyatt. Where is the horse?"

Wyatt sat up, his eyes suddenly wide. "Didn't you tie him up?"

"I thought you tied him up."

We stood at the same time and stared our accusations at each other, and then we ran in opposite directions, searching for horse tracks. Wyatt found them first.

"This way."

I picked up the rifles and joined Wyatt as we followed the horse's trail almost due south.

"He's weaker than we are. He couldn't have gone too far."

"Keep telling yourself that, Wyatt. Keep telling yourself that."

We walked for nearly three hours, best as I can figure it. My bare feet were cut and bleeding and stuck full of every kind of burr the south of California had to offer, but it was Wyatt who looked like he was on the verge of tears.

"God, Deke. I am so sorry."

Every fifteen minutes or so Wyatt apologized. With each new apology something new got added, until his *sorry*'s included things that happened before we ever met but could've, by some stretch of the imagination, had an effect on our current predicament.

"I shouldn't have turned down that internship with the bank back east. If I'd stayed and worked this summer . . . "

"We never would've met and I'd have missed out on all this fun. Just skip to 'I'm sorry for ever being born' and get it over with."

Wyatt turned his head away from me and wiped the back of his hand across his eyes. I stopped and turned him to me. I held his face and kissed him long and soft.

"And if you'd never been born I never woulda found out that heaven tastes like honey but looks a whole hell of a lot like hell." I took off his hat and pushed his sweaty hair back from his forehead. "Stop apologizing, Wyatt. This is probably the stupidest fucking thing I've ever said, but I'm glad we met. I'm glad we fucked and I'm glad that if I have to die out here in the middle of nowhere, I'm glad I'll be dying with you. So stop apologizing."

Wyatt laid his head on my shoulder and sobbed. "Oh, God, Deke. I'm so sorry."

I held him for a few minutes and let him have his cry, then I put his hat back on him and pushed him after the horse tracks. "If we're lucky, we can beat the vultures to the horse carcass and have us some more meat for dinner."

Wyatt sniffed and rubbed his sleeve under his nose. "Deke?"

"Yeah?"

"Did you mean I look like hell or this place looks like hell?"

I smacked him upside the head and watched his body smile from behind. I heard no more apologies from him.

It weren't too long after that we noticed a change in the scenery. The brush was getting greener and the ground a little springier. Up ahead, we could even see a grouping of what would pass for trees in those parts. Wyatt and I looked at each other but didn't dare curse our luck by saying what we were thinking.

Despite my chewed up feet we started walking faster. Soon we were running, or as close to it as I could manage. Our target was the pond, which we could clearly see now, the sun sparkling diamonds across its surface. The bay stood drowsing at the edge and he gave us a quick, uninterested glance before going back to his nap.

Wyatt and I fell into the water. We drank our fill, ignoring each other's warnings about making ourselves sick. We splashed and roughhoused until we were both exhausted, which didn't take too long, then we pulled our dripping, aching, grateful bodies out onto the dirt and laid down next to each other.

"Deke."

"Hmm?"

"It's your turn to tie up the horse."

I slapped his chest then he gave me a quick kiss before he got up to make sure our ride didn't take off again. I was asleep before he lay back down.

I was dreaming of sucking Wyatt's cock while he ate a banquet of dead animals when the sound of rifles being cocked woke me up. I opened my eyes to the sight of three Winchester barrels pointing at me. I checked to make sure that Wyatt was all right. He was awake and staring at the same three barrels. I looked back at the rifles.

My first thought, of course, was that the posse had caught up to us. It took me a few moments to realize that the rifles trained on us were being held by a woman and two children, one of which was a girl not too much taller than a newborn calf. They didn't seem likely candidates for a Harlan Jennings posse.

"What're you doing on our land?"

Wyatt and I looked at each other, then slowly sat up.

"Put up your hands."

The woman could've been twenty or she could've been thirty. Farming on land like this made a body's age hard to guess. I figured she must be doing it on her own to boot, otherwise her man would be holding a rifle on us, too. That meant she was a woman to be reckoned with. We obeyed.

She was no more'n five foot six with a slim body and long, buckskin-colored hair pulled back in a ponytail. Her eyes were green and I could tell that underneath the wear, she was a beautiful woman. She was smart, too, her eyes taking in everything and her mind sorting it out quick. I could almost see the wheels spinning in her head and I knew nothing much would slip past her.

"This watering hole is ours. You can't be drinking from it without permission."

I nodded at her. "We're sorry, ma'am. We didn't know. We've been lost out here for a spell."

"Our horse led us here. We'll pay you for it."

The woman and I both looked at Wyatt.

"With what, pretty boy? A lock of that golden hair of yours? I don't 'spect a couple of fellas with one near-dead horse and a single pair of boots between them would have much to offer in the way of payment."

I cut in before Wyatt could say anything else foolish. "We'll be happy to work it off, ma'am."

She looked at my swollen, bloody feet and lowered her rifle.

"Why is it God keeps sending me every pathetic stray this side of the border?"

The children lowered their rifles, too. Without the gun barrels in my face, I could see that the bigger one was a boy of about ten and the little girl couldn't be more'n six.

"Get your things. Toby, lead their horse for them. It's not far to the house."

Wyatt and I looked at each other, a little bewildered, then he helped me to my feet and we followed our captors. Or rescuers. I wasn't sure yet which they were.

The woman was right about the walk to the house. It was a short one, but the rest had given my feet time to realize what piss-poor shape they were in and the pain began pounding something fierce. By the time we got inside the tiny cabin, Wyatt was nearly carrying me.

"You'll have to sleep in the barn and clean up at the trough but I'll doctor your feet up first."

She pointed to a chair at the eating table and Wyatt sat me down in it. The woman pulled back the curtain to her pantry and began to rummage.

The cabin was only two rooms. We sat in the main room that served as kitchen, dining room, living room, and the children's sleep area. A bunk bed took up one corner and the table I was sitting at filled up the middle. One wall was lined with the stove, sink, and food-fixing table, and on the opposite wall, next to the only window, was a big, cozy easy chair with books piled on the floor, either side of it. I figured the other room must be where the woman herself slept.

Wyatt crouched next to me, his hand on my thigh, and smiled up at me. Without thinking, I ruffled his hair and smiled back. The woman stopped in front of us, her hands full of doctoring things and her eyes full of questions.

I jerked my hand away from Wyatt's head. Being lost alone with him had made me forget about the real world and how it felt about men like us. I was foolish to let things get as carried away as they had. I looked away from him, feeling his eyes on me. He knew what I was thinking and he was going to fight me every step of the way. He was fairly squirming now with the need to argue but it wouldn't do any good. We'd made our time in the desert into one of Wyatt's childhood dream adventures, but we were back among other folks now and our little pretend had to end.

"I'm Lettie."

The woman's voice pulled me back and I looked at her. The questions in her eyes were gone now. They were hidden behind a dead expression that she seemed to wear like a mask. Or maybe it was her real face, the face left to her by a life of struggling.

Wyatt stood and stepped behind me as Lettie prepared to doctor my feet. He was careful not to touch me and I could feel the effort it took him.

"I'm . . . Dillon." I offered her my hand but she didn't take it.

"John," came Wyatt's voice from behind me.

Lettie kneeled and examined my wounds. "Daisy, heat up some water. Toby, get out the extra blankets and take 'em to the barn."

Two *yes'm*'s replied as Lettie dabbed at the worst of my sores with a quinine-soaked rag. I held back my screams. My feet were on fire and every poke of the rag seemed to dig pins deeper into my skin.

"You got a lot of pricks what need pulling out. This might take a bit." She looked up at Wyatt. "Go to the barn with my boy and bed your horse down. Poor animal deserves some pampering."

"Yes'm."

I smiled in spite of myself. Wyatt's boyishness made my crotch tingle. There was something mighty appealing about that middle range of land between boy and man.

When Wyatt and Toby were gone and the girl was busy with her chore, Lettie fixed me with a stare. "I ain't going to ask you no questions 'cause I know I won't be getting the truth . . . Dillon . . . but I think it's only fair to warn you that if you bring down any harm on my children the rest of your body'll be matching your feet." She jerked her head toward the front door. "That goes for your pretty friend, too. Understood?"

"Understood. Thanks for the warning." I gritted my teeth as she went back to dabbing. "By the way, could you tell me where we are? We've been wandering for a bit."

"New Mexico Territory. Arizona, to be exact. And you may not be thanking me once you're done paying off that water you drank. Water's more valuable than gold in these parts."

"We'll earn it. Guaranteed."

Lettie shrugged and gave me one of her dead looks, but her hands on my feet were gentle and I was beginning to think her look was more mask than face.

When the water was ready Lettie cleaned my feet. She plucked and scraped whatever poked from my skin, then she bandaged them both up.

When Wyatt returned I could feel his uneasiness. He knew what I was thinking and he was readying his arguments, but I knew what had to be done. I'd known it all along but I'd gotten caught up in the pretending. I'd even let myself believe I had feelings for the boy. But it was time for me to pay heed to those warnings I'd been getting since first laying eyes on him. It was time for us to be splitting up.

Lettie fixed us a meal of cold ham, warm bread, and goat's milk, then she went to the barn to set us up for the night. The children sat and stared while she was gone, Toby's rifle lying across his lap. I had no doubt the boy knew how to use it. Wyatt paced. I wasn't looking forward to being alone with him.

Lettie returned carrying our rifles. "These'll be in here for safekeeping."

"Thank you, ma'am, for all your hospitality."

"You're welcome, John."

"We'll start working off our debt to you first thing tomorrow."

"I already have your chores lined up."

We said our goodnights and went out the door. It was barely closed behind us when Wyatt started spouting like a water pump.

"I know what you're thinking, Deke. You're wrong. We can do this. Nothing has changed."

"Not now, Wyatt. We'll talk tomorrow. We need sleep."

Wyatt grabbed my shoulder and forced me to stop.

"No. We need to talk about this now."

I jerked away and kept shuffling to the barn. I cursed my damaged feet for keeping me from running away from him.

"Deke, please."

I pushed him into the shadows outside the barn.

"Stop it. We've been living in a dream, Wyatt. A fairy tale. What we feel for each other has no place in this world."

"You're wrong. We can make a place for ourselves. I know we can." He tried to touch my face but I slapped his hand away. "Don't do this, Deke."

The pain in his eyes made it impossible for me to look at him.

"The world doesn't want us around, Wyatt. We've seen that firsthand." I slid the door part way open. "People can't accept men like us."

Wyatt squeezed past me and opened his mouth to continue arguing, but instead we both stopped and stared.

A lantern, a razor, and some towels sat on a barrel in a corner of the small barn. The light from the lantern cast a warm glow on the blankets arranged on a bed of straw. Instead of the two separate beds I'd been expecting though, Lettie had made them into one big bed, complete with side-by-side pillows.

Wyatt turned and smiled, smug-like. "You mean, some people can't accept us."

I admit I was a bit thrown, but it didn't matter. I knew I was right. "It doesn't mean anything, Wyatt."

He slid his hands across my cheeks and ears then up into my hair. My skin tingled to my torn up toes and I couldn't stop the shiver up my spine.

"It could mean she doesn't care, Deke. It could mean you're wrong about the world." He kissed me softly then started to undo my shirt. "It could mean she's a very nice woman who doesn't mind if two men fuck the shit out of each other in her barn."

I unbuckled Wyatt's belt, thinking it couldn't hurt to have one more night of loving. "You mean a very nice woman with two small children. Don't forget there are two small children sleeping right over yonder."

"I'll be very quiet."

"That'll be a first."

"You could gag me."

"I was planning on it."

We got each other down to skin and our hands started exploring. I'd done a great number of things to Wyatt's body but I didn't feel as if I really knew it well. Up 'til now it had been mostly fucking and sucking. I told myself that if I was leaving him soon I owed it to myself—and to him—to get as intimate as possible with as many of Wyatt's inches as I could. Lord knows I'd never get this close to love again.

I don't remember getting down into our straw bed, but we were suddenly in it and he was in my arms and my cock had found its way to his hole, and Wyatt whispered, "Please don't run out on me, Deke."

I kissed him and pushed back his hair. "I never make promises I can't keep."

"But you'll try. Promise me you'll try."

Being inside him and watching the shimmering in his eyes made it impossible for me to say no. I knew there was a growing part of me that wanted it as much as he did. "I'll try. For as long as possible, I'll try. But that could mean tomorrow, Wyatt. Don't forget that."

He seemed satisfied with that and I fucked him slow. I thought hard about the feel of his hands running over my body. I noticed how his ass squeezed my cock the hardest if I kissed him while I fucked. I saw for the first time that his face was different when my cock was pushing in than when it was pulling out; sort of blissful on the in stroke and surprised on the out. I felt his heartbeat when I laid my hands down near his cock, so I pressed him into a ball and laid my head down on his chest, listening to his heart with my ear while feeling it with my hands. His cock beat the same rhythm as his heart against my stomach, leaving his wet mark on me with every beat.

I'm not ashamed to admit that I made love to him that night. It wasn't just fucking. It was something more—more powerful, more satisfying, more frightening. More than once those premonitions tore at my chest, warning me to go, but I held Wyatt tighter instead. I promised him I would try, and I would. I wanted it to work. No matter how little of a chance we had, I wanted it to work.

We didn't do much sleeping that night. In fact, when the cow started bawling to be milked, I still had my cock deep inside of Wyatt.

"I suppose somebody's going to be coming in to milk that cow."

"Probably be best if your dick wasn't in my ass when they do."

"Probably. Not sure it's going to come unstuck on its own, though."

Wyatt scooted away from me and my dick popped free, his ass making a loud sucking noise at the same time. "I think we forgot to sleep."

"I didn't forget. I just couldn't squeeze it in between the cock sucking and the butt fucking."

Wyatt pulled on his jeans and I found myself sighing as his pretty pink cock disappeared from view.

"Well, my asshole sure feels like it's had more than the usual squeezed into it."

"Yeah. I'm hoping I didn't leave anything important in there."

Wyatt laughed, pulled me up to him, and slipped his tongue into my mouth. "Morning," he whispered.

"Morning."

A knock at the barn door jerked us apart.

"Ma says I need to make sure I can come in first. Can I come in?"

I snatched my jeans from the floor and jumped into them.

"Yes, Toby. Come on in."

Lettie's son came in lugging a bucket and a milking stool.

"Ma says she's got your chores ready for you." Without another word Toby settled in next to the cow and began milking.

"Guess we better get to work . . . John."

Wyatt leaned close to me. "What's your name again?"

My mind went blank. "Shit. I don't remember."

"It's Dillon." Toby didn't miss a beat with his milking.

"Uh . . . Thanks, Toby."

Wyatt shoved me out the barn door. "We fucking stink at being fugitives."

I looked around, checking for peering eyes, then I grabbed Wyatt by the back of his neck and gave him a kiss. "We'll get better. Just a few days ago you sucked cock like a starving gopher and now look at you."

I dodged Wyatt's backhand and we stepped inside the house. The fire was crackling and the smell of bread baking made my mouth water. The word "home" sort of seeped through my body and I couldn't help but sigh at the thought of sharing something like this with Wyatt; fairy tales and fucking for the rest of our born days.

"Good morning. How did you gents sleep?"

"Uh . . . good."

Lettie nodded at me. "How are your feet feeling?"

"Almost as good as new. You have the touch, ma'am."

"I prefer Lettie."

"Lettie."

"We'll have breakfast in about an hour. John, out back you'll find some wood that needs chopping. Dillon, I want you off your feet as much as possible for another day or so." Lettie motioned to the easy chair by the window. "And I got a mess of mending I need to get caught up on. So have a seat. Everything you need is in that basket next to the chair."

Mending clothes? "Be happy to, ma'am . . . I mean, Lettie. But first could I use the outhouse?"

"Out back, near the woodpile."

I went outside with Wyatt.

"Keep your mouth shut, boy."

"But, Deke. If we're going to make a life together one of us is going to have to do the women's work." I could hear the laughter trying to bust out from Wyatt.

"I tell you what, Sweetlips. When the day comes that you can pin me to the ground and fuck me to six straight loads like I can do to you, I'll consider doing the women's work."

Wyatt's laugh let loose. "All right, but I do have a hankering to see you in nothing but an apron."

I took one threatening step toward Wyatt but he jumped out of my way and headed to the woodpile.

"Be careful, Deke. I don't want you pricking yourself with one of them sewing needles."

"And I wouldn't want to see that ax handle shoved up your ass, but it just might happen if you don't keep your mouth shut." I opened the door to the outhouse. "And the name is Dillon."

I held my dick in my hand and tried to keep it soft enough to piss, but the sound of Wyatt whistling happily while he swung an ax made my dick want to grow. I finally squeezed out enough to make my bladder stop aching and stepped outside.

Wyatt stopped his whistling long enough to say, "See ya at breakfast," then he went back to chopping. The sun peeked over the horizon and Wyatt's hair picked up its bronze glow. I headed for the house so full of happy that I was actually looking forward to the mending.

CHAPTER 5

THE MENDING wasn't anything too difficult. Most cowboys are used to fixing their own torn clothes and damaged leather gear so I knew how to do some basic stitching. What I wasn't used to, though, was trying to do it sitting in a big soft chair with a stove fire toasting me, sleep pulling at my eyes, and the feel of Wyatt's body wrapped around my memory. Next thing I knew, they were waking me for breakfast.

"Daisy, go get John and call your brother."

Lettie took the mending from my lap. I was ashamed to see that I hadn't made it through the first shirt.

"I'm sorry, Lettie. I swear I'll have this all done today."

"You better. At this rate it'll take you a year to pay off that water."

I thought I saw the hint of a smile run across her face but it was hard to tell. There was something about her, though, that had me believing that if I was a man who craved women, I'd probably be falling for her. She was pretty in a hardworking, healthy way; not pale and breakable like most city women. I understood her way of hiding herself from others, too, since I'd spent my life doing the same thing. Lettie and I'd be a good match for each other, that's for sure. If, of course, I was a man who craved women.

I started to stand up but my feet were pounding again and I couldn't keep the pain from showing on my face.

"Sit back down. Let me change your bandages."

I started to protest, but she laid her hand on my chest and pushed me back into the chair, then went and got her doctoring things. Just as Lettie started working on my feet, Daisy came back with Toby and Wyatt. Toby sat the full milk bucket down on the fixin' table, then Wyatt and Toby washed up while Daisy laid the food out on the eating table.

"Smells like heaven in here, ma'am."

"Go ahead and help yourself, John. I have to tend to Dillon's feet first."

"Thank you."

The eating table was only big enough to sit four, so after heaping his plate full of bacon slabs, eggs, and fresh steaming bread Wyatt leaned against the wall to eat, leaving the fourth spot at the table for me.

I eyed Wyatt's overflowing plate and watched his cheeks bulge as he shoveled food into his mouth. "Don't be shy there, John. You might want to squirrel enough food away for winter."

Wyatt smiled at me, pieces of egg dropping out of his mouth.

"Sorry but I'm doing real work; not sitting in a comfy chair darning socks. I need me some grub to keep up my strength. I'll make sure I leave some tea and biscuits for you, though."

"And I'll make sure I save a swift kick in the backside for you once my feet get better."

Wyatt smiled big, his cheeks puffed out like a chipmunk's. One drop of sweat trickled down from his hair. His face glowed reddish from his outside work and the inside heat. The blue of his eyes was so bright he looked downright feverish. It was a hard thing not to admire something as pretty as him, and I think I could've been happy darning socks and admiring Wyatt for the rest of my life. Providing life would let me do that, of course.

"Your feet should be better tomorrow." Lettie finished tying off my bandages and stood. "Now if you two gents work as good as you jaw, I'll be calling us square on the water in no time."

"And what about the food and board? We owe you for that now, too."

"I'll let you know when we're even." Lettie went to the pantry to put her doctoring things away. "I have a feeling you boys'll be anxious to move on soon, though."

I sat down at the table between Daisy and Toby. Daisy started spooning food onto my plate before I could say a word. I smiled, thanking her, and she tucked her head shyly but smiled back.

"Well, we do have things we need to be doing," I said.

"How come you only got one horse and no saddle? What happened to your boots?" Toby had already perfected Lettie's dead expression. His voice gave no hint of what he was feeling. It was strong and unafraid and I could tell that he'd probably been the man of the house for quite some time.

"Don't ask questions that don't concern us, Toby. They'll pay us what they owe us. That's all we need to know."

"Yes'm."

"The truth is, Toby, that we started out with two sets of everything." Wyatt sat his dishes in the sink and started cleaning them up. "Our other horse was a palomino. Most beautiful horse you ever saw. She was seventeen hands high and so golden the sun would sometimes forget to rise, thinking it already had."

Daisy stopped eating and turned in her chair so she could watch Wyatt.

"Her name was Athena and she was as brave and loyal as any dog ever was."

Wyatt's voice had a way of drawing me toward it, like a bug to candlelight. Watching Lettie and her young ones, I knew it wasn't just me it affected that way.

"One night we'd made camp and were sleeping deep when the most fearsome roar—louder than thunder—woke us up. A grizzly, eighteen feet high, towered above us. His claws were like hunting knives and his teeth were longer than my forearm."

Wyatt put his dishes aside to dry and he crouched between Daisy and me. Toby tried to look uninterested, but he sat tall in his chair and his body leaned forward, drawn to Wyatt's voice. Lettie sat back in her chair and watched the faces of her children. I felt a little sad by the wishes I could see in her eyes.

"De . . . Dillon shot the bear square in the heart but the bear grabbed the rifle in one giant paw and threw it aside. Worst part was, Dillon was still a hold of the rifle and he ended up in the top of a nearby oak tree."

"Is that when he hurt his feet?"

"No, Daisy. He still had his boots on then. Cowboys always sleep with their boots on."

"How come?"

"Cause the smell of their feet would stampede the cattle."

Daisy giggled and Toby bit his lower lip to keep from smiling.

"Anyhow, there's Dillon high up in a tree and there I am on the ground, alone to face this beast."

By the time Wyatt finished his story of how we'd ended up in the state we were in, we'd battled everything from Indians to rabid porcupines (the real cause of prickles in my feet) and his palomino had died saving our lives. Daisy was sitting in Wyatt's lap, Toby was laughing so hard he was near to tears and Lettie's mask was slipping just a tad.

I stood and started clearing the table of our dirty dishes. "That was a powerful good meal, Lettie, and a right amusing tale, John. I thank you both, but I got a mess a mending that ain't doing itself so I best be getting back to work."

Wyatt kissed Daisy on the top of her head and set her on the floor with a swat to her backside. "Dillon's right. It's time to get back to work. Just point me in the right direction and I'll do whatever needs doing."

"Toby, show John the fences that need mending and where the tools are. Daisy and me'll clean up this kitchen."

Wyatt tossed me a smile and followed Toby out the door.

I sat down and picked up my sewing basket. By the time Daisy and Lettie were done, I'd mended four pairs of socks and one shirt. I was right proud of myself when Lettie pulled up a stool and examined my handiwork.

"Not bad."

"Thank you, ma'am. Don't think I'm quite ready for a quilting bee yet but I think that stitchin'll last a spell."

Lettie pulled one of Daisy's dresses from the pile and started threading herself a needle. "Daisy, go on out and play for a bit."

"Can I help John, Ma?"

"If you don't get in his way."

Daisy bounced out the door calling "yes'm" back over her shoulder.

"You've got fine children, Lettie. You must be proud."

Lettie nodded. "They're my reason for getting out of bed every morning."

We were silent for a bit as we worked on our sewing but I felt questions hanging in the air between us. What happened to Lettie's husband? How'd a beautiful woman and two little ones end up on this remote piece of sand trying to scratch out a living? And I knew Lettie must'a been wondering about Wyatt and me, even though she would never come right out and ask.

"That John . . ." Lettie paused. "There's magic in that boy." Her words caught me off guard; both the truth of them and the dreamy way she said them. "And I never seen a man as pretty as that one."

I nodded. An odd feeling close to anger started spreading through my body and I felt it coloring my face. It was the first time I'd heard anybody else admire Wyatt and for some reason it got my hackles up.

"He has a way with my young'uns, too." Lettie concentrated on her work. "They ain't never really had a man they could look up to before."

I shifted in my seat. Lettie must have known about Wyatt and me. After all, she'd set up our bed like she knew we'd be sharing our blankets. 'Course, like I told Wyatt, that didn't mean nothing. She could just have been saving on blankets or maybe she figured cowboys were used to sharing their body warmth. It made sense that Lettie'd be eyeing Wyatt for herself, though. He was a hard worker, good with her children, and the most beautiful fucking man in the world.

My face was hot and I felt a powerful need to stake my claim to Wyatt. I was feeling threatened in a way I didn't understand but then it suddenly hit me like a load of bricks. Kids, marriage, and a home. Those were things I could never give Wyatt. There probably wasn't another man on earth who could take Wyatt away from me, but a woman . . .

"If you fellas stick around a while, then maybe John and me . . . Well, you know . . . It would be really nice for the young'uns." Her voice trailed off.

I couldn't see straight. I looked at Lettie and opened my mouth, then closed it again. I felt sick in my gut. I think I was suddenly more afraid of Lettie than I ever had been of Wyatt's pa. Before I could get my thoughts straight, though, Lettie burst out laughing.

"You should see yourself. You look like a hooked catfish gulping for air."

That's exactly how I felt, too. Trapped and struggling to breath.

"I . . . I don't understand . . . "

Lettie went back to her mending, her laughter gone and acting like nothing had happened. "I was just teasing with you."

I was more confused than before. Did Lettie suspect about Wyatt and me or not? Was she setting her sights on Wyatt? Maybe she was interested in him and was poking around a bit, trying to get more information. I studied her face from the corner of my eye but her mask was tight in its place. I worked hard to keep my fingers from twitching as I did my mending. Hadn't I just been thinking how much Lettie and I were alike? If Wyatt wanted himself a woman, it would make sense that he'd pick one just like me.

Lettie looked up at me as she put her thread to her teeth, ready to bite through it. Her eyes bored straight into mine, challenging me. I raised my head a might and met her gaze. Putting thread to mouth, I got set to bite, too. Staring hard at each other, we snapped our threads in two. Gauntlets had been thrown. I knew when I'd been called out and I wasn't about to sit around and play games. I believed in getting the enemy out in the open.

"You know nothing about him, Lettie. We could be fugitives for all you know. Murderers, horse thieves, rapists. You going to tell me you want to take that kind of chance with your children?"

"Living the life I've lived there are two things that have kept me alive: my instincts and knowing how to take care of myself. I've had plenty of men come through here thinking they could get a piece of whatever it was they were looking for and thinking they could take it without a fight. The ones who figured out fast enough that they were wrong, left standing up. The two who didn't figure it out are buried out back where no one's ever going to find them." She paused to let her words sink in. "My instincts are telling me that John, or whatever the hell his real name is, is the kind of man I want helping me to raise my young'uns. And my eyes tell me he's the kind of man I want sharing my bed. Whatever you've dragged him into is of no concern to me."

I felt my face getting red again. "What I've dragged him into? What the hell makes you think I dragged him into anything? How do you know he didn't do the dragging?"

She shoved her sewing into the basket and dropped it onto the floor. "Don't tell me you're going to try and deny that that boy would walk through fire to be with you. I know you can see that look in his eyes as well as I can. It would take dynamite to pry that boy away from you. You two are in trouble—that's plain to see—and I'm guessing you're the cause of it and he's just in it to be with you."

That woman had a way of changing directions that kept me struggling to stay on my feet.

"But . . . You understand about us? I thought you just said you wanted him for yourself."

"I said he is the kind of man I want helping me to raise my kids. I didn't say it was going to be easy making that happen." Lettie pulled a small dress out of the mending pile and eyed me. "He may never love me like he loves you, but I'm guessing I got a lot more to offer him than just dick which, from what I can tell, is about all you got to offer him."

We didn't talk much after that. Her words hit a little too close to my heart. It gave me a full head of steam and I found putting words together tough to do. Besides, I had some strategizing to do and it didn't involve chitchatting with the enemy.

When it was time for fixing the noontime meal, Lettie put her sewing aside and stood up. She smoothed out the creases in her dress and undid her hair. It was thick and long and fell over her shoulders, framing her face like a picture.

"You do any cooking, Dillon? Maybe you could help me fix a really special meal. I 'spect John will be right hungry and he'll appreciate a nice, big, home-cooked supper."

Shit. Kids, marriage, and home-cooking. She wasn't planning on fighting fair.

I smiled as big of a smile as I could muster and said, "I'd be most happy to help in any way I can, Lettie, but I have to admit cooking ain't my specialty."

"Oh." I saw the twinkling glint in her eye. "All right then. You just rest your feet and I'll make him . . . " She stopped and gave me a fake look of apology. "I mean I'll make all of us something really special."

Bitch.

Lettie went to the door and called for Daisy, then she set about fixing supper. As she moved around the kitchen her curves seemed to show more under her dress than they had before. She took off her shoes and padded from sink to table in her bare feet. She hummed while she worked, her voice clear and musical.

Daisy came running in, breathlessly telling about helping Wyatt before she'd even made it through the door. She stopped long enough to admire her ma's untied hair.

"You look so pretty, Ma. You should keep your hair that way. I'll bet John'll like it, too." Then she went back to chattering about how much fun she had helping John.

I wiped at my mouth, sweat and pressure building up. Dick, dick, dick. There had to be something more I had to offer Wyatt than just dick. Think, think.

When the cooking was all done the house smelled just like a home should: the aroma of warm bread and stewing meat filling the air. Lettie's top two blouse buttons were undone, showing just a hint of breasts. I had a hankering to strip off my pants and have my dick poking out from behind an apron when Wyatt walked in, but

I knew there were rules in this fight and parading around naked in front of children would probably break a few of them.

Lettie checked everything once more, including her hair and buttons, then told Daisy to get John and Toby.

"His name's Wyatt."

Lettie looked at me, suspicion clouding her eyes.

"What?"

"His name is Wyatt. Not John."

She stared at me for a bit, trying to figure me out, then she said sincerely, "Thank you." She turned back to Daisy and said, "Go call Wyatt and Toby to supper."

Daisy, unfazed, ran out the door shouting for Wyatt and her brother.

I can't rightly explain it but I felt it was for the best if Lettie and I started out on equal ground. Knowing Wyatt's real name seemed a part of that. Lettie stood with her hands on her hips, watching me and wondering if she were figuring me right.

"And you? What's your real name?"

"Deacon. Deke, for short."

She nodded. "Nice to meet you, Deke."

I nodded back. I thought about those two men she claimed were buried out back and I was pretty damn sure she wasn't making it up. Lettie was going to be a tough enemy but if I was going to lose Wyatt to anyone, I couldn't have picked a better someone myself.

Daisy burst back into the house and I wondered if that girl's engine ever ran out of steam.

"John . . . I mean, Wyatt says he's got too much to do. He's going to skip supper."

Lettie and I both sighed "shit" under our breath. She pulled her hair back into a ponytail and re-buttoned her blouse. I hobbled back to my chair and sat down, suddenly realizing how hard my dick was. Not being with Wyatt when I was expecting to made my stomach do a quick drop. I'd been counting on seeing that look in his eye. I needed to see that look; the one full of admiring that Lettie had mentioned. That look was my greatest weapon and I needed to use it every chance I got. Still, I had to admit it as right amusing seeing Lettie poking at her food now like it was just an annoyance and not her own secret weapon.

Toby came in with a bucket half full of milk. I figured most of their morning's milking was stored in the well to keep it fresh. Wyatt and I would have to take a look at their well and make sure they had a good water supply. It struck me as funny that I kept worrying about Lettie and what was fair to her. Before I could ponder on it too long, though, it was time to sit down and eat.

Lettie served up the food while she told the children Wyatt's and my real name. They seemed to accept it without question. I imagined they'd grown up learning to trust and rely on their mother. Accepting us was part of that trust.

Lettie and I didn't talk much, and Toby watched us, sensing that something was happening, but Daisy chattered away, talking about Wyatt and making me miss him even more.

After eating and cleaning up, Lettie gave Daisy a plateful of food to take out to Wyatt. "Don't want that boy dropping dead in the middle of something."

We got back to our mending and we managed to exchange a few niceties, but the longer I went without seeing Wyatt the harder it got to concentrate. I thought less about the battle between Lettie and me and more about how my body was feeling. It ached from wanting to be with him; my chest and my arms and my legs, they all ached. By the time evening meal rolled around, I was near to shaking from missing him. When Wyatt didn't show for that meal, either, I got downright angry. How come he wasn't missing me like I was missing him? I sure as hell wasn't going to be the needy one in this relationship. I had a good mind to sleep alone and see how he liked not having my dick nearby.

We finished cleaning up from dinner and I was so pissed and shaky that I was prepared to clobber Wyatt the minute he walked through the door. Lettie could have him all to herself for all I cared. I didn't want any part of a one-sided love. Hell, I'd never really wanted any part of him from the beginning. And it wasn't actually love, anyway. I just couldn't think of a better name for it. Men didn't love men. Everybody knew that.

And that's when he walked in, sweaty and dirty and shirtless from working. His hair stuck out from under his Stetson the same way it had the first time I saw him on his palomino. His muscles were hard and his skin was freshly browned. His eyes, carrying the blue from outside into the house with him, went straight for me. Their hunger made me stop breathing and I knew I wouldn't be denying Wyatt anything tonight. It was for certain, too, it wasn't home-cooked vittles those eyes were wanting.

I got my breath back and tossed a glance at Lettie. We both knew dick would be winning this round.

Not one to give up easy, though, Lettie stepped between us, keeping her back to me. Her hair was down again and I wondered how many buttons she'd undone this time.

"I saved some food for you, Wyatt. Let me get it for you."

Wyatt snatched his hat from his head and held it in front of his bulging crotch. He looked over Lettie's shoulder and his eyes begged for me.

I smiled a smile that I reckoned looked as smug as I felt and said, "Wyatt looks a might worn out, Lettie. I think I best be taking him to bed."

She shot me a look full of spitfire then walked back to the table.

Wyatt, afraid he'd hurt Lettie's feelings, sputtered compliments about her cooking and how much he'd appreciated having it brought out to him. "But Dillon's right. I'm plumb tuckered but good."

"Deke. I know his name is Deke." She was pissed and taking no pains to hide it.

Wyatt looked at me and I shrugged. "I'll explain it later. Time to get you to bed."

I grabbed him by the arm and started pulling him backward to the door. He tried to keep his hat in front of his crotch but I saw the circle of wet forming at the bulge.

"I promise I got a lot of work done, though, Lettie. I'll show you in the morning."

Lettie rolled her eyes and I pulled Wyatt out the door. We were racing across the yard before the latch had clicked shut. A few feet from the barn Wyatt grabbed my arm and jerked me to a stop.

"We need to be farther away. Out of earshot."

I shoved Wyatt forward, not too concerned about anything other than reaching the barn. "I'll gag you so you can't scream."

He stopped and crammed his hand hard up between my legs, squeezing my swollen dick. "Who says I'm the one who's going to be doing the screaming?"

His mouth was almost on mine. His lips were parted and his breath came out in short, hard, sweet-smelling puffs. I grabbed him by the throat and pushed him the rest of the way to the barn. He hit the wall hard. I pinned him there with a thigh to his cock and kissed him so deep he choked.

"I love you, Wyatt. More than stink loves shit. But you ain't man enough to make me scream. Don't you be forgetting that."

His heart banged against my chest and an odd sort of whimper eked out of him before he gasped, "Pond."

We took off running, shucking clothes as soon as we caught sight of water. When the dirt turned soft between our toes we tackled each other, our bodies hitting the wet sand with thuds and grunts. We wrestled and rolled, trying to pin each other. Wyatt pinned me first, sitting on my stomach and forcing my shoulders into the ground. My cock was flattened beneath his ass and his balls draped themselves on either side of it. He half smiled, half snarled at me, and spit dripped onto my cheek.

"Sorry. Let me get that for you."

He licked up the side of my face, rocking on my cock and grinding it between us. He kissed me hard, making me choke like I'd done to him. My cock burned against his cock and slime from both of them coated my stomach. I struggled but Wyatt pressed harder, my shoulders sinking deeper into the sand and his tongue reaching deeper into my throat. He pulled his mouth away from mine but I followed it, not ready for the contact to end. Wyatt smiled and leaned forward to kiss me again, when something seemed to catch in his brain.

"Hey. Wait a minute. What did you say back at the barn?"

"I don't remember. Get your lips back to kissing me or I'm going to stop letting you win."

Wyatt planted his knees on my wrists, making escape near impossible. "Letting me win? Deke, you ain't getting shit tonight unless you repeat what you said back at the barn."

"That's funny, Wyatt. We both know your hungry holes start yawning the minute they see me. You couldn't squeeze them two shut with my cock poking at them even if you tried."

"Say it again."

" 'That's funny, Wyatt. We both know . . .' "

He slammed his hips into my stomach, setting my cock on fire.

"Okay. I said something about shit stinking."

"My holes are squeezing shut . . . "

"Goddammit, Wyatt, you know what I said and you know that it's true."

Wyatt's smug grin covered his face. "Yes, I do but I want to hear it again when I'm really paying attention."

"Oh, fuck. All right. Wyatt Jennings, I love you. I ain't never loved no one before in my life but I know that's what I feel for you. I feel like I've been mule-kicked since the first moment I laid eyes on you."

Wyatt's grip loosened as my words poured out. His eyes were going soft and dreamy. I was afraid I couldn't stop confessing things once I'd gotten started but it felt kinda good. Scary but good.

"You satisfied?"

He smiled and let me loose. "I would have settled for the stinky shit line."

He pushed off of me and landed on his back in the sand, his open legs an invitation. I climbed on top and worked my cock into him. His hands ran up my back and into my hair and I kissed him. His heels hooked the back of my knees and I rocked, kissing and fucking and forgetting everything but him. He pulled his mouth away from mine long enough to whisper "I love you, too," then we went back to fucking. Connected through Wyatt's holes we rolled in the wet sand until he was on top again. He laid his head on my shoulder and I held tight. I didn't move much after that because Wyatt started doing a slow dance with his body still held close to mine. His insides were hot and muscular, squeezing and releasing my cock like a soft hand milking it. I grabbed a fistful of his hair and buried my nose in it while Wyatt tortured me with his slow, snake-like fuck. When I finally came it wasn't in violent spurts but in a steady flow, thick and slow as honey. It didn't seem like it would ever drizzle dry as he kept milking me with his ass.

When the flow finally stopped, Wyatt pulled himself off me. He rolled onto his back and the lower half of his body went into the water. His hard cock, still jumping with heartbeats, poked out of the pond. I crawled to him and settled myself in the cool water between his legs.

Wyatt pulled slowly on his cock until a thick bead bubbled out of his slit and joined the beads of pond water dotting his cock head. Then, with his head back in the damp sand and his eyes closed, he aimed his dick at me. I gathered each bead, one at a time, with the tip of my tongue, saving the come drop for last. I twirled my tongue over and under Wyatt's cock head then slipped my lips down it. I found more beads inside his slit, and I sucked until he made a sound of pain, his hips rising up to meet my face. I slid my mouth down Wyatt's cock, half of which was below water. When my nose-tip touched wet, I took a deep breath and swallowed the rest of Wyatt's cock. I pumped him with my throat and the faster I went, the better my timing had to be for sucking air. Wyatt's fingers clawed holes in the sand and his body twisted beneath me. Waves rippled away and back, crashing together at Wyatt's cock and splashing water onto my face.

Wyatt came when my throat strokes were so fast that I no longer had time to breathe. I was simply holding my breath and fucking. Nothing mattered to me but the reward of feeling Wyatt's come ricocheting off the back of my throat and burning a trail down to my stomach. He finally grabbed the back of my head and held me under water as his come did exactly what I wanted it to do.

I must've passed out. When I came to my throat and lungs were on fire and the biting taste of Wyatt filled even my nose. Wyatt was on his side, still partly in the water, lightly slapping my face and smiling down on me.

"Thought I'd lost you."

I squinted up at his contented face and coughed up some come-water. "Yeah. You look real broken up."

"Sorry but it's hard to get too teary-eyed when I just shot the most incredible load of my life."

"Well, at least you got your priorities straight. I'll give you that much." I pulled myself up onto one elbow and faced him. "And I gotta admit, if I were going to pick my way to die . . . "

Wyatt's face kind of melted from contentment to pure bliss and he pushed me onto my back again. He laid his head on my chest and I fingered his silky, wet hair. The pond lapped so steadily I could scarcely separate it from the sound of Wyatt's breathing. Coyotes bayed and yipped, but it was far in the distance and sounded more like singing, not their usual crazed sound of mourning. The fragrance of sage and lilac and chaparral added to the burn in my nose from Wyatt's come. We stayed folded together that way, half in and half out of the water, until Wyatt started to shiver.

I rubbed my hands over his body and whispered to him. "Come on, Sweetlips. Time to go inside."

Wyatt moaned but got to his feet. We gathered our things and walked naked, back to the barn. I dried us both off while Wyatt swayed upright, eyes closed and face peaceful.

"You need to sleep tonight, boy. You ain't had any real sleep since before that night at the bunkhouse."

"God, how long ago was that?"

"I don't know any more. The days have all run together."

"Think they're still looking for us?"

"You know your daddy better'n me, Wyatt. What do you think?"

"I think he'll chase us 'til the day he dies. My pa don't like losing."

"That'd be my guess, too."

Wyatt stopped swaying and got down under the blankets. I slid in next to him.

"I'm sorry I got you into this, Deke."

I kissed the tip of his nose. "No you ain't."

Wyatt settled into his spot—head on my chest and legs wrapped round mine—and I felt his smile against my skin. "You're right. I ain't."

CHAPTER 6

MORNING CAME WAY BEFORE I wanted it to, but Wyatt was up and prodding me before the rooster had even crowed.

"C'mon, stud. No more lazin' around the house, chatting and sewing for you. Today you do a man's work."

I shoved Wyatt away and rolled onto my side, pulling the blanket over my head.

"C'mon, Deke. Toby's gonna be in here soon. We gotta get dressed." Wyatt tried to pull back the blanket but I held tight. "Deke, get your ass out of bed."

"If you didn't keep me up most the night fucking maybe I'd have an easier time getting my ass out of bed in the morning."

A hand slid under the blanket and found my morning hard-on.

"Well, if you can't handle it . . . "

I slapped his hand away. "Boy, you're nothing but an appetizer for me. I've slept through wilder sex than you."

Wyatt's fingers came back, curling around my dick in a way that proved he'd learned an awful lot about dick handling in the short time I'd known him. In particular, he'd learned an awful lot about handling my dick. I faked some snoring and tried to keep my body still but Wyatt's quick-learning fingers had me soiling the sheets in record time.

"Now get up. We got work to do."

I got dressed while watching Wyatt clean my come off his hand with his tongue. I was stumped trying to think of a better way to start my day.

We passed Toby in the yard on his way to milk the cow and neither Wyatt nor I could keep from ruffling his hair as we went by. Toby complained and tried to dodge us but his smile gave him away as he whistled his way across the rest of the yard.

We reached the house and the smell of coffee hit us before we opened the cabin door. Wyatt stepped inside, took in a deep smell, and announced, "Lettie, if I were the marrying kind I would marry you for your coffee brewing alone."

His words stopped me short and Lettie threw me a smile.

"What about me, Wyatt? What would you marry me for?"

Wyatt scooped Daisy up and stood her on a chair. He held her long braids straight out from the sides of her head.

"I'd marry you for your pigtails. I ain't never seen a prettier sight than these here pigtails."

"You have to finish your chores, young lady, before you can marry anyone."

Daisy giggled as Wyatt tied her braids together on top of her head.

"Yes'm." Daisy hopped down from the chair. "We made some coffee cake, Wyatt. Do you and Dillon . . . I mean, Deke, want some before you start your chores?"

"Deke's not doing chores today, Daisy."

Wyatt and I looked at Lettie.

"But my feet feel almost normal, Lettie. I'm ready to get out and help with the heavy work."

"And you'll be mending fences and building pens in bare feet, will you?"

I looked down at my scarred, naked feet. I'd gotten so used to being bootless I'd forgotten.

"You'll be bleeding and hobbled up again in no time."

"But we got the clothes mending done yesterday." I started feeling cornered. Besides needing to be outside working with Wyatt in the fiercest of ways, I suspected Lettie was up to something. "I'm sorry, Lettie, but I gotta get outside and do me some real work."

"I know. That's why you and I are going into town to get you a new pair of boots."

Wyatt and I looked at each other. Going into town was not something we oughta be doing. I had no doubt Lettie suspected we were wanted. Maybe her plan was to turn me in and keep Wyatt for herself.

"Deke's too weak still. The trip would be too much for him." Wyatt, not wanting me to go for his own reasons, blurted out an excuse before I could say anything.

Lettie set her fists on her hips and narrowed her eyes at Wyatt. "But he's not too weak to mend fences and chop wood?" Lettie shifted her eyes to me. "You gents wouldn't be afraid to be seen in town for some reason, would you?"

She knew the answer already. I saw it in her eyes and heard it in her mocking voice.

"Of course not." I answered quick before Wyatt could open his mouth again. "Going in for boots is a dandy idea but I got no money to buy them with."

Lettie smiled her smug smile and said, "I do. It's not a lot but it's enough to get your feet covered." She held up her hand to cut me off from protesting. "I'll add it to the list of things you have to work off."

"Then I'm going, too."

"No." Lettie and I both spun on Wyatt. If I were going to have a knockdown, drag-out with a woman over my man I'd just as soon not have Wyatt witnessing it.

"Wyatt, I'd really appreciate it if you'd watch Toby and Daisy for me."

I nodded in agreement. "I think that would be best, Wyatt."

His voice whined. "But I don't . . . "

"I'll bring back candy."

I shot a glance at Lettie. I had to admit she'd figured out some essentials about Wyatt pretty quick. Like the fact that he was more boy than man sometimes.

"Peppermints?"

She had him hooked. "If they have them."

Wyatt looked at me then nodded. "All right. I'll stay here."

We sat down for coffee and cake and decided my name would be Dillon Marshall, in case anybody asked. I would be Lettie's new hired hand and I lost my boots in a campfire accident. Of course, Wyatt couldn't leave it at that and he got us all, Lettie included, to laughing with his complicated story about the details of the campfire accident, which involved exploding stills, a hornet's nest, and a blind, drunken billy goat.

Once we were finished and ready to go, I pulled Wyatt into the barn and gave him a kiss. I felt one of them odd premonitions building in my belly and suddenly found it hard to let loose of him. We'd be apart from each other—truly apart—for the first time since it all began. There were more than a hundred things that could go wrong while I was away from him and there were probably two hundred more things I hadn't even thought of. I was beginning to think leaving him behind wasn't such a good idea after all.

"You all right, Deke?"

"Yeah, Sweetlips. I'm all right."

"Going to miss me, aren't you?"

"Probably. I had an aching tooth pulled once. Missed it, too, but got over it."

Wyatt pulled me close and we kissed again. He laid his head on my shoulder and sighed my name. "Deke?" His voice was soft and dreamy.

"Yes, Wyatt?" I pressed my nose into his neck and prepared to say the words I knew he needed to hear.

"You won't let Lettie forget my peppermints, will you?"

I slapped the back of his head hard. He yelped and I gave him one more peck then headed out to Lettie. I had no idea what she had planned for me but I hoped she knew she was in for one hell of a fight.

We hooked the plow horse up to Lettie's wagon and the two of us started toward town. Lettie said it would take close to two hours to get there and two hours back. That was more than enough time to get in some serious battling. I wondered if I should take the fight to her or let her make the first move. Since this war was her idea I decided the first move should be hers.

We traded nothing but pleasantries for the first few miles. Stretches of silence were broken up by comments about the weather, compliments for the children, and predictions regarding the size of Lettie's corn crop.

When I said, "Come spring you should have lots of little ones running around," after Lettie said, "I think I got me some good breeders this time, not just a bunch of layers," she decided to make her first move.

She took a quick breath and blurted out, "One of them little ones could be Wyatt's."

It took me by surprise and made my stomach churn, but I decided to play dumb and let her do all the rationalizing.

"I don't think Wyatt can get pregnant, Lettie."

She shot venom back at me. "No, and neither can you. But I can." She took a deep, steadying breath. "I can give Wyatt a child."

I took my own deep breath. "Wyatt's never mentioned wanting a child." It sounded weak, even to me.

"It takes only one look at him with my young ones to see . . . "She started to say more but didn't. She didn't need to. She'd made her point well enough.

We didn't talk for the next mile or so. Her silence wasn't smug. She'd won a small victory but it didn't seem to make either of us particularly happy.

She finally spoke the words that were filling my head.

"If you love him, Deke, you should let him go, because he'll never leave you on his own."

"That's kinda his choice, don't you think?"

I could feel her eyes on me but I kept looking away.

"The two of you . . . "She sounded as miserable as I felt. "People aren't going to leave you alone."

Lettie wasn't fighting fair. I'd expected her to pull some female tricks, call me names and tell me all the things she could do for Wyatt that I couldn't. I hadn't expected her to speak my own common sense at me; repeat the very truths I was always throwing at Wyatt. I wasn't expecting her to sound like she cared.

I finally mustered the courage to look at her.

"It's his choice, Lettie. I admit I don't have the backbone to give him up but even if I did, it's his choice. If I walk out on him with him still wanting me, he'll just keep looking for me and his chance for a real life will be gone." I looked back out at the desert, nothingness stretching to forever in all directions. "It's his choice, Lettie."

We didn't say another word until the tops of the town buildings showed on the horizon.

"I'm sorry for some of the things I said." Lettie wasn't used to apologizing and this one kinda caught in her throat. "I know you give him a world more than just dick."

I nodded. "I think that's his favorite, though."

She laughed then said quickly, like it wasn't important, "Folks in town aren't real fond of me."

It was a warning to me but I could tell it was a warning she had no intention of explaining. I nodded and watched the town grow bigger before us. I pulled my hat down tight on my head and tipped it lower over my face. The closer we got to people and telegraphs and jail cells, the lower I seemed to sink. Coming to town suddenly felt like a very bad idea.

Lettie pulled the wagon to a stop at the back of the general store. The town was small but the store was big, serving as the central point to many of the small towns in the territory.

Lettie's face, almost always mask-like, looked downright frozen as she knocked on the back door of the store. A church-looking lady, narrow and pulled tight, opened the door. She recognized Lettie, that was for certain, and her pulled-tight face went close to splitting.

"What do you want?"

"I need some things."

The woman looked at me. She had tiny eyes with no light in them and they felt like they were boring holes in me.

"Who's that?"

"My new hired hand." The woman's eyes slid down to my bare feet and Lettie said, "He needs some boots. I need a list full of things." Lettie held out a piece of paper and a handful of money.

The tiny eyes returned to my face and the woman's disgust was plain.

"What happened to his boots?"

"They accidentally got burnt in a campfire."

The woman crinkled her nose, took the money Lettie offered, and left without another word.

Lettie looked at me, straight-faced, and said, "When he got pushed in the fire by a blind, drunken billy goat being chased by a nest full of pissed off hornets."

I busted out laughing and Lettie giggled despite her best efforts at keeping serious.

The woman returned and we were instantly silent. She eyed us suspiciously but I imagined that was most likely the only expression she had. She put three pair of boots out the door for me to try on. I chose an ugly pair of light brown ones that I figured were the cheapest. They fit decent and that was good enough for me.

The woman picked up the other boots and went back inside. We waited by the wagon until two young boys appeared at the door with armfuls of supplies. I loaded them up and Lettie asked one of the boys for her change.

"There ain't none," was his reply, and both boys went back inside, laughing as they slammed the door behind them.

Lettie didn't answer my look. She just climbed in the wagon and said, "I need to stop by the doctor's place, too, and get a few more things."

I climbed into the wagon and sat beside her. She clucked at the horse and we moved forward, staying to the backs of the buildings.

The doc's office was at the end of the main row we were traveling behind. We stopped and jumped down from the wagon. I noticed there was a narrow alley between the doctor's office and the building next to it. Through it I could see the sheriff's office across the street. I stopped and stared, my mind full of wondering.

"I can go in and see what I can find out." Lettie saw where I was looking. "Course, I need to know what I'm looking for."

I didn't know what to do. I was itching to know if there were wanted posters out for us, or if Jennings's men had made it this far, but I wasn't completely sure I trusted Lettie yet. Besides, I didn't think it was right getting her and the children more involved in our problems. Still, if word had gotten this far about Wyatt and me, we needed to know about it.

"Let's get your supplies first."

Once again, instead of walking through the front door like most folks, Lettie knocked on the back door. This time she had to knock several times before getting an answer.

The door was finally opened by a very pretty young woman dressed in fine skirts and smelling of roses. As soon as she recognized Lettie her face turned sour, much like the woman at the general store.

"What do you want?"

Lettie handed her a list and some money, just as she had done at the store. The woman looked at me but asked no questions. A little girl appeared from behind the woman's skirts and the woman pushed her back so hard that the child almost fell.

"You stay inside." The woman's voice was angry but fearful, like the voice of a mother scolding a child caught doing something dangerous.

I looked at Lettie, who stood tall and silent, her face a blank. She stayed that way, not looking at me, not talking, until the woman returned with the supplies, which she shoved at Lettie before shutting the door in her face.

Lettie tucked the supplies under the seat of the wagon then turned to me.

"What have you decided? Do I go to the sheriff's office or not?"

I suddenly felt small for not trusting Lettie. It was clear to see she was more my equal than my enemy. Not all fugitives, after all, are on the run.

"It's not important, Lettie. Let's just head back to your place."

I turned to walk back to the wagon but she grabbed me by the arm and spun me to her. Her face was storming in the same way Wyatt's did when he was especially riled with me.

"You listen and you listen good, Deke. If you even think about pitying me I'll . . . I'll . . . I'll tell Wyatt you slept with me."

"Why . . . You little bitch." I tried to look shocked because, truth be told, that's what I was, but my life suddenly struck me as so funny that I couldn't keep my face straight. I was a dick-loving fugitive running for my life, in love with the cause of all my problems and stuck in the middle of a catfight with a woman over my man. I started laughing, and soon my laughing turned to sputtering with a lot of snorting thrown in and every time I tried to say something, my laughter would head off in a whole 'nother direction and the snorting would get worse.

Lettie watched me at first like she might watch a rabid dog coming too near, but when I started on my second round of snorts, each one setting me off worse than the one before, she started struggling to keep herself serious.

I managed to squeeze out, "He'd never believe you. You ain't man enough for me to fuck," and that was the end of Lettie's self control. We ended up doubled over, hanging onto the sides of the wagon, gasping to breathe, and throwing insults at each other when we could manage it.

It took a good long time to get ourselves to the point where we could talk without getting lost in laughter. Tears streaming and sides aching, we finally managed to pull ourselves together.

"Well," Lettie wiped at her eyes and took a deep breath. "I think I'll go see what I can find out at the sheriff's office."

I nodded, with no more thoughts of stopping her. I watched her from the little alleyway as she walked across the street with her exaggerated pride. A few people pointed and several stared, and I hurt for Lettie in a way that felt familiar. I didn't know the particulars of why people treated her the way they did, but I knew the how of it. I'd been on the receiving end myself. I couldn't help but feel again that we were equals, fighting the same thing and not each other.

Lettie disappeared into the sheriff's office. The longer she was gone the more nervous I got. What if they knew she'd been helping us and locked her up? What if Jennings was in there this very minute? I looked up and down the main street for any signs of Crooked J men or stock, but saw nothing. What if I'd been wrong about her and she was turning me in?

By the time Lettie came back out I'd worked myself into a lather. As soon as she was within reach I grabbed her arm and pulled her out of sight.

"Are you all right? I thought for sure they'd found you out."

"Settle down, Deke. I'm fine. I was in there for five minutes at the most."

I let go of her. "Really? That's all?"

She raised her eyebrows but only said, "The sheriff has all his posters up on the wall and I didn't see anything that matched you and Wyatt."

I nodded. "We must have thrown them off our track. For now, at least. I 'spect they'll make their way here eventually, though."

I could see Lettie wanted to hear more, but I climbed into the wagon and asked if she wanted me to do the driving on the way home.

"No." She climbed up next to me. "I can manage."

I knew I owed her some explaining, but it took me until we were out of sight of the town before I could come out with the words.

"Wyatt's pa is the one who's after us. He caught us . . . Wyatt and me . . . Together."

I knew the word "fucking" wouldn't shock Lettie, but it didn't seem a fitting word any more to describe what Wyatt and I'd been doing that night. It probably never was the proper word for it. At the time, though, it was the only word I could face.

"Anyway, he was planning on killing me but Wyatt stopped him. Somebody else got killed in the middle of it all and now Wyatt and me are on the run. His pa's not a man who takes well to losing so he's not likely to stop looking any time soon."

Lettie nodded, looking ahead at the road. "I sort of figured it was something like that. Wyatt looks like he comes from rich stock."

"And I don't?"

Lettie just smiled.

"We don't want any harm to come to you or the children, Lettie. We'll move on as soon as we're even with what we owe you."

Without batting an eye, Lettie said, "I still want Wyatt, Deke. Him being married and father to my children does more good for all of us than him running from the law with you." She looked me square in the face. "The only one who makes out otherwise is you."

It took me a beat or two to get a hold of what she was saying. I'd thought our battle was over and she threw me for a loop by starting it all up again. When I got my senses back, I grabbed the reins and pulled the horse to a stop.

"Lettie, I admire you." I nodded back toward the town. "Now more than ever. But what gives you the right to decide what's best for Wyatt?"

"My whole life, Deke. That's what gives me the right." I saw something fierce and ugly rising to the surface but she stopped herself before I could see too much. "How long have you and Wyatt been together?"

"I don't know for sure. We kinda lost track with all the running."

"Weeks? Months?"

"Days, I guess. Maybe a week." It surprised me to realize it was true and it sounded foolish coming out of my mouth.

"Days?" Lettie would've laughed if she hadn't been so angry. "Days? Is that all? And all of it on the run?"

I didn't answer. The truth of it was still sinking in for me.

Lettie started the horse up again. "You have no idea what you're in for. No idea."

"I ain't exactly a newborn, Lettie. I know what folks do to anything that's different. I've tried explaining it to Wyatt and he's seen some for himself, but everybody's got to learn on their own. Nothing can't just be taught. It's got to be learned, too."

"Then give him a lesson he can learn from. Leave. Run out on him. Break his heart. Be as mean about it as you can be."

"I told you I can't."

"And I told you if you love him you will."

I took the reins from her and steered the wagon off the road, pulling the horse to a stop and facing Lettie. I was more than a little pissed.

"Why don't you tell me all about this life of yours that makes you so fucking high and mighty that you can tell other folks how to live theirs? You got it rough, Lettie, that's easy to see. But Wyatt and me—men like us—we deal with things you can't even begin to understand. Love and happiness—those are just words to us. A joke, almost. Things we don't even let ourselves think about." I grabbed her arm and squeezed, finding myself wanting her to feel somehow the importance of what I was saying. "With Wyatt . . . " My voice kind of caught and I had to work at getting the words out. "With Wyatt, I find myself believing sometimes because he's so all-fired certain . . . It's not just for me, Lettie. It's for Wyatt, too. Maybe if more men like us try . . . "

I couldn't finish and we stared hard at each other, me hoping she'd understand and her looking like she was dead set against it. She finally pulled my fingers from her arm and spoke her words slowly.

"I've seen what happens when people want to believe, Deke. I've seen how meaningless love really is. I know you know the truth, too. Wyatt thinks love can make it all pretty and perfect and you want to make it that way for him, but you know the truth the same as I do."

I looked away, pissed at everything she was saying.

"Wyatt doesn't know the truth, Deke. He really is like a newborn and it's going to get him killed. His believing in things that can't be are going to get him killed. I'll say it again. If you love him, you'll keep that from happening."

I shook my head. It was one thing hearing myself say the words to Wyatt, but it was another thing hearing someone else say them to me. Trying to convince Wyatt to leave me was safe. I knew in my heart it wouldn't happen. So it was safe to act like the reasonable one, to tell him he couldn't make a life with me, to tell him to move on. But it was a whole 'nother story to put the doing on me, to make me the one who had to do the right thing.

"My pa . . . "Lettie started out still fired up, but she stopped and took a deep breath. When she blew it out, the angry seemed to go with it; the stubbornness she carried everywhere just sort of sighed away and she seemed suddenly smaller. And very weary.

"My pa moved here when I was just a baby. My ma had died of some fever right after having me. My pa was a gunsmith and we lived in town. He came to be respected, both because of his smithing skills and because of his way of wanting to make things better. He was always speaking out at town meetings and arranging things and trying to get folks to work together." She kind of laughed but not because of something she thought was funny. "Everyone called him a God-fearing man." She took another breath before going on. "When I was about six he married the widow Blaine. She'd been a widow for a couple of years and her husband had been a good friend of my pa's, so everyone in town thought they were the perfect match. Especially since she couldn't have children of her own. It seemed like God Himself had arranged it. My pa would get a wife, I would get a ma, and the widow would get a child." She stopped talking again. She seemed to watch something on the horizon but it wasn't something I could see. "I actually believe they loved each other. Really loved each other. My pa was kind of edgy at first but that was to be expected, given how long he'd lived without a woman. But soon, he was happier than I'd ever seen him. And I was, too. I liked the widow. It seemed natural to call her 'Ma'. Nice, even." She stopped again but this time she didn't start back up. She just sat and stared far ahead at that something I couldn't see.

I gave her some time but when she still didn't start back up, I said, "I don't understand, Lettie. Your pa . . . Was he like Wyatt and me? Is that what you're trying to tell me?"

She pulled herself away from the horizon and looked at me, confused; almost surprised that I was even there.

"What?"

"Was your pa like Wyatt and me?"

"No." She shook her head, looking a little annoyed that I wasn't understanding. "My pa was my ma."

Now it was my turn to look confused. "I . . . don't understand."

Tears suddenly rose up in her eyes and she looked away from me, embarrassed 'cause she knew I'd seen.

"About two years after marrying the widow, my pa got shot by a customer who didn't want to pay for a gun he'd ordered. He was only shot in the shoulder but he was out cold when they found him. They took him to the doc's office and Ma and I . . . "She wiped angrily at her eyes and cleared her throat. "I called her 'Ma' . . . We went there, too. We stood there watching as they took my pa's shirt off to take care of the wound. That's when we saw." She looked straight at me, almost like she was daring me. "My pa was actually a woman."

I was too stunned to say anything, even though my mind was spinning with questions.

She looked away when she saw that I wasn't going to do whatever it was she expected me to do, and she kept on with her remembering. "He was wearing these sort of bindings that kept his chest flat. I looked around, not really understanding what I was seeing, but I knew from the other's faces that they were shocked. Even my ma. It was clear she didn't know. And it was very clear, even as young as I was, that what they were looking at made them afraid. It made them sick and it made them very afraid."

I noticed Lettie's hands, which had been tight together in her lap, were starting to shake. It was a disturbing thing to watch a person reliving her life, and it was even more disturbing to see a woman like Lettie so close to falling apart.

"My pa came round while everybody was still trying to get a hold of what it was they were seeing. I remember the look on his face . . . the shame. He wasn't afraid, even though I'm sure he knew what was going to happen. He was just . . . embarrassed." She shook her head, upset at herself. "It was worse than that. It was as if he was disfigured and his mask had been torn away."

Her hands were shaking so bad she was having trouble stopping them, so I laid one of mine on top and she opened them up. I slipped mine inside and she closed hers shut over it.

"I wanted to tell him right then—more than I ever had—how much I loved him. I'd never before seen anyone so in need of hearing those words. He looked right at me, hoping that if anyone could . . . "Her head bowed, a regret she could never fix making it impossible for her to keep it up. "But the words just wouldn't come out. I loved my pa with all of my heart but I just couldn't say it. When he needed it most, I just couldn't say it." She looked at me and her pain was too much to see. She crushed my hand in hers and her eyes pleaded with me to make it right somehow. "They took me out of the room and I know they killed him and I know he almost wanted it because of the shame, but he died believing no one loved him and it wasn't true." I pulled her to me and she buried her face against my chest. "It wasn't true."

I let her cry against my chest, not holding her because it didn't seem right, but letting her use me to hide her face. She cried a long time but suddenly stopped and sat up, her mask back in place but the streaks down her cheeks and the red in her eyes telling the truth.

"It took me a long time afterward to even figure out what I should call him when I talked about him or thought about him. He? She? Ma? Pa? They wanted me to call him 'she' and I tried to for a bit, but whenever I did I felt like I was betraying him." She looked at me and she was sitting straight again. "They wanted to take even that from him—his daughter's memory of her father. That's how afraid they were. But he was my pa, Deke. He may have given birth to me like a woman, but at some point he decided to live his life the way he thought he should and he was my pa."

Lettie gathered up the reins and started the horse toward home again, looking as strong and in control as she usually looked. Watching her I knew she could survive just about anything. She really would be my choice for looking after Wyatt if anything should happen to me. It was scary and comforting at the same time. It made our battle over Wyatt even odder than it already was.

I didn't want to bother her any more but I was curious about her life after that. "What happened to you? After your pa . . . died? Did you stay with your stepma?"

Lettie's voice was matter-of-fact. No more guilt, no more emotion.

"My 'ma' had left town before I even made it home from the doc's office. No one else in town wanted to take me in. After all, a freak's child is still a freak. Finally, an old hermit from the desert agreed to take me home with him to help around his place. That's how I ended up on that little piece of heaven I got. I was eight then. Toby was born four years later. The old man died shortly after Daisy was born." She looked me in the eye with that unflinching dare of hers. "I know how to take bad and find the good in it. I got me the two most precious gifts I could ask for from that old hermit—Toby and Daisy. Wyatt is my chance to give them what they deserve. He's close to loving them both already and I think he can learn to love me, too. I know it will never be like he loves you, but it will be love. A truer love than my pa had with the widow because I already know what Wyatt is. And I can make him happy, Deke. I promise you I will. He'll have the kind of life he can never have with you." She stopped and looked away. "I'm sorry, Deke. You're a good man. I'm not trying to hurt you."

I looked away, too. I knew she meant it when she said she was sorry, but she was lying when she said she wasn't trying to hurt me. She'd meant to tell the truth and the truth brought the worst kind of pain.

"I'm asking you, please. Do the right thing, Deke."

CHAPTER 7

WHEN WE GOT BACK to Lettie's place, Daisy was serving up the noonday meal. Wyatt had just finished working on the henhouse and he was shirtless, sweaty and browned and smiling from ear to ear. Toby was with him, shirtless, too, and watching Wyatt's every move. They were laughing.

Both children ran to greet their mother. Wyatt moved toward me, his smile changing as he got closer, from little boy funning to grown-up sinfulness. I'd always loved the way Wyatt looked at me; desire and playfulness rolled into one, but now all I could think of were Lettie's words about me having nothing to offer but dick. I hated that her words might be true but right then I needed him to be wanting me, even if it was just for dick. I didn't care. I just needed him to want me.

He was a few feet away and I could feel my body loosening as it waited for his touch. I wanted to be believing all those things that his touch made me believe.

"Peppermints!" Toby's and Daisy's squeals made me jump. "Peppermints and rock candy."

Wyatt stopped, his eyes as wide as the children's. "You got peppermints? Really?" He turned away from me and went to Lettie, crowding around her with the two kids and holding out his hand for his share.

"I told you I'd get you some, didn't I?" Lettie seemed to be making an effort not to look at me.

"Yes, you did. You're a woman of your word, Lettie."

I watched them laughing and enjoying their candy for as long as I could stomach it then I headed for the barn. I wasn't normally one to waste time on self-pity, but I felt a powerful case of it coming on fast. I wondered how many peppermints it would take before Wyatt even noticed I was gone.

It was almost a disappointment when he came into the barn right behind me.

"You all right, Deke? How'd it go in town?"

"Fine. Doesn't look like the word's gotten this far about us."

Wyatt came up behind me and kissed the back of my neck. He pressed his body against mine and rested his head on my shoulder; then he sighed pure happy. I laid my cheek against his hair and thought about that contented sigh of his. I tried to think if I'd heard it more since coming to Lettie's, but with him leaning into me, and the scent of him and honey and peppermint filling my nose, it was hard to remember a time when we both weren't sighing that sigh.

"Wyatt?"

"Hmm?"

"You seem happy here."

"I am."

"How come?"

Wyatt raised his head off my shoulder. "What do you mean, 'how come'?"

"I don't know. Just what is it about this place that makes you so happy?"

Wyatt stepped around so that he was facing me.

"You all right, Deke? You sure something didn't happen in town?"

I pulled his face to me and kissed him. "I'm sure. I just like to know what makes you happy. That's all."

"You know the answer to that." His sin-filled smile was back and his hand slid between my legs. "This big old cock of yours is what makes me happy."

I kissed him hard and let him rub my cock to fullness, but I think it's fair to say that that was the first time I'd ever wished I didn't have a dick.

The rest of the day was normal enough. Wyatt and I worked outside together; Lettie and I were pleasant to each other. I studied Wyatt when he was around the kids and I watched his face when he talked with Lettie. He seemed to be always smiling. There were times when I'd swear he was wagging his tail. I had trouble following conversations 'cause Lettie's words were filling my head. I tried to picture myself sneaking out on Wyatt in the middle of the night, but it just wasn't a picture I could conjure. "Do the right thing" kept repeating in my ears but I honestly didn't know what the right thing was. There had to be some middle ground, some way to give Wyatt what he deserved without ripping his heart out in the process. There had to be some way to let me keep what I thought I'd never have. My mind couldn't find it, though, and I felt weary from the trying.

I took my leave early after dinner and Wyatt followed. We didn't say much. Wyatt seemed to know I wasn't in the mood for words. We got naked and into bed and he settled into his spot—head on my chest and legs tangled with mine—and he sighed that sigh.

"Wouldn't it be nice if this could be our home? We'd make a good family. You and me and Lettie and the young 'uns." He snuggled deeper against me, yawning as he drifted off to sleep. "People wouldn't even have to know." And he was out.

I wasn't far behind him. I fought it a bit because Wyatt's words were prodding at me, but the trip with Lettie and the work with Wyatt had worn me down and I couldn't keep my mind open.

I don't know how long I slept but the next thing I knew, I was looking down the wrong end of a rifle barrel. It took a bit of rubbing at my eyes to realize it was Toby at the other end of the barrel.

"What did you do to her?" Toby's hands were shaking a bit and his face was tight with the effort not to cry.

I shook Wyatt while I tried to sit up. Toby pushed the rifle closer and I stayed put.

"Toby, what's wrong?"

Wyatt mumbled, still asleep.

"What did you do to my ma?"

I shook Wyatt harder. "Wyatt, wake up."

There was real fear in Toby's eyes, and I knew something must be wrong for a boy like Toby to be so fearful. I ignored the rifle and tried to sit up again.

"What's wrong with your ma, Toby? What happened?"

I punched Wyatt hard in the arm and he came to quick.

"My ma's crying. I ain't never known her to cry before. Ever. It's gotta be something you done. She ain't been acting right since she got back from town with you." Toby put the rifle sights to his eye and aimed it at my head. His eyes were filling with tears. He was looking like the scared little boy he really was and not the grown man he'd learned to be.

I got to my knees and held out my hand. "Toby, you know I wouldn't hurt your ma. We need to go inside and see what's wrong. Put down the rifle, Toby."

His hands shook but he didn't pull away as I reached for the gun. I wrapped my fingers 'round the barrel and slowly pulled it toward me. Toby let go and I laid the rifle down. Wyatt held out his arms and Toby went into them, no longer fighting back his tears.

"Let's go see what's wrong."

Toby nodded and we headed to the house.

Once inside we told Toby to get to bed then we knocked on Lettie's bedroom door. We heard sniffling and throat clearing before she told us to come in. When she saw it was Wyatt and me, her face reddened and she wiped angrily at her eyes.

"What do you want?"

"Toby was worried. Said you were crying."

"I wasn't. I had a bad dream. That's all. He shouldn't have bothered you."

"He was scared. He's never heard you cry before."

Lettie suddenly burst into tears, water spurting like a sprung well. "I told you I wasn't crying. Now go away."

I moved closer to the bed. Comforting sobbing women was not something I was generally familiar with and doing it twice in one day was definitely a record. I looked over at Wyatt and could tell he was going to be less than useless.

"Lettie, if you could just tell us what's wrong . . ."

A stream of words squeaked and squeezed their way out between Lettie's sobs. She pointed at both Wyatt and me several times and blew her nose twice but there wasn't much of anything, words or gestures, that was actually decipherable. It was hard to believe this was the same Lettie I'd gone to town with: the rock solid woman who I'd been fearing would take my man. Even when she'd cried earlier, there'd been a kind of dignity to it and her story. This was just plain pathetic.

I looked at Wyatt again. "I'm not getting any of this. Are you?"

"I heard something about making babies and I stopped listening."

"Yeah, she mentioned something about wanting to give you one when we were on our way to town but I told her the peppermints would be enough."

A hairbrush sailed across the room and hit me in the chest. I looked at Lettie and she was struggling against both smiling and crying, but it looked like the smiling was starting to win.

Wyatt leaned close to me and whispered loud enough so that Lettie could hear, "Whose baby was she going to give me?"

A shoe hit Wyatt in the head.

"Get out of here, both of you. I'd rather face nightmares than you two jackasses."

Like clouds clearing from my head, an idea suddenly came to me. An idea so good I had to sit down on the edge of Lettie's bed.

"Do you know what Wyatt said to me, Lettie, just before he fell asleep tonight?"

She rolled her eyes. "I can guess but I don't think it would be proper for me to repeat it."

I could hear Wyatt shuffling at the foot of the bed and I imagined his face was all kinds of red.

I laughed. "No, he said we would make a good family. All of us. You, me, him, and the children. He said nobody would have to know."

Lettie looked hard at me and I knew we were thinking the same things, figuring the same problems. It was such an easy solution it took some getting used to. Nothing that easy could work was the way I generally thought, but there didn't seem to be any reason why it wouldn't work, at least as long as Wyatt's pa didn't track us down.

I could tell that Wyatt had caught on to some of what was happening, even though he knew that he'd been left out of something important somewhere along the way. He sat down on the other side of Lettie's bed and watched both of us watching each other. When Lettie finally said, "It might work," Wyatt whooped. A smaller but just as happy whoop came from outside of Lettie's door and Lettie shouted at Toby to get to bed.

Wyatt and Lettie wasted no time making plans and coming up with stories we could use. I sat back and listened. I felt happy and I shared their hopefulness, but there were so many distant warnings still nagging at my insides that it was hard to get as excited as them. The hopefulness felt good, though, and watching Wyatt's happy face made the naggings seem less important. Anything that made him so happy couldn't be a bad thing.

Morning came and we started our new life as a family. The plan for the time being was that Wyatt and I were hired hands, which was true enough. We agreed (well, Lettie and I did; Wyatt did a bit of protesting) that Wyatt and I should not be seen together and that Wyatt should not go into town at all, seeing as how he stood out so much. We would use our aliases, John Deacon and Dillon Marshall, and either Lettie or I would go into town once a week to make sure nothing had changed. In other words, not much was different except Lettie and I had a truce, and that truce quickly turned into friendship, and friendship was something neither of us had known before.

At the end of our first week at Lettie's, Wyatt and I were settling in for the night when Wyatt said, "I think we should build a room onto the barn. Something that's ours. So we have more privacy." He was stretched out naked on our bed of straw, arms under his head, watching his stiff cock as he tried to make it dance by squeezing different muscles.

"Probably a good idea, Sweetlips. Wouldn't want Daisy walking in and seeing you putting on your puppet show."

Wyatt laughed. "I'm serious, Deke. Hey! Look what happens when I point my right foot." Wyatt pointed his right foot and his cock bowed slightly to the left. "I woulda thought it would bend the other way, wouldn't you?"

I laid down next to him on my stomach. "I need my back rubbed."

Wyatt rolled over and started working on my shoulders. "Maybe you should go back to just mending socks. This man's work seems to be putting a strain on you."

"Maybe you should shut up before I bend your cock in a way it will never bend back again."

Wyatt kissed the back of my neck while he rubbed. He wedged his cock against my ass and rubbed there, too. He rocked his body slowly on top of mine.

"You know what I've been thinking, Deke?"

"If you been thinking you want to try and stick that thing in my ass you better make sure you have an army back there with you first."

Wyatt poked his tongue into my ear then blew lightly. "You know my cock isn't made for that, Deke."

My flesh tingled from my scalp to my toes. "Hmm. One of these days I swear I'm going to teach you how to use that thing."

"What I was thinking was I should start schooling Toby and Daisy. I can do it after supper. They're smart, Deke. They deserve some learning."

"Mmmm." Wyatt's touch had me floating away.

"Deke?"

"Hmm?"

"Do you ever think about having children?"

"What?" Wyatt's words snapped me back.

"Your own children. Have you ever thought about it?"

"No." I didn't like the direction his wondering was taking. "I can't say as I have. Why?"

"I don't know. I just always thought . . . I don't know."

The wishfulness in his voice made me roll over and look him in the face. The things I feared most were sitting right there looking back at me. I sat up.

"Wyatt, we've started something big here with Lettie and her kids. We're calling ourselves a family and I think it can work, but I need to know exactly what it is you're expecting out of all this. If it's babies and a wife you want, with me fucking you on the side, I need to know that now because I gotta be honest with you, I don't think that's going to be enough for me."

He looked hurt and tried to turn away from me but I wouldn't let him.

"Wyatt, look at me. This is important. We can make ourselves a nice life here together but we've gotta be wanting the same things. I love you, Wyatt, and you're all I want. I'm fine with the idea that we are never going to have children, we're never going to go to the town social together, and we're never going to be having tea and crumpets with the minister and his wife. This home we're making with Lettie . . . This is the closest we'll ever be to normal. And if your father hunts us down we're going to have to give it all up. Except for each other. Is that going to be enough for you? Am I going to be enough for you, or should I move on now and leave you and Lettie to raise some kids?"

He was angry and hurt and he didn't want to be listening. I squeezed his shoulder hard to make sure he was.

"Wyatt, please listen. I'm not mad and I'm not trying to be mean but I'm fast approaching the point where I might not be able to stop loving you even if I try. I need to know now that what I have to offer is enough for you. If it's not, you need to tell me and I'll ride out of here. You and Lettie can get married and have babies and you can be normal. But you owe it to me to be straight about it. Are my dick and my love going to be enough for you?"

He was fighting back tears and his voice was dry. "You know they are. I can't believe you would even ask me that. You are all I want or need. Yes, I love it here and yes, sometimes I do think about things I can't have, but I thought I could talk to you about them." He'd been looking down at the space between us, but now he looked up and into my eyes. "I didn't think I was going to have to spend the rest of my life proving to you how much I love you."

I brushed away the wet building up in his eyes. "It won't be for the rest of your life, Wyatt. You gotta remember this is new to us both and you gotta remember, too, that we haven't been together all that long. I see the wishin' in your eyes and I know the things I can't give you and I know the pain I feel when I even think about losing you. I gotta tell you, all of that gets pretty scary."

Wyatt looked pretty scared himself. He touched my face and looked me in the eye, and I saw some of what I needed to see. "I love you, Deke. I ain't never been surer of anything else in my life. Sometimes I admit I wish other folks could be different, but I've never wished we could be different. Not you and I. Never. Your dick and your love are all that I will ever need."

I let him push me back down to our bed. "And what if I lose my dick?"

He slid his body onto mine and our dicks settled in together. "Then I guess you will have to show me how to use mine."

He rocked on top of me, his dick sliding sometimes on top of mine, sometimes along next to it. I could feel its ridges dragging and bumping, not slick but not dry. I closed my eyes while he kissed down my throat and I tried to imagine those ridges bumping and dragging in and out of my hole. I shivered 'cause for a flash I could actually feel it.

I reached my hand down and found Wyatt's cock. It was stiffer, more solid in my hand than it had felt rubbing against my body. I found wet at the tips of both cocks and I used it to slick up Wyatt's. I twisted my hand down the length of it, squeezing medium hard and rubbing my thumb across the top every time I passed by.

Wyatt moaned so softly I had to open my eyes so I could see what he was feeling. His eyes were closed and his mouth was open just wide enough for a tongue to slip in. His face had more of a just-fucked look on it; more peaceful than excited. His lead-up-to-sex and during-sex face always carried a bit of pain with it. That was missing now.

He kept rocking even though my hand was doing the work. Watching his face, I started tightening my grip, slowly so he couldn't feel the change. When my fist was asshole-tight, I stopped stroking and let him do all the fucking. Pre-juice was squeezing out of his cock at a good rate and the stuff coming from mine was giving him more than enough grease to keep the pumping smooth.

I saw the bit of pain working its way into his face. His mouth was wider and his moaning louder. Sweat was starting to dampen his honey hair, making it stick to his forehead and across one eye. I knew how annoyed he tended to get with that strand of hair so I used my free hand to push it back into place, the sweat holding it there. Wyatt's eyes stayed closed but a wisp of a smile softened his look.

His hands were planted on either side of me and his arms were straight, holding him above me while he fucked. With my fist still making a tight hole for him, I brought my knees up through his arms and to my chest. As if he'd done it a hundred times, Wyatt shifted and put his hands on my ass. He slid them up the backs of my legs, straightening my knees as he went, until he had a hold of my ankles and had me spread wide. My fist and his cock settled against my hole and Wyatt fucked in earnest.

I felt a little trapped at first—pinned to a stable floor unable to escape—and I admit I had to fight the urge to throw Wyatt off, but I kept watching his face above me and I saw nothing there to be afraid of. His neck and shoulders strained with the effort of loving me, his cock pounded against my hole with the need to be a part of me, and his expression made him look as if he was soaring. It was one of the most all-powerful, flat-out beautiful sights I'd ever seen and I knew right then that things would be changing between Wyatt and me someday. Maybe it wouldn't happen for a long, long time but, Lord willing, they would be changing. And that didn't bother me none at all.

That's when Wyatt slammed forward with one final, wild-bronco buck. His cream shot out with mine right behind it, and we covered my chest and part of my jaw with spunk. I rubbed my hands in it, loving the way it felt, and loving the notion of where it came from and how it got there. I covered as much of myself with it as I could, and Wyatt just watched, half smiling, relaxed and satisfied.

When I was done, Wyatt lowered my legs then scooped up a puddle of juice from my belly. He carried it on two fingers to my hole and rubbed it on, pushing his come-covered fingertips in just far enough to leave me marked.

"That's mine," he said, matter of fact, and I didn't argue with him none.

He grabbed the sweaty shirt he'd worn that day off the nail in the wall and he cleaned my chest with it, then he laid down beside me and settled into his spot.

"You learn fast, Sweetlips."

I felt him smile against my skin and he snuggled deeper. I fell asleep, calmer than I'd been in a long time.

Not long after that Wyatt and I built a small room off the barn and made it ours. We furnished it with things we built ourselves and Lettie and the kids decorated it with some extra things they had, like a pitcher for flowers and a painting of some mountains that the old hermit had left. That little one-room house became something I could touch. It told me Wyatt and I had something real together and soon my worries about Wyatt's wishings, and the memories of his father, faded like nightmares.

We all settled naturally into our odd little family roles. I was the father figure, with Toby coming to me to learn about fighting and cowboying and Daisy coming to me during thunderstorms and all things scary. I didn't have the balls for scolding, though, so that was part of Lettie's job, along with the cooking and the doctoring and all things motherly. Wyatt was like a big brother to the young 'uns, or maybe an uncle. He played with them in a way neither Lettie nor I could, being as we kept such tight reins on ourselves. Wyatt wasn't like that. He had no concerns about looking foolish, and he had a way of enjoying things that was more childlike than I ever remember being, even when I was a child. Along with the playing, he started giving them lessons just like he said he would, and I admit it made me proud to watch him.

We got so comfortable with our new life that we started making grand plans. We were going to save enough money to buy a small herd and then use the money from the sale of the cattle to move all of us far away. Wyatt said Rhode Island would be the perfect place to go because his father had no connections that far east, but it was a part of the country he himself had grown familiar with after having gone to school in Boston. We could all change our names and Lettie and I would pretend to be married. We'd tell folks that Toby and Daisy were ours and Wyatt was Lettie's brother.

There was no denying, it was a pleasant dream. With each passing day the dream seemed more and more possible, and it became easier to ignore the warnings in my gut that cropped up now and then. I learned to stop worrying so much and to enjoy what I had; another thing I'd never had the knack for until Wyatt came along.

By the time fall rolled around, we felt liked we'd been farming with Lettie for most of our lives. To thank us for all of our help, she gave us some cash from the extra crops she'd been able to raise.

With the large harvest and the canning Daisy and Lettie had done, and the meat Wyatt and I expected to get on our upcoming hunting trip, we all felt we were going to have a pretty easy winter.

Our hunting trip was planned for the first week in October, and Wyatt and I were itching for some real time alone together. Even with our add-on home we sometimes felt a little crowded. We both longed for wide-open lovemaking, with lots of hollering and *oh fuck*'s screamed at the tops of our lungs. Wyatt especially missed the daylight fucking. He said nothing felt freer to him than having me plow his ass under a bright blue sky.

Wyatt and Toby both had birthdays the first week in October, so Lettie insisted on a party for the two of them before we left. It was hard to tell which one was bouncing more with excitement, Wyatt or Toby. They were chattering about it for weeks, poking around every nook and cranny looking for hidden presents and huddling together as they compared notes about secret activity they'd seen going on.

The party was planned for the night before the hunting trip. Wyatt could barely work he was so fired up. We knew Lettie and the kids had worked together on something for Wyatt because Daisy couldn't keep from giggling nearly every time she saw us. Lettie wouldn't tell me what it was for fear I'd let it slip to Wyatt.

Me . . . I was nervous as hell about my gift to Wyatt. I wanted to give him something special; something that had meaning for the both of us. I couldn't be spending what little bit of cash we had on birthday presents, but I decided to use a part of it to have the blacksmith in town fashion something I hoped would show Wyatt that I really did believe in a future together. I was worried he wouldn't get the meaning of it, though, and as stupid as it might seem, I knew my feelings would be bruised if he didn't.

Dinner that night was more a race between Wyatt and Toby than a meal. Lettie and I tortured them by carrying on a long-winded conversation while we poked at our food. Their calf-bawling and begging wore us down, though, and to loud whoops of joy Lettie finally announced it was time to open presents.

Toby got clothes from Lettie, mostly handmade things that she'd sewed together from left over cloth. Her big surprise to him, though, was a brand new pair of store-bought boots he'd longed for in town. They were black with some tooling down the sides and they were real wrangler boots, not farm boy work shoes.

Toby looked stunned as he held the pair in his hands.

"Ma . . . but where'd you get the money?"

"I've been saving up for a spell 'cause you're getting to the age where you need a man's pair of boots. When I saw you admiring these in town I knew they were the ones I wanted for you."

Toby stared at them for a few moments more before jumping into his mother's arms.

"Thank you, Ma. I ain't never had anything so fine."

"Hold on now, 'cause Deke and Wyatt haven't given you theirs yet." Lettie's eyes twinkled as she smiled at us.

Toby stood up from his mother's lap and looked at us, surprised. "You got me something?"

Wyatt held out a burlap sack. "It was too hard to wrap."

Toby straightened himself to as close to man-sized as he could get before taking the gift from Wyatt.

"It's so light."

"Open it, Toby. Open it." Daisy bounced and clapped, as excited as Toby to see what it was.

Toby opened the sack and looked inside. His eyes grew huge.

"What is it, Toby? What is it?" Daisy was beside herself.

Toby reached in and carefully pulled out a black Stetson.

"A man's hat to go with the man's boots." It was Wyatt's idea to get the hat after he saw the boots Lettie had bought. "Won't be long, Toby, and you'll be a real cowboy like Deke."

I have to admit it made me a little hard the way Wyatt and Toby thought of me as some kind of wrangling god.

Toby thanked us several times over, his face going from embarrassed to proud to cocky and back to embarrassed again as he paraded for us in his new boots and hat.

Lettie clapped her hands. "All right, now it's time for us to give you our present. It's actually for both of you. I know you know we been working together on it and we're sure hoping you like it."

"Close your eyes." Daisy was hopping like a trapped rabbit again. She grabbed both of us by a hand and pulled us toward Lettie's bedroom. I felt Lettie's hand on my shoulder as she helped guide us.

"OK. Open."

It took a few beats for me to realize what we were looking at.

"Lie on it. Lie on it."

I looked at Wyatt and he looked as confused as I was feeling.

"It's a bed, you mule heads. It's filled with down and feathers. We've been gathering and stuffing and sewing for weeks. We thought it would be a fair piece nicer than that corn husk one you sleep on now."

A feather bed. Visions of me fucking Wyatt on a soft, pillowy cloud flashed through my head and I was suddenly too hard and muddled to speak. Wyatt, on the other hand, was already backside down in it, oohing and moaning and doing nothing to ease my hard-on.

"Deke, you gotta feel this. It's like a cloud. Like lying on a cloud."

The damn vision popped back and I knew if I laid down next to Wyatt right then, Lettie and her young 'uns would see a whole lot more about man-loving than they ever bargained for.

"Ummm, it looks right heavenly, that's for sure, but I'm a might dusty still. I don't want to get it dirty."

Lettie laughed but covered it by clearing her throat.

"I tell you what. Why don't you boys take it back to your place and get it set up while Daisy and I get the cake ready?"

Wyatt and I lifted the feather bed off of Lettie's bed but had some trouble getting it through the doorways. It weren't heavy so much as it was big and floppy and right awkward to carry, especially with my dick sticking out like a third leg.

When we were clear of the house, Wyatt gave me his best look of innocence.

"I never knew you were so fond of furniture, Deke. I saw how hard you got the second you saw this here bed padding. You know, I saw a chair in Boston once that was so comfy it would have made you shoot your load just looking at it."

"Funny, Wyatt, but the second we're inside that door you better be on your knees and sucking or you ain't getting shit up your ass the entire hunting trip."

Wyatt laughed. "Sure, Deke. I'm worried. You couldn't go for more than eight hours without needing one of my holes to slide your dick into."

"Don't push it, boy. If you want to feel what it's like to fuck on clouds tonight I'd suggest you keep your mouth open for one thing and one thing only."

We struggled through our door with the bed, plopped it on top of the old one and Wyatt fell to his knees. In record time that boy unbuttoned my fly, pulled out my dick, and sucked me dry so that I was soft enough to be seen by children again.

He looked up at me, my cream covering his mouth, and said, "Did Lettie say she had cake?"

I pulled him to his feet and kissed his lips clean. I had a powerful rush of feelings for him all of a sudden and I said, "Don't ever make me live without you, Sweetlips. Promise me."

It startled Wyatt as much as it did me. "What's wrong, Deke?"

"Nothing." I cleared my throat. "Happy birthday, Wyatt."

We kissed a long, slow kiss and as Wyatt pulled away he whispered, "I promise," then we headed back to the house for cake.

The cake was good and the frosting was thick and creamy. Wyatt kept leaving globs of it on his lips so he could slowly lick it off for me when no one else was watching. Naturally, I was in pain by the time I hobbled out of Lettie's place. Wyatt laughed at me as I made my way stiffly across the yard.

"I swear to God, Lettie must spend half her evenings trying to explain you and your magical growing body parts to her children."

"Well you're a big fucking help." I grabbed him by the back of his neck and helped him along toward our room. "You like frosting so much, I'll give you enough tonight to choke a horse."

"Well if you didn't get me a present, cowboy, a horse is probably what you'll end up fucking tonight." Wyatt stopped and turned toward me. "I'm twenty years old now. This is the biggest birthday of my life and I'm expecting something pretty damned wonderful from you."

"Well, I was going to get you the most expensive saloon girl in town, but I took her for a test ride and she just weren't good enough for you."

Wyatt started undoing my fly. "I am pretty damn spoiled after you, that's for sure."

"Besides, I didn't think you'd know how to work her, what with her not having a dick and all."

Wyatt freed my cock and went to work unbuttoning my shirt. "Just how exactly does that work, anyway? If she's got an innie instead of an outtie, like I heard tell womenfolk do, how's she going to get it in my ass?"

He peeled off my shirt and I pulled his dick out of his jeans. I gave it a good squeeze and said, "I keep telling you to have me show you how to use this thing some time."

I pushed him through the doorway and we commenced to kissing every inch of each other while we shucked off the rest of our clothes. When we were both stripped bare I asked Wyatt what he wanted to do first.

"It's your choice, birthday boy. Do we try out the new bed or open your present from me?"

Without a second's hesitation Wyatt said, "Open my present."

"Wait here. I hid it up in the hay loft."

"The hay loft? But I looked there."

"Not good enough, I guess." I pulled my jeans back on and started out the door but stopped, suddenly nervous as hell. I turned back to Wyatt and said, "I'm not sure you could really call it wonderful . . . "

Wyatt's expression was so young and boyish I just had to hold him again. He laid his head on my chest and I kissed his golden hair.

"I was just kidding, Deke. You know that, right? I don't need anything but you." He let me hold him for a couple beats longer then he shoved me away. "All right, all right. Now go get my present."

"You sure? We could just lie on our new bed together and hold each other instead. Tell each other how much we love each other."

"I love you, Deke, more than life itself. Now go get my fucking present."

I smacked him on the ass and went out the door, no longer nervous.

I climbed the ladder to the loft and pulled the present down from the rafters. It was long and narrow and wrapped in a sack, much like Toby's hat had been. I carried it back to our room and handed it to Wyatt. He was sprawled out naked on our new bed, looking little boy excited and grown man fuckable all at once. He ripped the sack off and pulled out the branding iron I'd had made. It was a D over a W with part of the W twining 'round the D, all of it closed in a circle. I'd drawn the design myself for the blacksmith. I wanted it to show Wyatt how my life was so tangled up with his now that they couldn't really be separated any more. I wanted it to prove to him that I believed we had a future together.

He didn't make a sound and the longer his silence dragged on, the faster my nervousness returned. Finally, I couldn't stand it no more.

"It's a branding iron."

Wyatt nodded. He hadn't looked at me yet. He hadn't spoken. He just kept staring at the iron.

"It's . . ." I couldn't find the right word. " . . . kind of a symbol."

Wyatt nodded again.

Not knowing what else to say or do, I stripped off my jeans and got into bed next to him. I kissed him on the cheek, wished him a happy birthday, and settled back into the softness of our new bed. Wyatt tucked the iron under his pillow and took his position in my arms.

"Do you like it?"

Wyatt nodded and climbed on top of me. He pressed his face into my neck and I held him, while rain-like drops from him tickled down my skin. I smiled, knowing Wyatt understood, then I fucked him on our new cloud.

CHAPTER 8

WHEN I WOKE UP the next morning, Wyatt was gone. I checked under his pillow and the branding iron was gone, too. I pulled on my jeans and went outside to look for him. I found him hunkered down next to a fire, with the branding iron resting in the coals. The bay was tethered nearby.

I yawned, scratched my chest, and watched him. It was too early in the morning for more than a hint of light but it, along with the flames from the fire, were enough to make Wyatt glow. I ached like I always ached when I watched him, most of the pain settling in my heart and between my legs.

I went and hunkered down next to him.

"Have I told you lately that you're the most beautiful fucking thing I've ever seen?"

"Nope."

"Just checking. Whatcha doin'?"

Wyatt pulled the iron out of the fire and stood. "I'm wiping the old out with the new."

He took the iron to the bay and, lining the mark up just right, burned a DW into the horse's flank, wiping out his father's brand. I joined him as he stood back and admired his work. The smile on his face couldn't get any bigger without him tearing something.

"Ready to go hunting, Sweetlips?"

"Yup. Think we'll actually get any hunting done?"

"Don't know. Never fired a rifle before while my dick was balls deep in a man's rabbit hole."

Wyatt shrugged. "How tough can it be?"

I slapped him hard on the ass. "I don't know but I've got me a powerful need to find out," and I headed back in to finish dressing.

We'd readied our provisions the day before so we didn't have much to do but load up the horses. Lettie was letting us use her old gray plow horse as our second mount. He wouldn't do much good if we had to outrun a posse, but he was a willing worker and it beat riding double.

When we were all set, we went to the main house for a quick bite and to say goodbye. Daisy jumped into my arms as soon as I made it through the door.

"Going to miss me, Deke?"

"Like a bee misses honey, honey." She giggled and I kissed her on the cheek, holding her on my hip while I ate some biscuits Lettie had set out for us.

"So you boys think you'll be about a week?"

"Yeah. Game's pretty plentiful. I doubt we'll need more'n that."

"It's going to seem right odd around here with you two gone. Gotten kind of used to having you around." Lettie tousled Wyatt's hair as he guzzled milk straight from the can. "Annoying habits and all."

Wyatt put the can down and swiped the milk from his mouth with his sleeve. "Yeah, I know what you mean. Deke can be pretty annoying." Wyatt looked around. "Where's Toby?"

"Admiring himself in the mirror while he practices his quick draw."

"Got his boots and hat on?"

"Slept in them."

Daisy squirmed out of my arms and climbed into Wyatt's lap.

"What if you come across a grizzly again, Wyatt?"

"We'll just have to kill it like we did the last one."

"But you don't have Athena any more. Tell me again about how she saved you."

"All right, but then me and Deke have to get going. Deke's just itching to be poking around in some rabbit holes."

I slapped Wyatt upside the head as I passed behind him on my way to Toby's room.

"Keep it short, Sweetlips. I'm going to give Toby some tips on quick drawing and then we have to go. We're burning daylight."

Once we were finally on our way, we were barely out of earshot of the farm before we stopped and fucked for the first time. Wyatt wanted to be on his back so he could look up at the sun and sky. He screamed his usual moment-of-firing "Oh fuck!" at the top of his lungs just because he could and then we mounted up and started off to hunt. By lunchtime the urge to whip out our dicks was so great again that we had to stop. It was dinnertime before we put them back. By then there was no point in going any further so we made camp for the night.

Wyatt stretched out naked under a scrub oak, his arms under his head and our come, dry and otherwise, covering a fair portion of his body.

"I'm fucking beat. Never knew a hunting trip could wear a body out so."

"Yeah, and all you did was make like a hole. I'm the one what did all the work."

"Think we'll actually get some hunting done tomorrow?"

"We better at least try. Our manhood's going to be questioned if we go back with nothing but bowed legs and shit-eating grins to show for our week of hunting."

The next morning we got an early start, kept our hard-ons jeaned-up and had two mule deer by lunch. We made camp and spent the rest of the afternoon butchering our game.

After a satisfying dinner of venison and beans, we hung the rest of the meat as high as we could in a Joshua tree then bedded down for the night. Wyatt nuzzled close to me, his long legs tangled up with mine, and he sighed.

"I feel so good I don't even want sex."

"Funny, Wyatt. Your sense of humor's one of the things that keeps me loving you."

"I'm serious, Deke. I'd rather just lie here in your arms. I think fucking would kinda ruin the mood." I patted Wyatt on the shoulder and counted silently to twenty. At nineteen and a half Wyatt said, "Well, that was special." He slid down my body and just before swallowing my dick whole he said, "I think it's important for our relationship that we don't need sex every minute we're together."

I grabbed two handfuls of hair and forced his head tight to my stomach. "But then thinking was never one of your strong suits, Sweetlips."

In the morning we downed some reheated coffee and cornbread Lettie had sent along with us. We made sure the cache of venison was secure and headed out for our third day of hunting.

It was a couple hours past noon when we decided to hunt up a watering hole and take a break. We'd been at it all morning and had nothing to show for it but four rabbits. Up ahead we could see a cluster of huge boulders with lots of green growing around. We figured we'd find some water there for sure.

I knew we were close to the border of a ranch and I felt uneasy about riding up without making sure no one was around. Lettie and I had gone to a lot of trouble to make sure Wyatt didn't exist in these parts and I wanted it to stay that way.

"You wait here, Sweetlips. I'll go make sure it's clear."

"Come on, Deke. Stop being so jumpy about this shit."

"Stay here, Wyatt." My voice didn't leave no room for arguing.

I rode in slow, trying to keep downwind. The closer I got, the more nervous I felt. The hairs on my neck prickled and I thought about turning back. The horses needed water, though, so I tied the gray to a mesquite bush about fifty yards from the boulder cluster and went the rest of the way on foot.

I was almost to the base of one of the boulders when I heard voices. Something made me keep going, even though I had a powerful urge to run back to Wyatt and hightail it out of there. I climbed the boulder, my heart pounding in my chest, and when I got near the top I flattened myself against the rock. There were at least three voices and I shivered head to toe as the blood froze in my veins. The cackling laughter of one voice was no doubt Shorty's, the hand from the Crooked J.

I felt so panicked for a moment I couldn't focus on their words. I had to force myself to quietness so I could concentrate on what they were saying.

"We'll hang up more of these posters and talk to the sheriff about the ranches in the area."

"Checking the ranches is a waste of time. McAllister's not stupid enough to stick with ranch work."

"The kid's probably dead by now, anyway. Don't know why we bother with his picture."

"'Cause Saunders told us to. You want to tell Ray Saunders you think it's stupid to hand out a dead boy's picture?"

There was no answer to that and Shorty continued, saying they'd rest the horses a few minutes longer before heading into town.

I crawled back down the rock, afraid that even my breathing might be too loud. I trotted to the horse, running being too noisy and walking being too slow. In the distance I could see Wyatt waiting for me. The thought that he might get impatient and come after me or shout out made my body start to shake. I wanted to jump on the gray and ride like hell to Wyatt but I couldn't take the chance.

As soon as I got on the horse Wyatt did exactly what I didn't want him to do—he started riding toward me. I waved him back but he kept on coming. I didn't want to run the gray when I was still so close to Shorty and his men but finally I just had no choice. I was too afraid Wyatt would start calling out to me.

I rode hard to him and his smile faded as soon as I was close enough for him to get a look at my face. I rode right on past him and he turned the bay and followed me. I didn't stop until I reached some heavy scrub at the base of a bluff. I dismounted and got the horse out of sight.

Wyatt pulled up a few seconds after.

"What the hell's the matter?"

"It's them. Men from the Crooked J."

Wyatt turned white and slid off his horse. "Oh, God."

"They're headed into town. They got posters."

"We gotta get out of here; get back to the farm."

I shook my head, dreading what had to be done. "No. We gotta let 'em see us."

"What? Are you fucking loco?"

"Think about it, Wyatt. They show those pictures of me in town and the sheriff's going to send them straight to Lettie's place. We have to lead them away from there; keep them from ever reaching town."

"But . . . Deke we can't just leave without saying . . . We've got Lettie's horse." Wyatt was desperate. "We have to go back."

"They can't ever know about Lettie. Don't you understand? They ain't going to politely ask her some questions then walk away. We have to lead them away now. We can't let them near Lettie and her kids."

Wyatt looked back toward the boulders then toward Lettie's place. I saw tears burning in his eyes.

"There's one other thing, Wyatt."

He looked through me, too stunned to understand that there could be more.

"Saunders is still alive. They were talking about him."

Wyatt covered his eyes with his hand. "Oh, God. Oh, God." I was afraid I was going to have to slap him or something to bring him 'round, but as quick as he'd fallen apart, he pulled himself back together. He looked me in the eye and asked, "How do we do it?"

"We wait until we see them coming out from the rocks then we head away from Lettie, riding as fast as we can."

Wyatt wiped the last bit of wet from his eyes. "That gray's going to be pretty damn useless." He looked up at the bluff. "Why don't we take a position up there and pick them off?"

"Number one, I don't know how many there are and we wouldn't be able to hold them off forever. I guarantee they won't just quit.

Number two, I may be accused of being a murderer, but I ain't one. Those men think you are dead. I have no doubt your father told them and the law one horrible tale about what happened in the bunkhouse that night. If we get to the point where I have to kill to defend myself I will, but I ain't going to shoot no one like a duck in a pond."

Wyatt nodded, looking a little ashamed.

"Listen to me, Sweetlips. We gotta think clear. We won't have no time for discussing and deciding once we do this. Understood?"

"Deke, they're coming."

I pulled him to me and kissed him hard. "I love you, Sweetlips. Don't let nothing make you forget that. Ever."

He held me tight and I took a good, deep sniff of his honey gold hair then we got on our horses and rode out into plain sight.

"Make sure they see us then run like hell."

Their shouting told us what we needed to know. We kicked our mounts hard and headed away from Lettie's place; away from the only things we loved besides each other.

Looking back over my shoulder I counted at least ten in the posse. They weren't close enough to fire any shots, but it didn't take long before the gray was struggling bad, which meant they'd be in range all too soon. I was pretty sure that Jennings's orders would be to bring me back alive, so we did have that on our side. Whatever punishment I was to get, I figured Jennings would be wanting to give it to me himself, so they wouldn't be shooting to kill; but that didn't mean they couldn't shoot to wound or shoot our horses out from under us. We needed an advantage and we needed it quick.

Wyatt kept looking back at me, worry dug into his face, and every time he looked back I was a little farther away. The gray just couldn't keep up.

After a spell, Wyatt started veering east. I knew right away what he was thinking. There was a small river we'd crossed the day before. If we could make it to the river we might have a better chance of losing them. Only problem was, I seriously doubted the gray would make it that far. Shorty and his men were gaining on me already; not by a lot, but that would be changing the weaker my mount got.

"Split up, Wyatt. It's our only chance."

"Fuck you," he screamed over his shoulder.

That's pretty much the answer I'd expected but I'd needed to try.

Still miles from the river the gray stumbled badly, nearly throwing me from his back.

"I'm losing him, Wyatt."

Wyatt slowed down and let me get even with him. I handed him my rifle then jumped onto the bay, bumping into place behind Wyatt. I heard the gray stumble some more then he fell to the ground with a thud. I was grateful that he had no brands or marks that would lead the posse back to Lettie.

I looked behind me. They'd gained quite a bit of ground during our transfer. Looking ahead again I scanned the horizon hoping for something that would help us out, but there was nothing but desert in front of us.

The posse fired some shots, close enough now to try and kill our horse.

"Deke. Riders to the north."

I looked where Wyatt was looking. "Shit. Apaches."

There were eight or nine of them armed with rifles and bows. One split off from the group and headed toward us. The rest aimed themselves at the posse.

"There's no fucking way we can outrun that pony of his."

Not needing hands to ride, the Apache coming for us took aim with his rifle and got off two shots before his gun seemed to jam. He tossed it aside and pulled his bow into place. It was harder than hell for me to get proper aim, squished up and bouncing against Wyatt like I was, but I managed to get a shot off. The Indian let loose with another arrow and I fired again, hitting my target.

"Got him." I checked on the posse. They were fighting for their lives and had no time to bother with us. "This is our lucky day." I turned forward and got poked in the face by the arrow sticking out of Wyatt's left shoulder. "Shit, Wyatt, you're hit."

"Yeah. I kinda noticed that."

"Oh, God."

Blood soaked Wyatt's shirt. From the small length of arrow sticking out the back I could tell it was in deep; maybe out the other side. I reached my free arm around Wyatt and took the reins from him.

"Can you stay on?"

"For now."

I wedged my rifle between us and put both my arms around him. He leaned back into me, his blood soaking my shirt, too. The shaft of the arrow rested on top of my left shoulder but there was no way I could keep it from jarring on a galloping horse. It was hurting Wyatt something fierce and tearing the wound wider.

"We need to stop so I can cut the arrow down."

"No. I can make it. We need more distance."

It wasn't long after that the river came into view. It was too deep and fast to cross or ride in, so I headed the horse north along the bank. As soon as it narrowed and calmed I took the bay into shallow water and we kept heading north. I didn't stop until Wyatt slumped forward, unconscious.

I took us into tall brush on the bank and got Wyatt down off the horse. The tip of the arrowhead was pushing out the front of his shoulder. His face was so pale I was afraid to check his breathing. The thought of life without Wyatt rammed me in the chest with the power of a charging bull. I couldn't do it. I knew right then and there I'd reached that point. He'd become one of my needs, like air and food, and I would never be able to walk away from him.

I laid him out on the ground on his wounded side and took out my knife. I cut off his shirt and tried to ignore the tears stinging my eyes when I saw his wound. It was chewed up from the jostling of the arrow, like some rodent had been gnawing at it. I could see bone inside but thankfully it didn't look damaged.

I ran to the river's edge and filled the canteen, then took it back and rinsed Wyatt's wound. He moaned and stirred when the cold water hit him but he didn't come to. With my knife I sawed off the shaft of the arrow as close to Wyatt's body as I could. He cried out but stayed unconscious. I kissed his cheek and rinsed the wound again.

The rest of the arrow was a bigger problem. Only the tip was showing through the skin, so to pull it out the front meant tearing open a larger hole. Leaving it in meant a bigger chance for infection, or the chance it would be knocked loose and disappear inside him. Pulling it out the back was out of the question. The arrowhead would cause even more damage going out than when it went in.

I decided to take it out the front.

I scrubbed my knife with water and sand then pried Wyatt's flesh around the arrowhead, giving it more room and making it a little easier to get a hold of. Wyatt moaned and I kissed him again. I put my mouth to his ear and told him how much I loved him. I pressed my lips to his wound, bit down hard on the arrowhead, and ripped it out as fast as I could. Wyatt came to, screaming and fighting. I held his hands and talked softly to him, kissing his cheeks and eyes and lips. He said my name a few times then passed out again.

I tore up his shirt and bandaged the wounds, front and back, then I got his spare shirt from the saddlebags. That's when I noticed how labored the bay's breathing was. We'd run him hard, no doubt, but he should have been a little more rested by this time. I ran my hand over his body as I circled him. He was sweaty and warm like I'd expect him to be, but when my hand passed over his chest between his front legs, I felt a thick, sticky wetness. I got down on my knees and saw blood. Checking him some more I found a bullet hole in his left rib cage. From the way he was breathing and the noise coming from the wound, my guess was the bullet had gone into his lung or at least nicked it. I stood up and held his head in my hands, stroking his muzzle.

"Most any other horse would have gone down the minute he got shot. Not you, though, huh? You just kept lugging the two of us on your back." I put my nose against his. Blood was showing in his nostrils. "Thanks, boy."

I took the spare shirt back to Wyatt and put it on him. Then I wrapped him in the bedroll. I laid down behind him and fit my body into his curves.

"I gotta do something, Sweetlips, before I can stay here with you. I'll be back soon, though. I promise."

I went to the bay and unsaddled him. I ran my hands gently all over him and told him what a mighty fine horse he was. I listed all the times he'd saved our asses; all the things we'd been through together. He looked me in the eye and I knew he understood. I took out my knife and drove it hard and deep into his throat, then cut across, doing as much damage as quickly as I could. Wind rushed out of him like a sigh of relief and he fell to the ground. I remembered how Wyatt had done the same thing to his palomino to save my life, and I started to have an inkling of an idea of how hard that must have been for him. I remembered, too, the gray running himself into the ground to help save my hide, and I swore to God that my next horse was getting treated like a king.

I sliced open the bay's stomach and scooped out some of the warm innards. I took them to Wyatt and added them to the bedroll that covered him. I cut out the horse's heart and ate a good portion of it, hoping the Indian belief of gaining strength and courage from a strong heart was true. The rest of the heart I mashed up and mixed with blood and water. I got a little bit of that down Wyatt. After that, I set to skinning the bay so we could use his hide for a blanket. When I got to his rump where the DW brand covered the Crooked J brand, I fingered the scar and found myself crying. That brand stood for the life Wyatt and me almost had; the life we deserved to have together. I wasn't letting nobody take that away from me. As long as Wyatt was alive and loving me, I was going to make damn sure we were reaching for that dream of his; the dream that had slowly become my dream, too.

I took the hide to Wyatt and laid down with him, covering us both with the warm blanket. His fierce shivering soon died down. He moaned my name a few times and I talked to him quietly. He fell into a deep sleep and I followed shortly after.

That was my last real sleep for days. Wyatt was in and out of consciousness and I was too nervous to sleep. He was so weak and defenseless that I was afraid of anything and everything causing him harm. Animals, insects, infection, Apaches, the weather—all of 'em could make him worse. I spent hours circling our little encampment, keeping my eyes open for any sign of danger. The slightest breeze made me jump. The tiniest noise made me take aim. I knew I was edging close to crazy but I was too afraid of losing Wyatt to care.

I kept feeding him his horse blood and meat broth, putting in more blood and less water every day. I packed his wounds with a mash of cactus leaves and mud. Infection was probably the thing I feared most and the poultice was the only way I knew of to keep it away. I kissed his lips whenever he called my name, told him over and over how much I loved him, and begged him not to leave me. My voice seemed to calm him when he was delirious, and my touch seemed to comfort him.

I lost track of the days but I think it was on the fifth that Wyatt opened his eyes and looked right at me.

"Deke?"

"I'm right here, Sweetlips." I lay down behind him and fit my body into his.

"What happened, Deke? Are you all right?"

I took a deep breath and kissed the back of his neck. "I am now, Sweetlips. I am now."

CHAPTER 9

I FILLED WYATT IN on the details of what happened as he sipped on his horse blood broth.

"We ate horse heart, huh?"

"Yep. I think those Indians are onto something. I believe that bay's heart gave you its strength."

"Hmm. Explains my sudden craving for hay, I suppose."

"I suppose. I actually thought about eating some other body parts, just in case it isn't just the heart that can pass on its strength, but I figured I'm about as big as that tight little ass of yours can handle all ready."

Wyatt spit out his broth with a laugh then grabbed his shoulder in pain. "Damn, Deke, don't do that."

"Sorry, Sweetlips. I'll keep the joking to a minimum for a bit."

Wyatt took another sip of his broth.

"But what if I had eaten it? Can't you just see me trying to drag that thing along with us in the desert? I suppose I could try to tuck the end into my boot top but that would give me a fierce gimp, don't you think?"

Wyatt cursed me as horse blood backed out his nose. "Asshole."

I cleaned him up then checked his bandages. "I've missed you."

"I didn't miss you. I felt you right there the whole time." He slipped his good hand behind my neck and pulled me in for a kiss. Thanks."

"My pleasure."

We decided to stay put until Wyatt felt strong enough to travel. There'd been no sign of danger so far and there didn't seem to be a need to push him any sooner than we had to. I finally felt comfortable enough to get some shut eye once in a while, but I could never sleep long. Visions of Wyatt being dragged back to his father by Saunders kept waking me up.

Two days after Wyatt came 'round completely, I woke up with my cock down his throat. I smiled and pushed back his hair. "Feeling better, huh?"

He nodded, slurping and sucking and using his good hand to explore my balls.

"Well, as soon as you're finished down there we need to start walking. Think you're up to it?"

His hand and his mouth switched places. He grunted a "yes" before he swallowed my balls.

"'Course, I'm in no big hurry so you just take your time down there."

He came up for air again. "You sure you didn't eat anything else of that bay's? You do seem a might larger than I remember."

"You're just out of practice. Now get back to work."

We spent a good long time getting Wyatt reacquainted with my cock, then we gathered up the things we wanted to take with us and heaved the saddle into the river. Together we buried what was left of the bay and made sure there was no evidence of us to be found. Wyatt's left arm was still pretty much useless so his rifle was all he could carry; I would take the rest. I knew he'd be too weak to make it far, but I also knew he'd be too stubborn to say anything so I needed to keep a close eye on him.

We stood ready with our things, about to start trekking across the desert on foot, and Wyatt said, "Get the feeling we've done this before?"

"Yup." I hoisted the saddlebags onto my shoulder. "But at least this time we know where the horse is."

Wyatt could only travel for about an hour at a time before needing rest. I checked his wounds each time we stopped and made him drink lots of water. We followed the river, which took us more or less north. We figured we stood a better chance of survival with a constant supply of water and plenty of brush to hide in, even if traveling the river was the more predictable route.

On our first day I made Wyatt stop well before sundown. He argued, of course, but his face was the color of a toad's belly and blood was starting to dot his shirt. He gave in fairly easily, which told me he was feeling right shitty.

"Let's bed down a ways from the river. It will be warmer and we'll attract fewer critters."

"Where do you think we are, Deke?"

"Still in the New Mexico Territory, I 'spect. Other than that I couldn't really say."

Wyatt helped me spread out the blanket and bedroll with his good hand. "Maybe we should get out of the country, Deke."

"You mean Mexico or Canada?"

"No. Farther. China or India or England."

"I ain't too familiar with the Scriptures, but don't they say only Jesus can walk on water?"

Wyatt laid back on the blanket with a painful but grateful sigh. "I kinda figured a boat would come in handy."

I checked Wyatt's wounds one more time.

"It's a thought, Sweetlips. I ain't taking nothing off the table at this point." I brushed his hair back a few times and he closed his eyes. "Except for turning myself in. That one's not up for discussion."

"Kiss me, please. I'm fading fast."

I kissed him on his chapped but still sweet lips and he was snoring before I pulled away. I sat against a rock next to Wyatt and watched the sun go down. Getting out of the country was a good idea, but our first goal was to get some horses again. Stealing went against my nature but it was looking like our only real choice at this point. It would be best to keep following the river and see where it led. Hopefully something helpful would pop up along the way.

The sky glowed orange and I thought about Lettie and the

children. They'd be settling down for supper right about now. I wondered if they were worried about us. We should have been back from the hunting trip by now. It wouldn't take much longer before Lettie knew something was wrong. What would they do? What would they think? It hurt not being able to say goodbye.

I shook my head. I needed to get rid of those thoughts for good. They'd only make me miserable and cloud my thinking. I looked down at Wyatt's angel face. He was the only thing I should be concentrating on now. It was too dangerous to have it any other way.

We walked for three days. We saw a couple of spreads but the risk of sneaking in and stealing horses seemed too great. Wyatt was still weak and a pursuit on horseback would put him back where he'd started. The walking was slow going but at least we had control of the pace. The river gave us plenty of water and I even caught a couple of fish barehanded. Under the circumstances we were doing pretty good, so there seemed no sense in pushing our luck.

Wyatt kept wanting to talk about Lettie and the kids, but I wouldn't let him. I know he understood my reasons but it was hard on him. We had different ways of dealing, Wyatt and me. He needed to talk everything out, like draining dirty water from a trough. Everything he felt would just pour out of him and then he seemed to feel cleaner after, ready to start new. Me, I liked to crawl inside myself and find a nice dark corner to hide in until the bad started to fade. I'm not sure either way had an advantage over the other, but since I got more violent about needing to deal my way, that's usually the route we took.

At the end of the fourth day of walking, just as the sun was falling out of sight, a town came into view. We found a small cave along the sand cliffs, out of view of town, and camped down there for the night.

"So, you think you're strong enough to handle whatever might come along, Sweetlips? Or do you think we should skip the town and keep wandering a bit?"

"I think I'm ready. What's going to be our story?"

"Well, your story's going to be the truth—you got jumped by Apaches, took an arrow in the shoulder, and lost your horse. Managed to escape and you've been walking ever since."

"And what's your story?"

"I don't need one. I ain't going in. Leastways not so's I'll be seen."

"You're still worried about us being seen together?"

"Now more than ever, although I must admit all the desert-walking and fever-battling has made you look more human than angel, but you're still mighty beautiful. Which means you stand out. Which means folks are more likely to put two and two together if they see us with each other."

"That's assuming wanted posters of us have made it this far."

"Yep. That's assuming just that."

"And what are you going to do?"

"I'm going to find us some horses."

That night I fucked Wyatt for the first time since he'd gotten wounded. I took it slow and easy and made it last. Lately, every time I'd look at Wyatt or touch him, I'd get the notion that it might be the last time I was doing it. I knew it could be true, too, what with our situation being what it was. It was an odd thing, 'cause thinking that way made every little touch feel like an explosion. Kisses didn't feel like just plain kisses any more. They were whirlwinds of feelings, making my skin tingle and my heart feel like it would burst. It was right exciting and a little bit scary and a whole lot sad. The fucking that night, as gentle as it was, was like riding a bull in a tornado. I didn't know which way my feelings would land next. When we finally finished, I fell asleep with him in my arms, and part of me was still buried inside of him. When the time came, that's how I wanted us both to go.

In the morning we went over Wyatt's story four or five more times. He was to act sicker than he was so he could avoid answering too many questions. His arrival into town should cause a commotion, and I'd take that chance to sneak in and see what was around for easy pickings. We'd meet in the cave the next day, after Wyatt got some real doctoring.

"My wound's looking pretty good now, Deke. Don't you think they're going to get a might suspicious about that?"

"You'll just tell them the truth—that it happened several days back and you've been treating it with poultices. We better take your shirt off, though. Kinda hard to explain why you had an extra shirt after you tore up the old one for bandages."

"You think of everything, Deke. Brains and a dick. A man couldn't ask for more."

I gave him one last kiss and a swat on the ass. "Be careful, Sweetlips."

"Always. Love you, Deke." And off he headed.

The moment he was out of sight I went into a tailspin. What had I been thinking, sending him off alone like that? What if some Crooked J men were there? What if someone recognized him? What if he met someone new and I lost him forever? Being reasonable and being in love sure as hell didn't go hand in hand.

I pulled myself together and started to circle around the edge of town. I decided I'd find the best spot for sneaking in then wait for everybody's attention to be on Wyatt before I'd make my move.

The town was your basic two-block stretch of boardwalks and storefronts, almost identical to the one near Lettie's. I found the blacksmith's shop on the far end. There was an alley that ran between it and the hotel and I decided that would be my best bet for slipping in unnoticed. Besides, the blacksmith's shop was the perfect place to start looking for horses.

I stayed hidden behind tall brush and tumbleweeds until I heard someone shouting for a doctor. In no time at all there was all kinds of shouting and running going on. I ran to the alley and carefully made my way to the front of it so's I could peak out and see what was happening with Wyatt. I had to duck back in quick when some folks went hurrying by. I tried poking my head out again and this time all was clear. I could see a crowd gathered way at the opposite end of town but I couldn't see Wyatt. I slipped 'round to the rear of the blacksmith's and slowly opened the back door. I heard the usual sounds a body'd expect to hear in a smith's shop but no clanging of metal or voices, which I was hoping meant the place was clear of people. I went inside, pressed myself against the wall and listened some more. I still heard nothing. Only the sizzle of fire and the shuffling of penned horses.

The front of the smith's shop was open to the roadway. I watched for a bit but saw no movement outside of the shop. I moved along the wall, making my way to the horses. I was sweating and palpitating something fierce. I tried to forget the fact that I was about to become a horse thief. I'd gone over and over it and didn't see how Wyatt and me had any other choice.

There were three horses in separate stalls near the front of the shop. One was a heavy work animal and not what I was looking for in a getaway horse. The other two seemed to fit the bill, but there was no way to be sure of their soundness without walking them out a bit. Unfortunately, that wasn't a chance I was likely to be gettin'. I'd just have to grab them both and hope neither of them were there for lameness.

The horse closest to me was a small chestnut mare. She turned her head to look at me but didn't seem concerned. I touched her rump and talked softly to her as I eyed the area for tack. I knew getting saddles might not be a possibility, but we'd need headgear for sure.

I was just about to move on to the next horse when I heard footsteps outside. I crouched down and held my breath. The smithy came into view, a huge shadow-figure backlit by the sun. He had his hammer in hand, and he looked to be a good two inches taller than me and about a barn's width thicker. I didn't fancy my chances if I got caught sneaking around his stable. The smith went to his anvil, pulled a piece of white-hot metal from his fire, and went to work pounding it into a new shape. No doubt that's exactly what he would do to my head if he caught me there. I didn't have a lot of choice but to stay put and stay quiet.

I must have crouched there, afraid to move even the slightest bit, for somewhere's near to two hours. I started praying that he'd take a break or need a piss or keel over and die. It didn't matter. I just wanted to get the hell out of there. My legs were burning from the crouch, and everything seemed to itch but I was too afraid to scratch.

Someone finally called from outside and he put down his hammer and walked to the front door. He stood in the doorway, jawing with someone I couldn't see, which made escaping risky but not as risky as staying put.

I uncramped my legs and started inching my way toward the back when their words drifted to me. I couldn't make it all out but when I heard, "attacked by Apaches," I froze. I knew I should get the hell out of there, but if they were going to be discussing Wyatt I wanted to hear.

The bits and pieces I could catch told me that Wyatt was taken to the doctor, that everyone seemed to be accepting his story, and that no suspicions had been raised. Satisfied that Wyatt was safe, I took another step toward the back door but suddenly their voices seemed to be right next to me.

"Now let's take a look at that mare of mine."

I dove behind some hay bales and landed face first in a hill of horseshit. I held my breath but the stench still burned my nostrils. From what I could tell they were going over the chestnut. I was probably no more than eight feet from them, with nothing but hay and a two-foot-high pile of shit to protect me. The odds weren't looking good. The smallest movement on my part would probably give me away. 'Course that's when I noticed the rat. The fucker started out sniffing the little finger on my left hand then moved on to giving it a couple of test nibbles. Satisfied that I'd make a good meal, he began gnawing on me in earnest. It took every ounce of manhood I could muster not to run screaming like a girl from that barn.

By the time the owner of the chestnut pulled his horse out of the stall, the rat was drawing some serious blood. Both the customer and the blacksmith stepped outside to settle up and jaw some more. I did no hesitating or sneaking around this time.

I shook that rat off and ran out the back door without looking over my shoulder. I didn't stop running until I was in the high brush again and out of sight of town.

The side of my left hand was smeared with blood and my finger pounded and stung. I broke off a cactus leaf and rubbed the juice all over the wound. Once cleaned up the bite wasn't nearly as bad-looking as I'd expected, but it still gave me the shivers thinking about how I'd gotten it. I wrapped the finger in my bandana and thought about what would happen when I showed it to Wyatt. He'd be right impressed at me lying there letting the rat chew away, and he'd give me all the sympathy I wanted.

Wyatt. I sighed. I sure did miss that boy. It'd been three hours at the most since I'd last seen him and I was already aching over him.

I spent the rest of the day circling the town from a safe distance trying to spot a chance for horse thieving, but none ever came up. There were always too many people, not enough horses, or too little cover. I headed back to the river, discouraged and missing Wyatt.

I sat on the bank of the river and had a dinner of raw crawdads and roots. It made me long for the good old days of stinkbugs and cactus apples. I drank plenty of water to try and fill up all my empty. When the sky was good and black, I snuck back to the edge of town to give the horse hunt another try. I started worrying about Wyatt again. Was he being taken care of properly? Was the sheriff questioning him at that very moment? Was he thinking of me at all and missing me like I was him?

I looked down at myself. What a sorry body love had made me—covered in shit, chewed on by rats, and mooning like a female. It was plumb disgusting. I needed to get myself back on the man side of the fence right quick, before it was too late.

I was having a stern talk with myself about just that thing when a jackrabbit shot by and I remembered the time I squashed the rabbit under me when we were horseless in the desert the first time, and I couldn't help but picture Wyatt doing his imitation of me and, before I knew it, my mouth started twitching at the corners and I felt warm all over.

Damn, I missed my Sweetlips.

The nighttime activity in town was as busy as the daytime. It was going to be near impossible to steal a couple of horses until early morning. It would be best to head back to the cave and get a little shuteye for the time being. I looked around a bit longer for any sign of Wyatt but saw none, so I made my way back to our camp. I curled up with the bedroll and tried to sleep. It was going to be right hard to do without Wyatt's warm body pressed up against mine.

I closed my eyes and pictured myself finding two beautiful horses, saddled and ready for the stealing, their saddlebags filled with jerky and hardtack and ammunition. Wyatt would look at me in that hero-struck way he had and he would fret something terrible over my rat bite, then we'd fuck until stars were exploding and the heavens were a openin'. I fell asleep smiling like an idiot.

I woke up hours later to a biting burn on the right side of my face. I shot out of the bedroll, slapping and scratching at my face. I looked down at the ground and saw what I was afraid of seeing—a mangled, dying black widow spider twisting in the sand. I felt the side of my face and a hot welt was already growing.

Shit, shit, shit. I'd been widow bit before and it had made me sicker'n a dog. I couldn't be sick. Wyatt was depending on me to get horses and maybe some supplies. He'd risked getting caught walking into town to be my distraction, and I was going to waste it by curling up in a ball and puking on myself.

I had to act quick. The last time I'd gotten bit it took a while for the poison to hit my stomach. If I got into town now and found some horses, I might be able to get back to the cave and be waiting for Wyatt before my stomach started turning itself inside out. The burning and itching on my face were already unbearable, so I packed some wet sand on it before going. The sand helped with the burning some but I could feel my face swelling as I headed toward town. By the time I reached the edge of it, my right eye was half closed.

I crept behind and between buildings, looking for unattended horses. I was heading for the saloon, which I figured would be my best bet, but I had my one good eye open for any possibilities along the way. I tried to ignore the dizziness I was feeling and the bile pooling in my stomach. The spider venom was acting much faster than I remembered, but since my belly was damn near empty this time, it sorta figured.

Outside of the saloon there were four saddled horses tethered to the rail, but they were square in front of the doors and lit up by the glare of a street lamp. There was no way I could slip up unnoticed and steal away with two horses.

While I was figuring what to do, I heard an odd wheezing noise in the alley to the side of the saloon. I made my way slowly through the shadows until I could see into the alley. There, wheezing and braying softly, was a pint-sized donkey loaded down with mining gear. An old, sick, dog-sized jackass was useless to me, but at least I might be able to get some supplies off of it.

I neared the critter, talking softly. It eyed me in that stubborn way donkey-types do, but it seemed willing to give me the benefit of the doubt. I held my hand out and it reached its muzzle toward me.

"There you go, little donkey. Easy. Easy."

I could see she had plenty of supplies that Wyatt and I could use. Maybe my luck was finally turning. I reached out to touch her and was just about to make contact when my stomach swelled and flopped. I covered my mouth and doubled over. I tried to run but my belly squeezed tight and I heaved, sounding something like a bellowing buffalo. The donkey screeched and hawed, raising a bigger racket than me and my heaving stomach. I tried to say something comforting to her but all that came up was a mess of raw crawdads and chewed up roots. I ended up on my knees and the donkey screamed one last hee haw before kicking me square in the ass. I landed face first in my own mess, my ass exploding in pain.

I heard someone shouting, "Rosie, Rosie. I'm coming, sweetheart." I scrambled to my feet and I made it to the back of the alley where I hid behind a water barrel. The miner and some drunken cowboys showed up and tried to calm old Rosie down.

"What the hell you been feeding that ass of yours, old timer? That's some of the nastiest shit I've ever seen."

"And the stink. Jesus Christ."

"She's not feeling well. Just leave her alone. Go on and mind your own business."

The cowboys returned to the saloon, laughing and carrying on about nasty donkey shit. The miner led his Rosie away, clucking and fretting over her.

I heaved a few more times, doing my best to keep the noise down and not pass out, then I decided to call an end to my horse thieving career and stumbled out of the alley. On my way out of town, I spotted a steaming pie cooling on a windowsill. The mere thought of pie made me want to heave some more, but I just had to have something to give to Wyatt when he came back to me. It weren't as good as two horses but it was better than nothing. I snatched the pie from the sill and managed to make my way back to the cave before passing out.

CHAPTER 10

I WOKE UP WITH daylight filling the cave and the most god-awful stench filling my nose. I was disappointed but not real surprised when I figured out the stench came from me. My face was on fire and my right eye was about the size of an 8 ball. My ass throbbed like it had been hit by a train and not some donkey with one hoof in the grave. My little finger on my left hand was puffy and chewed up and my stomach felt like someone had hooked it up to a hand pump and pumped it dry. But the worse pain of all was knowing that I'd let Wyatt down; that we'd be stuck wandering through the desert again, horseless and hungry.

I knew he'd be worried and looking for some sign of me so I pulled myself to my knees, ready to head back into town. I couldn't make it past my knees, though, and knelt there swaying.

"Deke?"

I tried to stop the spinning of my head so I could listen better, not believing I'd really heard Wyatt's voice.

"Deke? Good God, what the fuck is that smell?"

Wyatt stood in the cave entrance. He had on new duds and his clean, fresh, just-washed smell cut through the stink of my shit and puke. His left arm was in a tidy white sling, looking cozy and rested like a patient tucked into a hospital bed. He looked like some rich rancher's son all dressed up for Sunday school, not like the worn down, torn up fugitive he'd been yesterday.

I retched bile on his new boots.

"Deke, what happened to you?"

I held up my left hand. "Rat bit." I pointed to my face. "Black widow." I put my hand on my backside. "Ass kicked."

Wyatt never admitted to it, but I saw him bite his lower lip to keep from laughing.

I pointed to the pie on the ground, which was now covered in ants, and said, "But I got us something to eat."

"Oh, that must be the pie Mrs. Maynard made for me."

Through my swollen eye and returning nausea I tried to focus on Wyatt's face. "Mrs. Maynard?"

"The doc's wife. Nicest woman. She baked a cherry pie for me but someone stole it off the windowsill. Must have been you."

I looked at the bug-covered mess that was no longer fit for eating. "Sorry."

"Doesn't matter. She baked me apple and rhubarb ones, too. They were delicious."

It was hard to tell, what with the spider venom in my veins and all, but I think I was starting to feel a might peeved with the whole situation right about then. I probably would've shot off a couple of choice words for Wyatt and his pies if it weren't for suddenly remembering that I'd failed to get horses for us, which had been the whole point of Wyatt going into town and being my distraction. I started feeling ashamed of myself for begrudging him his pampering.

"Wyatt? I'm afraid I got some bad news."

"Worse than the way you look?"

"Well, it kinda has to do with the way I look. See, I tried to steal us some horses but shit kept happening and well, we'll still be walking, I'm afraid."

"That? Oh, don't worry about it. Come on. I got something to show you." Wyatt helped me to my feet, trying his best to not actually touch me, and led me outside. The bright sun and my swollen eye made it hard for me to believe what I was looking at but there just weren't no doubting it. Tethered to some scrub oaks were two horses, saddled and loaded with supplies.

"They were all just the nicest folks, Deke. I wish you coulda met them. I told them my little brother and sister and my grandpap were waiting for me to bring them supplies when I got jumped by the Apaches. I told them I managed to escape by playing dead but the Apaches took everything I had. Everybody in town pitched in to help me out so my family wouldn't starve. Isn't that wonderful?"

I squinted at the horses in disbelief. One of them was the little chestnut mare from the blacksmith's shop. While I was lying face down in horseshit getting devoured by man-eating rats, Wyatt was downing pies and being showered with gifts by everyone in town. I was definitely feeling more than a might peeved now.

"Gee, Wyatt. I hope your worrying about me and missing me didn't sour the taste of your cherry pie none."

"Apple," Wyatt corrected me. "Apple and rhubarb. You stole the cherry, remember?"

I opened my mouth to cuss Wyatt out but my stomach lurched and all I managed was a hacking bray that sounded a lot like Rosie. I fell to my knees, too weak to stand. Wyatt kneeled in front of me, getting puke all over his new jeans while he fingered my spider bite.

"I did miss you, Deke. So much. Everybody was so nice but still, all I wanted was to come back to you." He kissed my swollen eye. "And to think that the whole time you were going through such hell. All for me."

I looked away from him. His hands felt real nice on my fevered face, so I didn't jerk away or nothing, but I didn't want to look at him right then.

"Even as delicious as those pies were, I wished I was eating stinkbugs on the trail with you, not sitting by the fire with the Maynards and the minister's family. And the mayor. He was there, too."

"You got to sit by a fire? While I slept in a cave?"

"Believe me, Deke. I would have rather been in the cave with you."

He lifted my left hand to his lips and kissed my pinkie. "Nothing feels right without you."

"Bet you never even thought of me." I cursed the poutin' that came out with my words.

"I mean it, Deke. I thought of you every second. Even when the doc's daughter gave me that rubdown, it was your hands I was wishing were on me."

I leaned to the side a bit and touched my bruised ass. "Did you get to sleep in a bed?"

"A great big feather one." Wyatt bent and placed five kisses on my backside. "But that only reminded me of our bed at Lettie's and I missed you so much I couldn't sleep a wink."

Wyatt started undressing me to get me cleaned up. I studied him close while he got me naked.

"You slept like a fucking log, didn't you?"

"Oh, my God, Deke. It was incredible." Wyatt busted at the seams. "They had to drag me out of bed this morning. And the food . . . Holy fuck. I thought Lettie was a good cook. These women were amazing; dish after dish of the best eatins I've ever had. I brought some leftovers for you. Not many 'cause I finished most of what they put in front of me, but it's enough to give you an idea of the spread they put on for me. And cookies and pies . . . Well, you know about the pies. And . . . Oh! Oh! I got to bathe in a real tub. Mrs. Maynard boiled up gallons of water and I got to soak my whole body in it. Smell me." Wyatt shoved his neck under my nose. "Lavender. Mrs. Maynard put lavender from her garden in it. And the mayor himself gave me cash to tide me over." Wyatt pulled a wad of paper and coins from his pocket. "See?" He took a deep breath and let it out with a sigh. "You would have loved it, Deke."

As much as I didn't want to, it was plumb impossible not to smile at him. "I missed you, too, Sweetlips."

Wyatt looked suddenly shy and sheepish. "I do have one very special thing I saved just for you, though."

"What's that?"

Wyatt stood and dropped his jeans. His hard cock stood straight up and his balls seemed to dangle a bit lower than usual.

"Nobody gets this but you."

"Hmm. Surprised they didn't offer you their daughters to take care of that."

"They did. Had a whole string of beautiful young women they paraded in front of me, but I don't give my load to anyone but you."

"As romantic and generous as that is, Wyatt, I couldn't keep down water right now, much less your load."

Wyatt kneeled again and held my dick, which was drooping as bad as the rest of me. "That's all right. I may have got pie and casserole and pot roast and cookies but there was only one thing I was craving that whole time," and Wyatt sucked me down, bringing life back to my limp and battered body.

Fifteen minutes later I was munching on a bread roll, giving Wyatt's throat a healthy pounding, and feeling happier than a buzzard in a slaughterhouse. That was life with Wyatt. Wonder piled on top of wonder.

When we both had as much as our stomachs could hold, I got dressed while we talked about our next destination.

"Deke, I know what your answer is going to be, but why can't we stay here for a little bit? These people are not at all like the ones you and Lettie described in that other town. They're really nice here. And generous. We can work for a while; give ourselves a rest and earn some money."

"And who will I be? Your grandpap or your little sister?"

"What?"

"Wyatt, you lied to these good folks. You told them you were on a mission to save your poor, starving family. You think they are suddenly going to accept you and your cowboy fuck partner and let you settle down in peace?"

Wyatt looked wounded.

"And have you forgotten how recently we were almost caught by your daddy's men?"

He dug his toe into the sand and shook his head. "No. I just kinda wish . . . "

"I kinda wish, too, Sweetlips. You know I do. But we can't. We can't live a normal life right now. Jesus, Wyatt, we've gone over and over this and you keep telling me you understand. We may never be able to live a normal life. Ever."

"But why can't we just try? You seem so dead set against it all the time. You didn't want to at Lettie's, either, and look how that turned out."

"Yeah, look how that turned out. We both almost got caught, you almost got killed, and we put Lettie and her children in danger."

"But sometimes I feel like . . . "

"Like what, Wyatt?"

"Never mind."

"Tell me." I knew I was getting too angry. The boy had a right to have his say. It wasn't his fault my old worries about not being enough for him were springing back to life. Things had been so good at Lettie's that I'd stopped fretting over all the what-ifs, but now it was staring me in the face again.

Wyatt shook his head. "Let's just get going."

"Wyatt if you would rather stay here with your pies and warm fires and beautiful young women, I'm not holding you back. I've told you all along you could go home. Your father will forgive you. I didn't want you to come along in the first place, remember?" I regretted it the moment it came out.

Wyatt looked me in the eye and his jaw tightened. "Yeah. I remember. Sorry I've been such a burden." He got on the chestnut and turned her north. "Let's try Canada." Then he rode away.

Why was I such a fucking idiot?

I got on the other horse, a big handsome black gelding, and followed him. We rode in silence most of the day. Twice we stopped and ate some of the leftovers Wyatt brought, but they didn't have much flavor for me. They weren't going to last long, either. The truth was, no matter how big the risk, we were going to have to start earning some money if we expected to make it all the way to Canada.

The next break we took, I settled down next to Wyatt. He scooted away a bit.

"I've been thinking about what you said. Maybe it is time we started getting work here and there. Never stay long in one place but earn enough to buy ammunition and food at least."

"Let me guess. We can't both work at the same place at the same time. We can't be seen together."

My first reaction was to lay into him, but I made myself stop. "No. We can't be seen together. I think we've tossed that topic around enough times, Wyatt. Do we really need to get into it again?"

"And I suppose you're going to be the one working while I'm . . . what? Hiding in the bushes somewhere, darning socks until you come back?"

"What the fuck is up your butt?" But he was already on his horse and riding off.

I couldn't figure out what had suddenly gone sour with us. It had to have something to do with that damn town. Maybe the whole fugitive life was getting to him. Maybe he was missing Lettie and the kids. I didn't know and worse, I didn't know how to fix it.

That night we fucked and sucked and nothing on the surface, seemed, to have changed, but I felt a toughness to his loving that hadn't been there before. Truth be told, it didn't harm our loving none but it wasn't real romantic. It seemed more like competition than sex, and being that Wyatt and I were both fond of winning, it made for one powerful grand finale.

The next day we got on our horses and started riding again in silence. I knew Wyatt wanted to talk things out, but I'd shut him down so many times before I guess he wasn't going to bother trying any more. I thought about how things were between us; how we always did things my way—fought my way, traveled my way, fucked my way. That was bound to wear a little thin no matter how much a body loved another body. Wyatt was too much of a man for me to be treating him like a boy.

I gave the black a kick and rode up next to Wyatt, who had been riding ahead of me most of the morning.

"Hey, Sweetlips."

"Hey."

"I'm an asshole sometimes."

"Yeah, you are."

"Forgive me?"

He shrugged.

"I promise the first town we come to you get to work first while I hide in the bushes darning socks."

He turned his head slightly away from me. "And you'll stop rubbing my face in how not normal we are?"

I grabbed his reins and made his horse stop. "Is that what this is about? I can't do that, Wyatt. I can't stop telling you that you're not normal because you're not normal. You're special, Wyatt. You're different. There isn't another person in this world who comes close to you. You're not anywhere near normal and you never will be. That's why I can't stop loving you. That's why I am so fucking terrified of losing you." My voice rose as words poured faster and harder from my mouth. "I can't give you everything you want and that stabs me like a knife. I feel like I'm failing you sometimes and it kills me, because you give me more than I could ever ask for. I'm more man for loving you than I ever thought possible. So no, Wyatt, I'm sorry, but I won't stop rubbing your face in how not normal you are. I can't."

We stared at each other, both a little surprised by my outburst, then Wyatt nodded and said, "OK. I was just asking."

After that, things were good between us again. In fact, I'd plumb forgotten how all-fired annoying Wyatt could be on the trail when he was in a good mood. It was a rare moment indeed when that boy's gums weren't flapping.

"I told you, didn't I, that the doc couldn't believe how good the wounds looked without any real doctoring?"

"I do believe you mentioned it once or twice."

"Any more pie left?"

"No, Wyatt, I haven't had time to bake another one since you asked me the last twelve times."

"How long is it going to take to get to Canada?"

"That answer hasn't changed, either, since the last twelve times you asked it."

"I'm sorry, Deke, but I get so bored on the trail. When are we going to come to another town? I hope it's as good as the last town. That sure was fun."

"Yes, it was a barrel of laughs. I can't decide which part I enjoyed more—the rat chewing or the black widow bite."

"How about the ass kicking? God, I bet that was funny to see."

"Wyatt?"

"Huh?"

"You might want to be shutting up now."

"Shit." I looked up at the sudden change in Wyatt's voice. "Riders coming."

I followed his gaze. "Holy shit."

"Cavalry."

"Damn. They've seen us already. Stay calm and let me do the talking."

An entire regiment rode toward us, moving like one long snake of horses and riders. Their precision made me itchy even from a distance. I forced myself to relax. This wasn't necessarily a bad thing. In quieter times the Army might be better informed about civilian criminals, but with all the Indian troubles in the territory it was possible they didn't have time to be looking at wanted posters. I needed to stay calm.

The regiment commander called a halt and the snake of riders stopped in unison.

"I'm Captain Jones, United States Cavalry. Where are you men headed?"

"We're headed north. Is there some kind of problem, Captain?"

"We've had several recent attacks by hostile Apaches. There have been reports that a major uprising is in the works. We're advising everyone to stay close to home and be prepared."

"We'll get out of the area as soon as possible, sir. Thank you."

The Indian scout rode up to Jones and whispered in his ear. I felt mighty uneasy about the way the captain's eyes were studying Wyatt and me while the scout was whispering to him. When the scout was done, they both looked at us.

"Well, gentlemen, it seems you'll be coming with us."

I held down my panic and kept myself from looking at Wyatt. Seeing the fear that I knew he was feeling would only set me off.

"I don't think that's necessary, Captain. We'll take our chances with the Indians."

"Mr. . . . "

"Marshall."

"Mr. Marshall, the recent uprising is due to the death of one of the chiefs' sons. He died from wounds he received while chasing two white men. Before he died, the brave told his father he had wounded one of the men with an arrow through the shoulder. The brave described the injured white man as a 'palomino boy.'" The captain looked at Wyatt and paused to let his words sink in. "It appears you two gentlemen are responsible for an Apache uprising. I have no choice but to take you into protective custody. So if you'll come with us we'll take you back to the fort."

I let myself look at Wyatt. He was as white as he'd been after getting shot with the arrow. I smiled a little, trying to calm him, but it weren't much of a smile and I think it only made him feel worse.

"Oh." We both looked back at Captain Jones. "You'll be happy to know that one of the other men in your party survived the attack. He's being treated at the fort."

One of the other men in our party?

I looked at Wyatt again. No luck holding the panic down this time. The captain had to be talking about one of the Crooked J men. We couldn't let them take us back to the fort if there was someone from the Crooked J there. Somehow we had to figure out a way to escape from an entire regiment of cavalry soldiers. We'd worry about the entire Apache nation later. I felt my stomach drop. Canada was looking farther away every minute.

Wyatt, who up to that point had done a real good job of shutting up, picked now to open his mouth. "Captain Jones?"

"Yes?"

"There were no other men in our party. We were being chased by a band of outlaws when the Apaches attacked. Maybe he's one of the outlaws."

I held my breath. There was no telling how much the Crooked J hand had already told the Army. Maybe Captain Jones knew the whole story and was leaving that part out to get us to go to the fort, peaceful-like.

"If that's true, we'll make sure he is turned over to the proper local authorities, although I think he's been punished enough. For the time being, though, the two of you need to come with us."

We didn't have much choice. Captain Jones signaled with his arm and four soldiers rode up, boxing Wyatt and me between them. The captain signaled again and we became part of the cavalry snake, off to the fort to face one of Jennings's men. Boxed in and being herded by soldiers made it impossible for Wyatt and me to talk or plan. Even looking at each other might give something away, so I kept my eyes forward and tried not to think about what was going to happen when we reached the fort.

We rode for nearly an hour before the fort came into view. As soon as it did the regiment picked up speed, picking us up along with it. I heard a bugle call announcing our arrival and could soon see the sign at the entrance to the fort. Fort Craig. I'd heard about it. It was a fairly new fort used mostly for keeping the Indians under control. As far as I could recollect, it was a fair piece into the New Mexico portion of the territory, which meant we'd made it farther than I thought. It was still too close to California, though, and still too far from Canada.

Craig was an impressive fort, I had to admit. It was made of adobe and rock instead of the usual log buildings I'd seen, and they'd dug a trench around the outside of the entire fort for extra defense. Once inside the gate I was surprised at the size of it. It looked like there was room enough for two full companies of men to parade down the center.

We halted outside what I figured was the commanding officer's quarters, and then we had to wait in our box of soldiers for the regiment to do its regimenting. The Army wasn't big on doing things simple-like. There were all kinds of hoops the soldiers had to jump through before being allowed to dismount. Made me start to itch again.

When the show was done, our four guards dismounted in unison and marched Wyatt and me into the commander's office, right behind Captain Jones.

Jones sat down at a desk and got out a pen and some paper. He didn't invite us to sit and he didn't dismiss the soldiers guarding us.

"I'll need to ask you men a few questions, then we'll see if you can identify the man who was attacked with you."

I wasn't looking forward to answering a bunch of questions, most of which I was going to have to answer with lies, but if it kept us from coming face to face with someone from the Crooked J, I was willing to do it.

The captain pointed his pen at Wyatt. "Let's start with you, palomino boy. What's your name?"

"John Deacon."

"What is your relation to Mr. Marshall?"

"We're, uh . . . cousins."

It was a very small pause, but it was a pause. Jones showed no reaction, but I knew a man as rigid and spit-polished as him would notice it.

"What did you do to provoke the Apaches to attack you?"

"We didn't do anything, sir. I told you we were being chased by outlaws when the Indians appeared. Most of them went after the outlaws but one came after us."

"How did you escape?"

"De . . . lon shot the one who was following us. The others never came after us."

"How did you get injured?"

"An arrow hit me in the shoulder."

Jones did not look up once. I felt sure he knew more than what he was letting on to knowin', but why pretend? If he knew we were wanted men, why hide it? Why not just throw us in the stockade until the local lawman could come and get us?

Jones aimed his pen at me. "Your name again?"

"Dillon Marshall."

"Do you have anything to add, Mr. Marshall?"

"No, sir."

Jones waved his hand. "You men are dismissed."

Wyatt and I sighed in relief and turned to leave. One of the soldiers put his hand on my shoulder and stopped me.

"He was talking to us."

"Oh."

Once the soldiers were gone, Jones stood and walked toward the door. "Follow me. I'll take you to the infirmary. I'm sure you're anxious to confront the man you were running from."

Anxious weren't exactly the word I was shooting for, but I took a deep breath and followed Jones out the door. I scanned our surroundings as we crossed the parade grounds. Fort Craig was a mighty busy place, crawling with both soldiers and civilians. We were going to have one hell of a hard time escaping from it. I looked at Wyatt and he was watching me, eager for some sign that I had things under control—maybe had a plan brewing in my head already. I gave him a smile but I'm pretty near positive it was just as weak as I was feeling, so it didn't do much to ease his worries.

We went into the infirmary and a soldier exchanged salutes with Captain Jones, then Jones continued to the rear of the building. I stopped in my tracks when I saw the man lying in a bed in the far corner of the room. It was Shorty.

CHAPTER 11

TO BE EXACT, it was Shorty without the top part of his head. I'd seen a scalping victim once before and it made me lose my stomach, just like it was doing to Wyatt now. He doubled over and I put my hand on his back while he retched and gagged.

Shorty looked close to death, but when he saw Wyatt and me he tried to sit up. He waved his hands weakly and gurgled some strange sounds.

Captain Jones ordered a woman changing hospital beds to clean up Wyatt's mess. He watched Shorty for a bit then he looked at me.

"He seems to recognize you. Of course we'll never know for certain. The Apaches cut his tongue out and we've been unsuccessful in getting him to write anything other than an x. Do you recognize him, Mr. Marshall?"

"Yes." My voice croaked. Watching Shorty, with the top half of his head peeled off, and listening to the pitiful, god-awful noises he was making, made me feel bad for what I was about to say but I had no choice but to say it. "He's one of the outlaws who chased us."

"Would you like me to notify the local authorities?"

"No." I was feeling right filthy about myself. It just weren't right to accuse a man of something when he had no way of defending himself. "I think you're right, Captain. He's suffered enough already." I put my arm around Wyatt's shoulders as he came up for air. "I appreciate your worrying for our safety, sir, but we really would like to get a move on now."

"I'm afraid that's not possible, Mr. Marshall."

"Are we under arrest?"

"No, you are not."

"Then how come we're being held here?"

"Because we may need you and your cousin to help avert the Apache uprising."

I didn't like the sound of that and the itching started up again. "But how can we help?"

"By turning yourselves over to them. Our scout has been in negotiations with the Indians. They are willing to call off their attacks in exchange for the men who killed their chief's son."

Now I was the one who felt like heaving. "And if we don't volunteer?"

"Then we'll turn you over to them. It's two lives versus possibly hundreds of lives. I'm sure you can understand that, Mr. Marshall."

Fuck no, I don't understand. I was trying to get just those words to come out of my mouth when Wyatt spoke up.

"I'll go. I'm the one they're looking for. There's no need to send my cousin, too."

I punched Wyatt in the face as hard as I could. He was unconscious before he hit the floor. I turned back to Jones.

"I'm the one who shot the chief's son. John had nothing to do with it."

Jones studied me. "I'm impressed with both of you. I hope you understand this isn't something I look forward to doing, but we have a territory full of people we're here to protect. If we have a way to keep the casualties down to one or two, we have to take it."

"Fuck no, I don't understand, Captain, but I do understand I'll do anything to save my cousin's life. I'll be your sacrifice as long as John stays safe."

Jones nodded. "I'm not sure the chief will be willing to accept a deal that does not involve the 'palomino boy' but I'll send my scout to find out."

"And, Captain? The kid's going to be right pissed when he wakes up. You might want to lock him up."

Jones called for a soldier and, like magic, one appeared. "I think it's best if we keep both of you locked up for now. Can't take the chance that my bargaining chip might disappear."

I started to argue but knew it was no use. Jones was a smart man and in his position I'd lock us both up, too. The soldier and I hefted Wyatt off the floor and I half carried, half dragged him out of the infirmary. Shorty was still gurgling and waving when we left.

Jones put Wyatt and me in separate cells. I was glad to see we were the only prisoners and that we were closed off from the stockade office; it would make planning things a whole lot easier. Not to mention that I didn't want Wyatt's cussing and screaming at me to bother anyone else once he came to.

Jones stood outside my cell after locking us up and apologized again.

"If there was any other way, Mr. Marshall, I'd give it a try."

"How 'bout giving the Indians back their land?"

Jones squinted at me as he tried to figure out if I was joking or not. "Yes. Well. I'll send my scout to talk to the chief. As soon as we get word I'll let you know."

"I'll be waiting."

Jones squinted again and added a little twist to his mouth. I think his admiration for me was fading fast. 'Course men starched as tight as Jones usually had trouble appreciating my sense of humor.

Jones turned and left, leaving me alone with Wyatt who was still unconscious, lying on his cot. I was a little worried about his shoulder and how it was holding up to all the throwing up and knocking down.

"Hey, Sweetlips. Can you hear me?"

Wyatt moaned and lifted his good hand to his face. I'd missed his nose when I hit him but I could see the purpling and swelling starting around his left eye.

"Hey, you. Still love me?"

Wyatt bolted up. "What the . . . "He turned and saw me. "Deke. You goddamned motherfucking son of a bitch. You can't do it. I won't let you."

Wyatt stood up to come toward me but dizziness knocked him back to his ass.

"I'm sorry, Wyatt. I didn't know how else to shut you up."

Wyatt hesitated, poking at his bruised eye.

"You mean you have a plan?"

"Besides sacrificing myself to the entire Apache nation? No. You just been annoying me lately and I wanted to shut you up."

"Goddamn it, Deke. This isn't funny."

"Jones doesn't seem to think so, either."

Wyatt stood slower this time and walked to the bars separating us. He curled his fingers around the bars and the fear in his voice made me a little weak. "I won't let you do it."

I curled my fingers over his and kept my voice gentle. "You may not have a lot of choice, Wyatt. Besides, you were going to sacrifice yourself for me."

"But it's me they want, Deke."

"No, it ain't, Wyatt. I'm the one who did the shooting. You're just the one everybody remembers. That's what I've been trying to tell you all this time." I reached through the bars and ruffled his hair. "Palomino boy."

Tears rose up in Wyatt's eyes. "Its not funny, Deke. Please don't do this."

Wyatt's tears set me to burning—my chest and my throat and my eyes. I stepped away from him and cleared my throat.

"I'm not saying I'm going without a fight, Wyatt. I'm going to try and think of a way out of this, but you need to accept . . . "

"No!" Wyatt slammed the cell bars. "I won't accept and don't you even fucking try to tell me to." Wyatt grabbed the bars again and stared hard at me. His words came out slowly, one by one. "Do not leave me here while you go off to die."

I stared back into those beautiful, shimmering sky blue eyes. I pictured myself living as the one left behind, alone and missing him, and I knew he was right.

"Okay. I promise, Sweetlips. If we go, we go together."

He hung his head and sighed. "Thank you."

"Now. We need a plan."

Several hours later when Jones returned with his scout, Wyatt and I were still plotting. We shut up quick and stood to hear the verdict.

"Well, Mr. Marshall, the chief has agreed to accept just you but he wants to see you, too, Mr. Deacon, so he can be sure the right man is paying for his son's death."

"And I suppose self-defense was already argued?"

Jones ignored me. "You are to be turned over to him at sunrise tomorrow."

Wyatt sat down on his cot like the air had been let out of him. We'd been hoping for a little more time than that to pull off our escape. To keep back my own fear, I put my concentration on our plan and the captain.

"I was wondering, Captain Jones, do I get all the same rights as a condemned man?'

Cause after all that's what I am."

He pondered that idea for a bit before asking, "What did you have in mind?"

"You know—last meal, last request. Those kinds of things."

Jones pondered some more. "I suppose that would be appropriate. What is your last request, Mr. Marshall?"

"A woman."

"I'm sorry?"

"A woman. I want to spend my last night in the arms of a woman. Can't think of a finer farewell. Maybe I'll even get lucky and leave behind a little Marshall. Carry on the family name and such."

Jones looked like he was smelling something bad but the scout was a grinnin'.

"If you are suggesting I get you a prostitute, I'm sorry but I don't allow that in my camp."

"You know, that doesn't surprise me one bit, Captain, but we both know there ain't an Army base in this fine country that doesn't have women near it to provide aid and comfort to our fighting men. For a price, of course."

Jones was not pleased but he nodded. "I'll see what I can find."

"Oh, and I'd like to have her somewhere else but here." I whispered to Jones while I pointed to Wyatt. "Not exactly the kind of thing you want to be doing in front of your baby cousin."

Jones walked out with the scout, who was trying not to laugh, following.

Wyatt stood up, looking a heap livelier than before. "All right. That's done. Now what's next?"

"We wait until they take me to my woman."

Wyatt nodded. "Good. I think we need to go over some things again. I just want to make sure we are clear on everything. So, tell me if I've got this straight. You're not actually going to have sex with this woman, right?"

"I don't know. I was thinking if I do end up dying it might be kind of nice to try something new before I go."

Wyatt's expression was starting to look a might like the captain's. "How 'bout I bite your dick off the next time I'm sucking it and you can never fuck anything again? That will be new and different, won't it?"

"Wyatt, for the twentieth time, I will not actually fuck this woman."

"All right. Jesus. I just wanted to be clear. No need to get all pissy about it."

"Come here." I reached my arm between the bars separating us and got a hold of Wyatt's shirt. I pulled him to me and kissed him. "For my last supper I'm planning on eating you."

Wyatt smiled. "I don't think Captain Jones would approve of that."

"Bullshit. I ain't never seen a man more in need of some dick up his ass than our Captain Jones. Hell, he's probably got a corncob up there right now. That's why he walks so stiff; he's trying to hold it in."

Wyatt started laughing and I had to kiss him again.

"No matter what happens, Sweetlips, don't ever forget you're the best fucking thing that's ever happened to me."

Wyatt laid his forehead against my fingers, which were curled around the bars. I put my lips to his hair and closed my eyes, smelling him and feeling him and remembering him. If we failed, there was a good chance we were going to die without ever holding each other again, so I needed to get as much of him now as I could.

We didn't talk any more and about an hour later Jones returned with two soldiers at his side.

"All right, Marshall. You're getting your last request."

He unlocked my cell door and I stepped out, then looked back at Wyatt.

"Remember, John, you promised to raise my son as your own, if'n I produce one tonight."

Wyatt smiled and Jones pushed me forward in disgust. I surveyed the stockade office as I passed through. I was pleased to see that with only the two of us as prisoners, Jones had only one soldier on duty.

I had a guard on each side of me and Jones was behind me as we walked across the grounds of the fort and on out the front gate. Scattered around the outside of the fort in all directions were the kinds of businesses that catered to the needs of Army men. One of those buildings, about a hundred yards from the entrance, was a two-story house with lots of horses tied up out front. My guess was we were headed there.

And I was right. When we reached the porch, Jones gave his men their orders.

"You two men stay with him. I want a post outside the room door and one in the back of the building. Is that clear?"

"Yes, sir."

So far so good. A fair-sized house of ill repute was just what I'd been planning on.

Jones left and the soldiers led me inside. We were greeted by a rather large woman in a dress that exposed her two largest assets.

"So this is our condemned man? Honey, you are a tasty morsel. And a big one, to boot. It will definitely be my pleasure to grant you your every dying wish."

I watched the soldiers from the corner of my eye. I'd suspected that they'd be less rigid with Jones gone, and they were. In fact, their attentions were on the half-naked women running all over the place and not on me.

The woman who greeted us cuddled up to me. "The name's Wanda, hon. Let's go get started."

Wanda led me up the stairs while one of the soldiers left to keep watch from outside. The other soldier followed Wanda and me. At the top of the stairs, I heard groaning and moaning from every direction and I gotta admit it made me a little hard. I'd always been partial to the sounds of a man delivering his load and there did seem to be a mighty lot of delivering going on in that house.

Wanda took me to a room half way down the left side of the landing. She opened the door and smiled at the soldier following us.

"Are you planning on watching, young man? If so, you're going to have to pay."

"I'll be staying out here, ma'am."

"I feel so much safer knowing that." She gave the soldier's crotch a quick squeeze then led me into the room, shutting the door behind us.

Wanda didn't waste any time. She unfastened the one button that was keeping her assets reined in and they popped free like a couple of plump pink piglets being birthed. I fumbled with my hand in my front pocket as I tried not to look at them. I'd never been so close to unclothed female parts before and it was more than a little unsettling.

Wanda and her piglets came closer.

"My, my. You are a shy one. There's no need to be bashful, honey. You're going to be dying soon. You don't want to waste any time."

I pulled my hand out of my pocket and with it the wad of bills Wyatt had given me; his gift from the mayor. I held it up in front of the advancing parts.

"I got a job for you, Wanda."

"Does it involve sex?"

"Nope."

"Ah. My favorite kind of client." Wanda took the money then wrestled with her breasts for a bit as she tried to get them corralled again behind that one button. Once they were more or less out of sight I was able to look Wanda in the eye.

She surveyed me from head to toe then said, "You're not a woman-fucking kind of man, are you, hon?"

"No, I'm not, but I must say your . . . " I waved my hand in the general direction of her chest, " . . . are very impressive."

"Thank you. Most of us girls got a glimpse of that 'palomino boy' they brought in with you. He's pretty damn impressive, too. Is he yours?"

I nodded.

"Something as pretty as him would be hard to pass up, whether you're a man or a woman."

"And if we get turned over to the Apaches . . . " My voice suddenly stopped working. I struggled hard to keep back the tears I felt coming on. I felt all-powerful foolish breaking down and crying in front of a female, but the only thing I could see in my mind's eye was Wyatt with his scalp peeled off and his tongue cut out, and my voice just wouldn't work. It was plumb embarrassing.

Wanda's hand went to her throat and I saw some shimmering in her eyes, too. She handed the money back to me. "Honey, love's not something I see much of in my line of work. I don't want your money. Some things are worth doing for free."

I took back Wyatt's money and stuffed it in my pants, still embarrassed but very grateful.

"Thank you, Wanda. If I ever do decide to mount the horse from the other direction, I'll be headed straight to you."

Wanda laughed and held out her hand. "It's a deal, honey. But promise me we'll do more than just stick corncobs up your chute. I get enough of that with old Tightass Jones."

I shook Wanda's hand, laughing hard and thinking how I couldn't wait to tell Wyatt I'd been right about Jones.

"So, what do you need me to do, honey?"

"I need two uniforms."

"Easy. There's a half a dozen empty ones scattered all down the hallway."

"I figured as much. Once I get the uniforms I'm going to need some kind of distraction to get the guard away from the door."

"That'd be Mimi. Best damn distraction I've ever met. She holds the house record for getting soldiers to abandon their posts."

"Is there a back entrance to the fort?"

"Nope. Just the main one. You've seen that trench they've dug and you've met Captain Jones. Not much gets in or out of that place unless they want it to."

"Well, can you tell me where the stables are? I need to know where both the civilian and soldier ones are. Where are they from the stockade?"

Wanda described for me where everything was inside the fort, including the armory, and when she was done I gave her a kiss on the cheek. "You are as near to perfect as a body can get, Wanda."

She blushed and I imagined that was an unusual happening for her.

"Sure you don't want a freebie, honey, just to see how the other half fucks?"

"Don't tempt me. I'm running out of time."

"Stay right here then. I'll be back in a bit with your uniforms."

Wanda stepped outside the door and closed it behind her. I put my ear to it so's I could her talking to the guard.

"Got me a lively one, Junior. I need to get some accoutrements to take care of this one. Don't let him get away, 'k?"

I went over and over the plan while Wanda was away. If the rest of the pieces fell into place as smoothly as they did with Wanda, Wyatt and I would be back on our way in no time.

Wanda's humming told me when she was about to return. I put my ear to the door again and heard what sounded like a slap then she scolded the guard. "No peeking, Junior. I plan on using these things on you next time you visit. Wouldn't want to spoil the surprise now, would you?"

Wanda opened the door and stepped in carrying a burlap sack. She took it to the bed and dumped out two complete cavalry uniforms, including boots and suspenders.

"The gents who usually wear these will be occupied for the rest of the night so they won't be missed until you're, hopefully, long gone. And I talked to Mimi. Told her to give us ten minutes then she's going to work her charms on Junior out there. Molly'll come tell us when the coast is clear."

"I don't know how many times I can say 'thank you', Wanda."

"Just save up for one great big one right before you leave."

I started stripping off my clothes and Wanda jumped onto the bed backside first, making it squeak something fierce before it slammed against the wall. The entire time I changed clothes Wanda moaned and wailed and bounced on the bed. When I could manage to keep from laughing, I'd throw in an "eeyah" or an "oh God" of my own. I was sitting in the chair pulling on my cavalry boots when the door opened and a tiny wisp of a girl younger than Wyatt came in.

"All's clear, Wanda. Mimi's got him in the tub room."

"Thank you, Molly. Now go and see if you can make sure the other guard stays put in the back while our friend goes out the front."

"Yes, ma'am."

I put my own clothes in the burlap sack with the extra uniform and I held out my hand to Wanda. She took it and I pulled her to her feet. I slipped my arm around her waist and pulled her as close as I could given the size of her bosom. "You, Wanda, are a true lady and a mighty tempting distraction yourself." I gave her a good long kiss on the mouth.

She finally pushed me away and, with cheeks flushed and hot, said, "You better hurry on now, honey. That beautiful boy of yours is waiting on you."

I gave her one last peck and a final thank you then peeked out into the hallway. All was quiet except for the sounds of fucking, so I made my way down the stairs and out the front door.

With no rear entrance to the fort, I had no choice but to go back in through the front gate. I was tempted to take a horse right then because moseying the hundred yards to the gate on foot with the sentry watching didn't make me feel real comfortable, but I didn't want some soldier leaving Wanda's and starting up a racket about his horse being stolen.

I started my moseying, staggering a little to make it look good. I figured the chances were good that the sentries were used to seeing soldiers coming out of Wanda's bow-legged and liquored-up. Sweat dripped down my back and my heart pounded as I fought to keep myself from breaking into a run. That hundred yards was going to feel like a mile. The huge double gates were standing open, but I knew they could be closed in seconds with a warning from a sentry. I concentrated hard on a spot just inside the gates. I figured if I could just make it to that spot, I'd be home free.

I finally made it the full distance and was just about to step through the gates to that spot I'd been staring at, when I heard a shout from above.

"Hold it, soldier! Ain't you forgetting something?"

Shit. There was probably some secret word of the day every soldier needed to know to get in through the gate. My heart stopped as I looked up toward the sentry. I prayed that in the darkness and from such a distance he wouldn't be able to recognize me. I thought hard for something clever to say but all that came out was, "What?"

"You need to salute. Whether you're on duty or not. Captain's orders."

My heart started beating again and I let out the breath I'd been holding, then I threw him a sloppy salute. I made it through the gates and headed straight for the stables. I only passed three people on the way—two soldiers and a civilian—but I saluted them all just to be on the safe side.

Everything was just where Wanda said it would be. I reached the supply warehouse first and hid in the shadows of the building. The stables and barn were the next building over, and on the other side of them was the enlisted men's barracks. The armory would be next and it was mighty tempting to sneak over to it and get some extra weapons, but the chances were good it was being guarded and I didn't have the time or the luck to be dealing with more than I needed to be dealing with. I was none too happy as it was, what with the barracks being next to the stables. Doing what I was planning on doing while there were more than a hundred soldiers sleeping nearby was risky enough for my taste.

I was nervous as hell but I had no time to hesitate. The girls at Wanda's wouldn't be able to keep those guards distracted forever and Jones would be heading to fetch me soon. And Wyatt was counting on me to rescue him. That was my biggest reason of all.

I could see two guards posted at the front of the barn, and two guards wandering through the corrals out back. With all the Indian problems and the Apache's appreciation of fine horses, Jones was making sure the Army mounts had plenty of protection.

Entering the barn through the corral area was my only hope unless I planned on facing off with the two armed sentries at the front, so I watched the guards in the corrals for a few minutes to see if they were patrolling in a pattern or at random. It fucking figured Jones would be having them patrolling at random. That meant I couldn't time my run across the open area between the warehouse and the stables. I would just have to take the first chance I got at sneaking across, through the corrals and into the barn. There was no telling when I would get a second chance.

I watched them for what seemed like an hour but probably wasn't much more than a few minutes. The guards never patrolled far outside the corrals, which was making my plan nearly impossible to carry out. Just when I was about to give up, go get Wyatt, and take our chances at escaping without the plan, one of the guards whistled softly. The second guard joined him and I saw one pull a tobacco bag from his pocket. They whispered for a few minutes, then headed off to a far corner of the corrals and disappeared into the darkness.

I put my bag of clothes down in the shadows, took a deep breath, and crouch-ran as fast as I could across the distance between the warehouse and the back corner of the barn. I pressed myself into the wall once I got there and listened. No one was shouting for back ups and no one was firing any shots. So far, so good. I settled my breathing down a might then I climbed through the corral bars. There were mazes of fenced pens on both sides of a walking aisle that led from the barn door to the back wall of the fort. I made my way to the aisle and slipped into the barn.

I stopped to let my eyes adjust to the moonless dark. Once they adjusted it didn't take me long to find what I was looking for. In times of trouble, like the ones Fort Craig was dealing with now, it was common for a full company's worth of horses to be left tacked and at the ready. Then, if all hell broke loose, the men could pretty near just jump on their mounts and ride. Those were the horses I was looking for, and I found them at the front of the barn in some special stalls made just for them. That meant I was going to be doing my work with the other two guards just a doorway away.

My plan was to fix it so that once I broke Wyatt out of the stockade, he and I were more or less guaranteed a bit of a head start.

I figured the best way to do that was to make it hard for them to follow us. Since U.S. Cavalry ponies were some of the best-trained creatures on four legs, sabotaging the gear seemed the way to go.

The horses, as calm and used to being handled as they were, accepted me without so much as a snort. Moving as quickly and quietly as I could, I loosened either the saddle or the headgear of all fourteen waiting horses. As soon as that was done, I snuck back to the rear of the barn and looked around for any sign of the smoking guards. The coast looked clear, so I made my way back through the pens and across to the warehouse. I took a few seconds there to let my heart slow down, then I picked up my sack and started off for the civilian livery. I made it there without passing a soul, going over in my head exactly what I wanted to say to the stable hand.

Inside the livery, I found the stable hand sleeping on a cot just on the other side of the door. I steadied my hands then shook him awake.

"I need the prisoners' horses."

He jumped to his feet, mumbling and groggy. I pointed to the chestnut and the black who were standing drowsily in their stalls.

"I need the prisoners' horses," I repeated. "We're getting them ready for transport."

"Yes, sir." The stable hand, a pixie-sized man in his sixties who barely came to my chest, stumbled to the saddle racks. "Are you part of that group that just transferred here from Texas? I don't recognize you."

"Uh, yes, sir. I just got assigned here."

"You think this is really going to work? Do you think the Indians will leave us alone for a while once we turn those two men over to them?"

"It's not my place to say. I'm just following orders."

The old man moved slower than a tortoise in a windstorm. I wanted to jump in and help him with the saddling but I knew he'd be expecting a soldier to just stand by and wait. When he was finally done I told him I'd be needing the prisoners' belongings, including their rifles. He opened a chest and pulled everything out for me. I loaded our things onto the horses, thanked the old man, and led the horses out of the stable. I tied them up behind a building near the stockade and readied myself for the riskiest part of all—breaking Wyatt out of jail.

CHAPTER 12

I KNEW THE SOLDIER inside the stockade would recognize me, so I had to get in and knock him out fast before he had a chance to call for help. Jones would be fetching me soon from Wanda's and there was no time for complications.

I pulled my hat down over my eyes and stumbled into the stockade office, singing "The Yellow Rose of Texas" in the drunkenest voice I could muster.

"What the . . . ?" The soldier came out from behind his desk as I fell to my knees, retching and coughing. "Don't do that. Shit. Jones will have my hide if he comes in here with the place smelling like puke."

He touched my shoulder to help me up and I rose fast, throwing my head back and butting him in the face. He stumbled backward and I punched him. He hit the wall and slumped to the floor. I got the keys off his belt and dragged him into the cell area.

"Jesus Christ, what took you so long? You fucked her, didn't you? I reckon you're going to tell me you had to just to make it look convincing."

I dragged the unconscious guard into an empty cell then retrieved my sack from the office. I handed it to Wyatt through the bars and told him to put the uniform on.

"Take off the sling. You're going to have to manage without it."

"Shit. I can smell her perfume on you."

I took the guard's bandana off of him and gagged him while Wyatt started stripping.

"Tell me the truth, Deke. Was she better than me or just different?"

I got shackles out of a cupboard and put them on the soldier's wrists and ankles.

"I guess there's nothing I can do to compete with a pussy, but what about the sucking? Was she better than me at sucking?"

I took the soldier's pistol out of his holster and tucked it in the front of my pants.

"Oh, God, Deke. You don't think you really could have gotten her with child, do you?"

I unlocked Wyatt's cell door and opened it up. "No, Wyatt, I didn't fuck her, but if you don't shut up, I'm going back and doing just that because she was a hell of a lot less annoying than you. Now let's get the hell out of here."

We looked outside to make sure the coast was clear then we hightailed it to the waiting horses. Even with the uniforms on I wasn't anxious to be running into any other folks, so we led the horses from building to building using the shadows for cover. Once we were near the front gate we mounted up.

"We do this slow and calm-like, Sweetlips. And salute. Don't forget to salute. Now these horses don't exactly look like cavalry mounts so if anyone yells out or sounds extra excited, ride like hell and don't look back."

Wyatt nodded. "Was she young and pretty?"

I shook my head, giving up, and nudged my horse toward the gate. I saluted without looking up and passed through the gate. I could hear Wyatt following close behind.

We'd made it about fifty yards when I heard someone shout, "Stop those men!"

I kicked my horse hard and headed east at a dead run. I looked back just long enough to make sure Wyatt was doing the same. Rifle shots kicked up dust all around us but nothing important got hit.

We rode hard until close to midday. We never heard or saw another soul once we were out of sight of the fort, so when we came across a small creek we decided it was safe to stop and let the horses rest and drink. I dismounted and Wyatt was right behind me.

"Did she make you come, Deke? That's all I want to know."

I pushed Wyatt to the ground and peeled off my uniform shirt. "I did not fuck her." I pulled off my boots. "Since first laying eyes on you I have thought of fucking no one else." I undid my soldier pants and let them fall to the dirt. "Even the women at the whorehouse envied me because you were mine. I love you, goddamnit. Why can't you get that through your thick skull?"

"You told the women at the whorehouse about us?"

I stood above Wyatt, naked, hard, and annoyed. "Yes, Wyatt. I told them about us."

His body wiggled with an all-over smile as he undid his pants. "Deke?"

"What is it now, Wyatt?"

"Would you mind putting those soldier boots back on before you fuck me?"

We didn't have time for much more than sticking it in and making it come, but it was enough to shut Wyatt up and to steady my nerves. I hadn't realized how tightly I'd been wound until I'd gotten off my horse and found my legs shaking.

When we were done I put on my own clothes and we buried the uniforms.

"Can't you keep the boots? Don't know what it is about those shiny black boots but they do get me a goin'."

"Air gets you going, Wyatt. Besides they're kind of a dead giveaway. Cowboys don't generally ride around in knee-high dress-up boots."

"How far you think they'll be willing to chase us?"

"I honestly don't think they'll waste much time on us. Jones has got the Apaches to deal with and all we're really guilty of is stealing a couple of uniforms and knocking out a soldier. I'd be surprised if Jones had the right to hold us like that, so once his temper cools down a might I think he'll realize he's better off just forgetting the whole thing."

"Are we going to keep heading east or start north again?"

"North again, I think. I like the Canada idea."

Wyatt stretched and yawned then started putting his clothes back on. "I like how the land is changing. It's getting greener and prettier. I think we'll have an easier time finding food and cover."

"I think you're right. And I don't know about you, but I'm ready for a change of scenery."

"Me, too." We got on our horses and turned them north. "So what exactly did you do with that woman, Deke?"

I heaved a sigh. "I rode her like there was no tomorrow. In fact, I sampled each and every one of them whores. There must have been about twenty of them."

"I knew it!"

I shook my head and moved the black to a trot.

"But you still came back and got me. Hey. That must mean I really am the best." Wyatt kicked his horse and tried to catch up. "You really do love me, don't you, Deke?"

"Is there any answer that's going to shut you up?"

"Probably not."

"I was afraid of that."

We rode for a couple of days, with the land getting greener and the weather getting colder. At night we had to use both bedrolls and the bay's hide, which Wyatt had insisted on keeping because it bore our brand, to stay warm. 'Course the fucking helped quite a bit, too.

On the third day we rode up over a crest and there beneath us lay a valley so beautiful and green we both had to sit and admire before riding down into it. We found a stream bubbling out of some rocks and we let the horses rest there. The sun was bright and the air was clear but there was a definite bite to the breeze. Wyatt stretched out next to a boulder that shielded him from the wind and closed his eyes.

"The sun feels so good, Deke, I could lie here the rest of the day."

I leaned back against the boulder and looked up at the sky. There wasn't a cloud to be seen. I followed the flow of the stream with my eyes and saw that it emptied into a sizable pond further down into the valley. Some movement caught my eye and I whistled.

Wyatt sat up. "What?"

"Looky down yonder."

Wyatt stood and looked where I was pointing. Coming toward the pond was a herd of mustangs at least fifty strong. Bringing up the rear and guarding them was a stallion as pure and honey-golden as Wyatt's old mare. His mane and tail were almost white and he had pure white socks on all four legs. There was a white blaze on his face so bright we could easily see it from where we were. His body was powerful and it was easy to tell he was a stallion few others dared to challenge.

"Deke. He looks just like her."

"I know."

The distant look in Wyatt's eyes made me almost wish I hadn't shown him. There was a lot of pain and a lot of wishin' in that look but there was an excitement, too. For a moment it scared me, because he seemed to be off somewhere else where I could never go with him. That mare had been a huge piece of Wyatt's past; probably the only happy part of Wyatt's past. He had belonged to her long before he belonged to me, but he had chosen me that night with the grizzly, and in a strange way I felt like the mare had accepted that. I felt I owed it to her to stay out of their memories.

"I've never seen another horse that even came close to her before."

I watched a mess of things going on behind Wyatt's eyes, and it made me realize I didn't know shit about his life before I showed up and turned it upside down. I hadn't even known the mare's name was Athena until he told the story to Toby and Daisy. I'd never bothered to ask him what he studied back east or how long he'd lived there. I didn't even know about his mother—was she alive or dead; was she loving and caring or as cruel as his father?

To be honest, it didn't even seem right to me that Wyatt had a life before me. I felt stupid for thinking that way but it made me ache that we hadn't always been a part of each other. My own past seemed unimportant now; hard to remember even. It was as if everything else before that moment in the tack room was just me killing time, waiting for Wyatt to come along and bring me to life. I couldn't help but wonder if it felt that way for him, too.

I guess it boiled down to the same old problem that kept cropping up between us. Wyatt didn't love me any less than I loved him, but Wyatt didn't need me. At least not like I needed him, and that was mighty hard medicine to swallow for a man such as myself. It was a medicine I hadn't quite gagged down all the way yet. Wyatt had a talent for loving and a way of finding home wherever he was. Without me, he would be sad—sadder than sad—but he would survive and he'd make a new life. But me without Wyatt . . . That was a picture I couldn't bare to look at.

I watched him watching the stallion and it suddenly hit me. Wyatt would never really be mine unless I kept giving him the chance to choose to be mine; like him killing his mare. If I kept him from loving anything else, he would forget how much he loved me. I'd end up being the only thing he loved, instead of the thing he loved the most, and I didn't much like that idea.

"I was thinking, Sweetlips . . . "

"Yeah?"

"Maybe we should travel with the herd for a bit. It'll help hide our tracks some and I'm sure that stallion knows all the best hiding spots around. A horse that special has probably been chased more than once and, obviously, he's not been caught. Or at least he's not been kept. It might be worth a try to follow them for a bit."

Wyatt looked at me, wide-eyed and boyish, and he was mine.

"Could we, Deke?"

"Don't see why not."

"God, I would love to try and make friends with him."

"Wyatt?"

"Yeah?"

"Were you actually born, or just dropped straight down from heaven?"

Wyatt looked surprised then flustered. He shrugged and looked down at his feet, his face reddening. I ruffled his hair and gave him a kiss.

"My money's on heaven. Now let's go see if we can join the herd."

We got on our mounts and very slowly approached the herd. The stallion picked up our scent and warned the rest of the horses with a high-pitched, drawn-out whinny. The mares lifted their heads and spotted us. They looked to the stallion for direction. He made a short, threatening advance toward us and we stopped. He trotted back and forth, tossing his head and snorting. We waited a bit then moved slowly forward again. The stallion went to his mares and moved them out. We followed, matching our pace to theirs. We kept a comfortable distance but stayed close enough that the stallion could see us and smell us.

The stallion would drop back from the herd occasionally so he could get a closer look at us. We would close the gap a bit then stop. He would put on his king-of-the-harem display then return to the herd.

We followed them until nightfall, when the stallion stopped his mares on a grassy knoll. He checked on us then went to the highest point to keep guard over his herd. Wyatt and I dismounted and walked our horses closer to the mustangs. As soon as the stallion started whinnying threats we stopped and made camp.

"I want to walk up closer to him. I want him to hear my voice."

"Go ahead. I'll see if I can find us some food."

Wyatt took off on foot. I watched his body change as he got closer to the stallion. He seemed to shrink, as if he was making himself less threatening. He took off his hat and his hair got stirred by the breeze. He wiped at his face and I knew which curled lock of hair had just fallen across his forehead, annoying him. I could see it as clear as if I were right there with him. His eyes would be wide, the whole world reflected in them, and his mouth would be slightly open. His skin would be flushed and glowing, giving him that fevered look he got when he was excited. I smiled at the picture and knew that if anybody could tame that animal, it would be Wyatt.

He didn't get too close that first night but he stayed up on the knoll for a good spell, talking to the horse and getting it used to his being near. When Wyatt came back to me he was as worked up as a kid at Christmas, full of talk of everything that happened between him and the stallion. I couldn't keep from smiling as I listened to his voice, and I couldn't keep from wondering if Wyatt would ever stop being a source of wonder to me.

We followed the herd for days. As we hoped, the horses began to get comfortable with us. The stallion led us to the most fertile spots, giving us plenty of water and easy game. We made snares to catch rabbits and quail, which saved our ammunition and kept us from spooking the horses. No longer as worried about having someone on our trail, we built fires and cooked our meet, a first for us while on the run.

Every night after eating, Wyatt would walk up alone to talk to the stallion. I watched them and saw the changes in both of them. Wyatt stood taller and was less afraid of spooking the horse. The stallion moved easier and his whinny began to sound more like a greeting and less like a threat. He even let Wyatt move among the mares and foals.

Somewhere along the way, when I wasn't paying attention, I stopped fearing the horse and the feelings Wyatt had for it. My time alone became something I looked forward to. I could see Wyatt and

I liked that he was near, but I was alone and I liked that, too. And watching him from a distance let me see Wyatt as himself, without me. Together we had a natural way of behaving with each other, a way that couldn't be broken; like the stallion with his herd. He led the others and protected them. They trusted him and followed him. That's how they behaved with each other and it wasn't likely to change. The stallion might have a different way of being with Wyatt or another stallion, but with his herd, he was always the same. That's what I got to see when watching Wyatt in the distance. I got to see his different way of being. Without me he seemed more man than boy, more equal than faithful pup. Not that I ever thought of him as just a faithful pup, but that's what he usually reminded me of when we were together, eager for love and needing my attention. There weren't no way I could say the same thing about the tall-standing man I watched taming a wild stallion. Everything about the way he moved said he was a man who knew what he was doing and was easy about doing it. It made me proud straight through to my bones. The pride tended to settle in my crotch, but then just about everything I felt about that boy eventually settled in my crotch.

After spending time with the horse Wyatt would come on back to camp and I'd watch him change as he returned to me, grown man to happy pup. He'd settle into my arms and, between kissing and licking, he'd tell me about some new happening with the horse. I'd listen to his voice with my eyes closed, and I could hear what he was feeling. I'd feel, too, the softness of his lips on my body and the eagerness of his loving, and I was right glad we'd crossed paths with that stallion.

One night after we'd been traveling with the herd for a good many days, Wyatt climbed under the bedroll beside me and I could tell some sadness was mixed in with his usual happiness.

"He comes within a few feet when I call him now. I think I'll be able to touch him soon."

"But . . . " I knew there was something more waiting to come out.

"But he's changing directions. With the herd. He's going to start heading them back, isn't he?"

"Most likely."

He paused. I knew what was coming. This was the part where I was going to have to tell him he had to give up something he cared about. This was the part I'd been avoidin' thinking about.

"It's so beautiful here. I wish we could stay. This would be great country for a ranch."

"That it would be." I kissed the top of his head, dragging out the inevitable and acting like I didn't know where he was heading with his wishing.

"Guess we can't head back with them."

"No. Heading back to certain imprisonment or death would probably be a bad idea." My edginess was creeping into my voice. I felt that old anger at that usual argument building inside of me and I was mad at myself for letting it happen. It was my idea to travel with the herd. I had no one to blame but myself for the fight that was about to break out.

Wyatt propped himself up on one elbow and bent down to kiss me. "Thanks for giving me this time with him, Deke. There's no way I can tell you how much it's meant to me. It's no wonder I love you so much." Then he laid back down and snuggled against me.

His words kinda threw me, but I had a head of steam building and it was too late to stop it. I pushed him away from me and sat up.

"What the hell does that mean?' It's no wonder that I love you so much'?"

"It means you give me everything I want, even things you don't really think I should have. And I love you for that."

I just didn't have nowhere to go with that. I hemmed and hawed but nothing much came out. He laughed and put his hand on my chest, pushing me back down to the bedroll. He laid his head on my chest and tangled his legs up with mine.

"You're not going to fight me and beg me to let us stay with the herd?"

"Why would I fight you when I know you're right?" His hand slid down my belly and teased my cock head.

"You won't blame me for making you leave something you love?"

"But I'll be with you and you're the something I love the most." His thigh bumped my balls and humped them a little while his fingers worked my cock. "How could I blame you for that?"

My thoughts started drifting in different directions. Some were trying to stay with Wyatt's words and the argument I kept expecting, but some were giving themselves up to his loving. Wyatt's mouth was near to tasting my dick when my thoughts came together.

"This is a trick, isn't it?"

Wyatt took one good slurp up my cock then asked, "Is it working?"

He swallowed my cock, his lips hitting my hairs, and I couldn't answer, what with the moaning and all that I was doing. But we both knew the answer. It was working just fine and we'd be staying with the herd for a little while longer.

CHAPTER 13

THE DAYS WE FOLLOWED the mustangs turned into weeks. The stallion was smart and tough. He protected his herd well and he seemed to accept us now as part of that herd. He took us to the choicest feeding grounds, kept us hidden from other men, and fought off predators like cougars and wolves. I even saw him stomp a rattler once when it got too close to a colt.

Wyatt called the stallion Sun and they developed a friendship like I'd never seen before between man and animal. Wyatt had no desire to ride the horse—he said a creature like that wasn't meant to be saddled—but the horse loved Wyatt's touch. I watched from my silent, distant spot as Wyatt ran his hands over the stallion's muscled body or as they nuzzled face to face. The horse followed him, head over Wyatt's shoulder, as they strolled and talked alone or among the mares. I never went near the horses although I'm sure they would have tolerated me. I liked my distant spot much better.

We were able to fire our rifles by this time without spooking the mustangs, so when our snares and traps didn't work we could still get food. We rigged together a shelter from branches and animal hides that we could put up and take down easily so we always had shelter with us, which came in handy with the wetter weather.

Like I did at Lettie's I started to feel a sense of home. Even though we never stayed in one spot for more than a couple of days, it felt like a place where we belonged, Wyatt and I together. But along with that sense of home, I started getting that uncomfortable feeling of something wrong on the horizon. I was getting itchy and edgy and my skin prickled sometimes for no reason; the hairs on the back of my neck would shoot up when I was least expecting it. Something was coming, but I didn't know from which direction or when it would be arriving or even what it was. I was having a harder and harder time, though, keeping my uneasiness from Wyatt. That's why one evening, when the stallion led us across a well-traveled road, I decided I would be heading into the nearest town the next morning and seeing if I could hear any news about us. The tricky part, of course, would be keeping my real motives from Wyatt and convincing him he needed to stay with the herd while I went into town.

That night the rain came down hard and thunder rumbled in the distance. The stallion was as uneasy as I was and wouldn't stay put long enough for Wyatt to touch him. Wyatt came back to our shelter looking worried.

"Must be a bad storm brewing. Sun's jumpier than I've ever seen him."

"He's a smart animal, Sweetlips. I reckon he'll be staying put with his mares tomorrow. Not a good idea to be traveling in such bad weather."

Wyatt stripped off his soaking wet clothes and climbed under our warm hide with me. I pulled him close and rubbed his arms to chase away the cold faster. Wyatt's hand settled on my dick, like it so often did, and he played me into half-hardness without even thinking.

"Is it the storm that's been making you so jumpy lately, Deke?"

"You noticed, huh?"

"I noticed."

"It's not exactly one thing that's been making me edgy. It's a lot of little things, like an ammunition supply that's running out fast. I need to get to a town, but you know how nervous they make me.

We passed that road earlier and I was thinking tomorrow would be the right time for going in and getting supplies. The herd won't be moving and folk's will be too distracted by the weather to pay much attention to a stranger."

"You mean two strangers."

"I mean one stranger."

"Forget it, Deke."

"Use your head, Wyatt. We need bullets. Not just for food but for protection."

"Then I'm going with you."

"No. You stay with the herd just in case they do move on. And your stallion's going to need your help. What if lightning spooks some of them babies? You need to be here to help them."

"Sun's managed without me all this time. I think he'll be okay without me tomorrow."

"No."

I wasn't in the mood for arguing and my simple 'no' let Wyatt know that. His body was tense in my arms. His hand wasn't playing with my dick any more.

"You think something's up, don't you? You're getting worried about my pa or something again."

I sighed. Trying to hide from him was near impossible.

"Please stay with the herd, Sweetlips. Please don't argue with me about it none."

He was quiet. His body stayed tense but his hand went back to its playing. There was more purpose in his fingers, though, and I knew there was something brewing in his head.

"Then I'm staying put until you get back."

"Not if the herd moves on, you're not."

"I'm not going to take the chance that you can't find us."

I took a deep breath and counted until the chance for explosion passed.

"Wyatt, I want you to stay with the stallion. I know it sounds crazy but I think that damn horse would kill to protect you." I ran my fingers through his hair. "It won't be for more'n a day, I swear. And I need to know that you're somewhere safe."

Wyatt's hand squeezed my cock and I got all the way to hard.

"I need to know that you're somewhere safe, too," he whispered, "But that doesn't ever seem to matter. How come?"

"It does matter, Wyatt, but I'm in charge and I'm telling you to stay put."

It popped out before I could stop it. I held my breath and waited for him to let loose.

"All right. But I still don't like it."

I let a little of my breath out. "Is this another of your tricks?"

"Nope." He kissed my lips. "I trust you, Deke. I argue a lot because I don't always like the way things have to be, but I know you're always right. That's why you're in charge." His lips started working their way down my body. They stopped at the hairs growing up to my belly. He looked up at me, his baby blues pure innocence. "You protect me, Deke. And I like it that way. I'm a man and you usually treat me that way, but I gotta admit, it feels nice being your boy."

The warm spread up from my dick to my heart and then out in all four directions. I nodded. "I like it that way, too." I pulled him back up to me and kissed him deep. "I treat you like a man because that's what you've proven you are. I respect you, Wyatt, and . . ."

His eyes suddenly grew wide. "Ooh, since you're going into town, can you see if they have some peppermints? And licorice. But if you can't get both, get peppermints. And if you can't get either, see if they have rock candy. But peppermints first, 'k?"

". . . And now we know why you're my boy."

I swatted his ass and pushed him back down to my dick, but instead of swallowing it like I was expecting him to, he popped one of his fingers into his mouth and worked it like a cock. I knew there was only one use for a slicked-up finger like that and I was interested in finding out which of our holes he was planning on putting it in.

That interest was playing second fiddle, though, to my interest in the finger-sucking he was giving himself. While he worked it in and out of his tight, sweet lips, his cock was humping my leg, making itself hard and a little bit slimy. My cock was standing tall now and the head was dragging up and down Wyatt's chest and belly with every rocking hump of his body.

He pulled his finger out of his mouth and spit dripped onto me. Wyatt bent his head down and nibbled at my chest, finding his way to my left nipple, where he started sucking hard. My cock was mashed between us and Wyatt's cock was between my legs, nudging at all my good parts. I closed my eyes and something somewhere in the back of my mind wondered about that slicked-up finger of Wyatt's, but the sucking and the mashing and the nudging made everything else kinda unimportant. I felt twinges in my dick that matched the rhythm of Wyatt's nipple-sucking and I could feel my hole, far, far below, squeezing and unsqueezing with the nudging of Wyatt's cock.

"I want you to feel this."

And Wyatt's mouth was gone from my chest, and my cock was rubbing nothing but air. His cock stopped nudging and I figured out fast where he was planning on putting that slickered-up finger.

I started to say something like "don't" or "stop" but my cock suddenly slid down his throat and "stop" was the last word on my mind. I held his head with both hands and lost my fingers in his golden-soft hair. Wyatt's free hand slid up my body and started twisting my right nipple, soft at first but with some surprisingly hard tweaks thrown in here and there.

His finger down below played at my hole, never trying to go in but keeping it edgy and tender and wondering. I was surprised at how much feeling was in my asshole, and I found myself wondering what a tongue would feel like running against it. That thought made my hole start puckering even more at Wyatt's touch. The skin there felt wet and soft sometimes, dry and tight others, but any time I thought about something going inside, my hole clamped up quick.

The longer Wyatt sucked and played, though, the more my body loosened. The hard pinches to my nipple came more often but started feeling less like pain. The twinges from chest to cock were steady pulls which stretched my cock tight and made Wyatt's throat feel like a closed fist.

When my body was on the verge of stretching in two and the feelings of pleasure were so powerful that they were closer to being pain, Wyatt's finger slipped into his mouth along with my cock. He slicked it up good again, then poked it into my hole before I could think. For a second I was on fire and I started to push him away, but the second was over and part of Wyatt was in me. The fire cooled down to warm and Wyatt worked his finger gently, loving my cock with his mouth and rubbing my chest with his hand. I had trouble telling which of us was which, and I held his head tight with one hand and his arm tight with the other. I suddenly, fiercely, wanted him inside of me. His whole body inside of mine. Not just his finger or his tongue or his cock, but him. All of him.

Wyatt's finger was in deep and it found a spot against my belly; he worked that spot hard and my cock started pumping and just as I blew, the face of Wyatt's father reared in my mind. I felt fear so powerful it shook my body. Come was everywhere but all I saw was blood and I think maybe I was crying. Wyatt kissed me, over and over, and for a flashing moment everything that was going to happen to Wyatt and me, everything that would come of our love, it was all there. I knew how it was all going to end. But the flash was gone before I could hang onto it and all that was left was the fear.

Wyatt held me tight, and if he knew what I was feeling or saw what I had seen, he didn't say a word. We held onto each other until morning and I didn't close my eyes once.

The worst of the storm was nearly on us when we got out of bed, making sunrise almost as dark as evening. I saddled up the black, feeling like it was a mistake to leave but feeling, too, like I had no choice. Whatever was going to happen, whatever I'd known for that brief instant, had to happen. It was as if I couldn't stop myself from throwing the saddle on the horse's back, cinching it tight, and swinging onto it.

Wyatt and I didn't say goodbye. We didn't say anything. He stood next to my horse looking up at me, his hand on my boot. I ruffled his hair, then touched his cheek and ran my thumb across his lips. He kissed it lightly as it passed, then I turned the horse and rode away.

I felt dazed as I looked for the road we'd passed, the heavy rains making it hard to see much at all. I felt dreamlike, nightmarish; half asleep and still stuck in the nightmare, and half awake, trying to take control. With every step I fought the urge to go back to Wyatt and run, but run to where? It had to have an ending. Good or bad, it had to have an ending, and I knew that this was the beginning of that end.

I found the road and decided to follow it northeast, since that's the direction the stallion had seemed more nervous about. Once on the road it took about two hours before I came across the town. The whole trip I argued with myself and fought to keep a handle on the nagging pain in my belly and the voice that urged me to go back.

Lightning was crackling across the sky when I rode into town and rain was coming down in buckets. The few people out were scurrying like mice from cover to cover and, just as I had hoped, they were uninterested in a stranger riding in.

I rode straight to the general store and stepped inside, drenched and shivering.

"Good Lord, mister. Ain't you got a slicker?"

A boy of about fifteen stood behind the counter. A chaw the size of my fist filled his right cheek and, although he had the face of a boy, his body was near to manhood.

"A slicker's one of the things I'm here for."

"Well, we got some. Right over there. Just take your pick. What else is it you're needing?"

"Rifle shot. Jerky. Beans. The usual trail needs."

"Where you headed?"

"North."

"Ain't never been there before. Heard tell it's nice."

I gave him a smile and took a better look at him. He was already Wyatt's size but that's where the resemblance ended. His hair was cropped tight to his head and was nearly black. His features were heavy but not ugly. The plug in his cheek made his smile lopsided but it was a good smile. A friendly smile.

I thought nothing of it until another customer rushed in from the rain. As soon as the bell at the door rang the boy busied himself at the end of the counter, as far from me as he could get. I'd seen that reaction before. Hell, as a kid I'd had it myself more than once when I was watching a man and thinking things about him. At that age, when the thoughts are popping into mind stronger and faster than a boy can handle, it seems like everyone can peer inside and see the unnatural things going on.

I gathered the supplies, put them on the counter, and surveyed the jars of candy.

"Give me a handful each of peppermints, licorice, and rock candy."

The boy could barely look at me now that someone else was in the store. He grabbed the candies I asked for, stuffed them in a sack, and mumbled how much I owed him. When I handed him the money, he risked raising his eyes to my face and I saw something flash in them. He stared hard at me, his hand stopped inches from mine, color rising in his cheeks.

"You can set the money on the counter," he said. "I'll get your beans for you."

He disappeared into the back room and I laid my money on the counter. The hairs on my neck were standing tall and I wanted to get out of town quick. I wanted to get back to Wyatt but I needed to poke around a little first to see if we had a need to be moving on from the herd, to start running again.

The boy returned with the sack of beans and dropped them on the counter. I gathered up my purchases and headed out the door.

The rain had gotten even worse so I set everything down on the boardwalk and put on one of the new rain slickers as quick as I could before stepping out from under cover. The other customer came out of the store, covered her head with her package, and ran out into the mud.

I was just about done tying everything onto the black when the boy came out of the store. His cheeks were still flushed and I could tell his heart was beating hard by the way the sides of his head kept jumping. He fidgeted in front of me, looking up and down the street before speaking.

"I know who you are, mister."

I stared at him, not knowing what to think but thinking the worst.

"My pa's the sheriff. I look at his wanted posters every day."

That was the worst I was thinking. I froze. The whole world seemed to freeze. I saw Wyatt in my mind looking up at me and I hated myself for riding away. Fuck the ending. I just wanted to be with Wyatt.

"If I were you, mister, I wouldn't stay in town."

I couldn't understand what he was telling me, my thoughts were so stuck on Wyatt. "I'm . . . not sure what . . . "

"Please, just go. Before my pa sees you."

The boy went back inside.

It took a few beats before my brain thawed out and I was able to get on my horse and ride. I looked back at the general store and saw the boy's face in the window, watching me leave, and I knew it was that powerful need not to be alone in the world that made him do what he'd done for me.

I decided not to head back to Wyatt right away just in case guilt made the boy tell his pa about me after all. I would circle around and catch up to Wyatt later. I was feeling better, knowing the warnings I'd been feeling were played out. Soon I would be back with Wyatt and we'd move on once more, to some place where the posters hadn't reached. This hadn't been the real ending after all. This was just another fork in the road for us. It was true I was still feeling a might queasy, but that was just from having such a close call. Everything would feel fine once I was back where I belonged.

I was about a quarter mile out of town when I came to what was probably a medium-sized creek normally but with the heavy rains it was now a rushing river. I saw pieces of a washed out bridge on the far side of the water and I knew I was going to have to either leave the road and follow the river or head back to town. Following the river, even as risky as it was in such bad weather, sounded a whole lot better than heading back through a town where I'd been recognized.

I turned my horse and was about to leave the road when through the downpour, on the other side of the creek, I saw what looked like a horse lying in the mud, its hind legs in the rushing water. I rode until I was opposite the animal and I could see that it was saddled and alive, but barely. I scanned the banks and the water. A saddled horse meant a rider. I spotted him about fifty yards down the river, wedged against some branches.

I calmed the black, who was getting skittish because he could sense the dying horse. I called out to the figure in the water but got no answer. I'd never had to test the black's skills as a cowpony but I was about to find out what they were. I leaned forward and talked to him gentle-like, urging him closer and closer to the river's edge. As soon as his feet started sucking when he raised them out of the mud I backed him up a bit.

"You're doing good, boy. You're doing good." I patted him on the neck. "Do this for me and I'll slip you a bit of Wyatt's rock candy."

I uncoiled my lariat and tried not to think about how long it had been since I'd worked a rope. I sent it flying and missed my target. The black pranced backwards and threw his head.

"Ho, boy. Rock candy. Remember?"

I gathered in my rope and set it sailing a second time. It dropped over the man's shoulders but got a sizeable branch in there, too. I was just about to jerk the rope back to me for a third try when I saw the man struggle to lift his arm. He pulled the rope off of the branch and slipped it under his armpits.

I tied my end of the rope to my saddle horn and started urging the black backward very slowly. The man broke free from the branches and I pulled him to the bank.

"Ho, Black. Stay put."

I kept the rope tied to the saddle, figuring the horse would be stronger than me if the man slipped back into the water. I reached the poor fella and pulled him out of the river. We both sunk pretty deep in the mud, making it hard for me to get him very far. The black proved himself to be one fine cowpony, though, and started backing up on his own, keeping the rope taut and helping me drag the man to solid ground.

As soon as we were clear of the mud, I slipped the rope off the stranger. He was shivering too hard to talk and seemed close to passing out. I carried him to my horse and slung him across the saddle then I squeezed on with him. I felt bad about leaving his mount behind but knew it was close to dead anyway.

I headed back to town, voices screaming in my head that I was a fucking fool, but sometimes the right thing to do's not always the smartest.

Since I only knew one person in town, I rode straight back to the general store, but before I could make it there a huge mountain of a man stepped into the road and stopped me. I didn't need to see the badge to know he was the boy's father. The sheriff.

"What happened?"

I wiped water from my eyes and tried to cover my face a bit.

"The bridge was washed out. I found him in the river."

"The doc's office is this way. Follow me."

We turned back the way I'd come and went down a wide alley, almost big enough to be another street. At the end was the doctor's office. The sheriff helped me carry the man into the office and we laid him on a bed.

"Take his wet clothes off and wrap him in some blankets. I'll go see if the doc's upstairs."

I did as I was told even though every muscle in me was leaning toward the door.

The sheriff and the doctor came down before I'd finished my stripping. The doctor started examining his patient and the sheriff helped me with the undressing. He didn't look at me. His attention was on the half-drowned man and I knew if I could slip away I'd soon be on my way back to Wyatt with no one on my tail.

Once we had the man wrapped and warming up, I waited until the sheriff was busy helping the doctor then I headed for the door.

"That's far enough, McAllister."

I froze. I heard a gun being pulled from a holster and I raised my hands, turning to face the sheriff. A thousand pictures of Wyatt raced through my head and most of them included me riding away.

"Didn't think I recognized you, did you?"

It was a stupid question and I had all kinds of smart-ass answers for it but I was too busy fighting the pain of a breaking heart to bother with them.

The doctor looked at me then at the sheriff. "What is this, Henry?"

"He's a wanted man, Doc. I can't even recall all the things he's wanted for but rape and kidnapping stick out in my mind."

"Well get him out of my office. And send Bessy Williams over here. I need a nurse."

The sheriff took me to the jail at gunpoint. Down the street I saw the boy step out of the general store and watch us from the boardwalk.

"Get inside."

I stepped into the office and a deputy came out from the cell area. "What's going on, Henry?"

"Go get Bessy Williams and tell her the doc needs her."

"Yes, sir."

"Into the back, McAllister."

The sheriff locked me in the cell then stood and studied me, questions filling his head.

"Can I get some dry clothes, sheriff?" I was freezing to death but mostly I was stalling. I needed time to think.

"You have any in your saddlebags?"

"No, but I got money."

He didn't answer me. He was too busy trying to answer his own questions.

"Pa, what happened?"

The boy from the general store walked in. His face was still flushed and he didn't look at me.

"Ty, what are you doing here? Why aren't you at the store?"

"I saw you leading this man at gunpoint, Pa. I wanted to see if you were all right."

"You never been worried about me doing my job before."

"Well . . . I . . . He was in the store earlier. I was just curious."

The sheriff straightened to his full size, which was an inch or two taller than me. His body tensed. "You saw this man in the store? You waited on him?"

Ty looked down at the floor.

"Look at me, Ty."

The boy obeyed.

"You study every wanted poster that comes in this office harder than you study your school work. You know most of them better'n me. You're going to tell me you waited on him in the store and didn't recognize him?"

"Pa, it's . . . It's not a very good likeness of him."

The sheriff's voice rose to a near yell. "It looks exactly like him, Ty. I took one glance and knew it was him." He grabbed the boy's shoulder. "How come you didn't tell me?"

Suddenly the sheriff spun and looked at me. Something close to fury was building in him. He turned back to his son.

"Did he touch you, Ty? Did he hurt you?"

The boy looked at me and I saw it in his face—the chance to escape his father's questions by putting the blame on me. I was a wanted man, guilty probably, and saying I'd hurt him could keep his pa from asking questions that might give away some secrets.

But Ty had more balls than most grown men and he told the truth. "No, Pa. He didn't do anything. I just . . . I remember you said the man doing the accusing was a dangerous, lying, snake in the grass and you'd trust any man he accused before you'd trust him."

The silence was so loud it drowned out the banging of my heart against my chest, but the sheriff suddenly busted out with a laugh. "I did say that, didn't I? And it's true. Ray Saunders is a hired killer and if this man, Jennings, has him working as his foreman chances are he's a piece of shit, too." Just as suddenly the sheriff got serious again and shook his son's shoulder. "But you can't make those decisions on your own, Ty. Do you understand me?"

"Yes, Pa. But he saved Mr. Owens, didn't he? I saw you two take him to Doc's. He can't be bad, Pa. He came back even though I warned . . . " Ty cut himself off too late.

The sheriff's voice made it all the way to yell this time and there was no mistaking the fury. "You warned him? What do you mean you warned him?"

Feeling the need to help the kid I tried to get his pa's attention back on me.

"Excuse me, sheriff. Could I get my dry clothes now?"

"You shut up. Saunders was just here two days ago. It won't take long at all to get him back here."

My stomach dropped and I grabbed the bars of my cell.

"Ray Saunders was here two days ago?"

"That's right. That's why your face stood out so clear in my mind. He's got Indian trackers with him. Said they knowed you escaped from Fort Craig recently. They followed your trail but lost it in a mustang herd or something. They know you're around here."

Wyatt. Alone.

"Sheriff, please. You have to let me out. Please." My voice broke. I shook the cell door. Wyatt. Alone with Saunders. "God, please. I need to get to Wyatt."

The sheriff stared at me. I could tell some of the questions he'd had bouncing around in his head were starting to get answers. Without looking at his boy he said, "Ty, go into the other room. And shut the door."

Ty looked at me then obeyed his father.

The sheriff stepped close. I was so sick with fear I thought about grabbing him, snapping his neck through the bars, and taking his keys, but something in his eyes told me I might have a chance at making him understand.

"You didn't kidnap that boy, did you?"

"No, sheriff, I didn't, but please, we've got to find him before Saunders does."

The sheriff looked to the office where his boy sat, framed in the window of the door separating the office from the jail. "Jennings's son wanted to go with you, didn't he?" He turned back to me. "Did Jennings know? About his son?"

I nodded, the steam running right out of me. This was the ending after all. This was where it had all led and it was over now.

"Jennings caught us together."

The sheriff squeezed the bars between us with both hands. "I'm a lawman. Do you understand? There is nothing in this world that means anything to me but this job and my family." He took a deep breath. "I'm going to ask you some things and I want the God's honest truth. Did you do anything to my boy?"

"No, sheriff. I did not do anything to your son."

"Why did you save Owens? Why did you come back here knowing you'd been recognized?"

"What the hell would you have done? Let him drown?"

The sheriff was quiet for a good long time. I felt weaker and sicker with every second that passed.

"I need to know something, McAllister. If . . . "He bowed his head, struggling with his words and with what he was feeling. "If a boy is . . . like that . . . What kind of life can he expect to have?"

I looked out at Ty sitting in a chair, hands in his lap, looking awkward and confused. He might be one of the lucky ones. At least he had a father who cared enough to ask, and that was a good start.

"A lonely one, sheriff. Unless he gets lucky like me. Or if, unlike me, he has a family who sticks by him. But I ain't going to lie to you, sheriff. Either way it's not likely to be an easy one he's facing, but I'm guessing living the truth is always going to be better than living a lie."

The sheriff watched his son while he considered my answer. "Do you think Jennings would actually harm his own boy just because he couldn't . . . accept him?"

"He already has hurt him, sheriff. And Jennings's not even here, is he? He always sends Saunders to do his dirty work and if Saunders finds Wyatt I swear to you he will do what he wants to him and worry about explaining to Jennings later. And the saddest part is, I can't honestly tell you if Jennings would care or not." I looked the sheriff in the eye. "I'm guessing that Ty's a hell of a lot luckier in the pa department than either me or Wyatt was. At least that's what I'm hoping."

The sheriff turned and left without saying another word. Through the window I saw him grab Ty by the arm and pull him out of view.

I sat on my bunk and covered my face with my hands. I tried to tell myself that Wyatt was safe with the stallion and his herd.

The rains would make tracking impossible, even for the best trackers. But I didn't believe myself. The weakness in my bones told me the truth. Saunders had Wyatt. While I'd been saving the life of a stranger, I'd been sacrificing Wyatt's. I felt the burn of tears but I was too empty for any to spill. Wyatt was lost to me and the fight was all gone.

But love's a stubborn thing and it wasn't ready to let me give up. It took only minutes for me to decide that even if Saunders did have Wyatt I wouldn't be quitting until Wyatt was in my arms again. Dead or alive, I'd be holding Wyatt again, and I knew that if I had to snap the sheriff's neck to make that happen, then snapping the sheriff's neck was what I'd be doing.

I heard the outside office door open, then close, and I stood up from my bunk. I readied myself for whatever needed to be done. The door from the office to the jail cells opened and the sheriff came in, but instead of having to kill him I saw I might have to hug him. He was carrying a pile of new clothes and sitting atop the pile was a gun belt, complete with gun. He unlocked the door and handed me the pile.

"I'd like to ride with you but I can't. I'll probably lose my job as it is."

"Sheriff . . . "

"Before I change my mind."

I was stripping before he finished talking and I ran out the door, still dressing. The black was tied up out front. I jumped on him, turned toward Wyatt, and ran that horse as hard as I could.

CHAPTER 14

THE FARTHER WEST I got the lighter the rain fell. When I reached the spot where I'd last seen Wyatt, the rain had stopped and the sun was visible on the horizon just as it was disappearing for the night. I let the black lead the way. We'd traveled with the mustangs long enough that our horses considered themselves part of the herd. The black would find them faster than I could. I knew the chances weren't good that Wyatt was still with the mustangs, but it was the best place to start.

It didn't take the black long. Less than a mile from where I'd last seen Wyatt, we found Sun's dead body. He'd been shot more times than needed to kill a horse, and the ground for yards and yards around him looked as if a battle had been fought. There were three dead men scattered around, too. One I recognized from the Crooked J and one looked like he might be one of Saunders's Indian trackers. Two of the men had been shot and the third had his face torn up and both his legs broken. My guess was Sun had stomped him like I'd seen him stomp that rattler. Wyatt and his stallion had put up quite a fight, that was for damn sure. I prayed none of the blood I saw soaking the ground was Wyatt's, but I couldn't help remembering when I'd fired my load last night. The come had seemed like blood.

It suddenly hit me like a bullet to the chest. Last night might have been the end for me and Wyatt; the very last time we loved and fucked and held each other.

I choked back some bile, struggling to get air in my chest. I couldn't let myself think those things. I couldn't fall apart. I needed to find Wyatt and I couldn't do that if I was lying in the dirt crying like a baby.

I got myself together and kneeled on the ground to take a closer look at the tracks. There were hundreds of prints and puddles of blood, and it was going to take a bit to sort them all out and find the right ones that would lead me to Wyatt. I stood up and started following some, my legs shaking so bad it was hard to walk. I finally separated the shod hoof prints from the unshod ones and found where the shod ones left the fight. They were headed west.

I was just about to get back on the black when a pile of brown about ten feet away caught my eye. I went to it and stood staring down, seeing and understanding but not accepting what it was. I felt tears making their way down my face as I bent to pick up a piece. It was the hide from the bay, cut into dozens of pieces and pissed all over.

My plan for a future with Wyatt was burned into that hide. The horse that carried it had saved our lives more times than I could count and he had died doing it. That hide kept Wyatt warm when he was fevered and covered us when we were loving. That hide stood for our future and Saunders had figured it out. It was his message to me.

I drew my gun and went to the dead men lying in the dirt. I emptied my six-shooter into their faces then I dropped to my knees and retched up my stomach. Before I could pull myself out of the dirt, though, pain tightened my chest. It was a strange pain, real but not real. It felt kind of like all those times when Wyatt's thoughts had mixed with mine. The idea that I was feeling Wyatt's pain forced me to my feet. I took the guns off the dead men and grabbed the two pieces of hide that bore our brand, then I got on the black and started following the tracks. I had no idea what I would be finding at the end of those tracks, but I knew I'd be doing a hell of a lot more than just pissing if I found Saunders and his men.

The tracks were still fairly clear, having missed the heaviest of the rains, but it took nearly two hours in the cloud-broken moonlight before I found the end of them. They led me to an old mining camp, protected by boulders and rock hills. I tied the black to a tree a good distance from the entrance and snuck in closer. When I was near enough to get a good look at the layout, I hunkered down behind a rock and started counting. There were thirteen horses scattered around the camp, including Wyatt's little chestnut. The chestnut and about six others were tied up outside what looked like a huge cave. The opening to it had been blasted wider and was shored up with timber. I was guessing there were several mineshafts inside of the main cave. Next to the cave, almost built into the side of it, was an office. In front of it were more horses and a buckboard.

My thoughts were coming at me faster than I could sort them and the strange pain in my chest was pounding, getting worse every mile I'd gotten closer to Wyatt. I was trying to settle everything down so I could come up with a plan, but I never got the chance. Something slammed into the back of my head and I was out.

I came to in what I was guessing was the office I'd seen on the side of the cave. I was tied to a chair and Harlan Jennings was staring me in the face. I spit, hitting him in the mouth, and he hit me so hard it knocked me and the chair over. Jennings grabbed me by the hair and sat me up again. I started to cuss him but he slapped me hard again before the words could get out.

"Don't give me any more reasons to kill you, McAllister. I've got plenty already and believe me, there's nothing I'd like to do more right now."

I looked around the office hoping to see Wyatt but there were only two other men, neither of which I knew.

"Where's Wyatt, Jennings?"

He slapped me again.

"Shut the fuck up or killing you is exactly what I'll be doing."

"If you were going to kill me you'd be doing it right now. What's the matter, Jennings? Where's Wyatt?"

Jennings stared hard at me, the hate so bad I could taste it. Or maybe it was my hate for him that I was tasting.

"I think you're the lowest piece of shit this world has to offer, McAllister. I don't know what you did to my boy to turn him like you did, but you done a good job. No amount of threatening or hurting will convince him he's not meant to be like you."

I struggled against the ropes, almost knocking myself over again.

"Where is he, Jennings? What have you done to him? I swear to God, I'll kill you if you've done anything to him."

Jennings laughed. "That's good, McAllister. You're the one who did something to him, not me. I'm just trying to show him the truth. The truth about you and the kind of life he'd have if he keeps on acting like . . . " Jennings turned away, too disgusted to finish.

"Like what? Like he's in love? How the fuck would you know what love looks like? The power to love ain't even inside of you. You don't give a shit about Wyatt, Jennings. You just don't want people knowing your son loves another man."

He spun to face me again. He gripped the arms of the chair and put his nose almost against mine.

"I'm not going to discuss my feelings for my son with you, but you're damn right that I ain't going to have nobody thinking I sired some kind of sideshow freak. No son of mine's going to be playing pussy for no one. I won't have it. I won't have people whispering behind my back. That boy is mine, same as my cattle and my ranch. He carries my name, like my cattle carry my brand. He's going to live his life like the man I want him to be or he's going to die trying."

Not being able to do anything else, I spit again. He hit me but this time it was with full fist. He cocked back his arm and was aiming to do it again when he stopped, some sudden figuring going on in his head.

He lowered his fist and stood straight. "If I kill you it's only going to fuel this fire Wyatt seems to think he has for you. I haven't been able to convince him you're a piece of shit. Or Saunders hasn't, to be exact."

My stomach flipped and my skin crawled at the mention of Saunders's name. Wyatt was with Saunders. Jennings was still having Saunders do his dirty work for him, including trying to beat love out of his one and only son.

I didn't like the smile that was growing on Jennings's face. "Since Saunders can't convince him, maybe you can." Jennings pulled back my head, hanging onto my hair. "You're going to let Wyatt know what a piece of shit you are, McAllister."

Jennings let go of me and went to some saddlebags sitting on a broken down desk. My mind was racing with ideas of what Jennings might be up to. He reached into the bags and pulled out a wad of cash.

"There's $10,000 here, McAllister. It's yours. All you need to do is tell Wyatt that it's all been a game to you, then get out of his life. I'll call off the law and you can find yourself some other little pussy boy to fuck with."

I let loose with a string of swear words, not finding one that was foul enough to fit my feelings for Jennings. When I ran out, he pulled out another wad from the bags and held it up.

"I'll make it $20,000."

"Jesus Christ, Jennings. You just don't get it, do you? There ain't anything you can pull out of them fucking bags that could take me walk away from Wyatt. Now let me see him, you motherfucker. I want to see Wyatt."

"You want to see Wyatt? Fine. I'll show you Wyatt. I'll show you what you've done to him. You can see exactly what it is you have to offer him."

Jennings waved his hand at me and his two hired men dragged me in the chair over to a large picture window.

"Take a look, McAllister. See what your love has done for Wyatt."

The window looked down into the cave that I'd seen from the outside. It was a huge cavern, lit by lanterns and torches, and down below were Saunders and several hired men. And Wyatt. Wyatt was kneeling on the ground, naked, with his arms spread wide and his wrists tied to posts. Saunders was whipping him.

"Each of those men has had a turn with Wyatt. I told Saunders to do whatever it took to make Wyatt hate you and everything about you." Jennings voice cracked a little and I wondered if even an animal like him might not be feeling a little sick at what we were looking at. But Jennings's hatred of things that didn't fit into his world was planted too deep. And the more Wyatt resisted, the stronger Jennings's hate became.

I leaned my head against the glass of the window, no strength left to hold it up. Wyatt's cries, faint through the glass, echoed in my ears. I heard Saunders's voice, "You ready to feel McAllister's dick again? You want more of that man-fucking?" and I was dizzy. One of the men got up and undid his jeans. I was defeated.

"If you don't convince him, McAllister . . . If I can't take Wyatt home with me knowing he'll be a man, and marry and have kids and make me proud . . . Well, I'd rather have him dead. I cull weakness from my cattle herd, McAllister. I'll do the same thing to protect the Jennings name. You're leaving me with no other choice."

I wanted to believe he wouldn't. I wanted to believe that little crack in his voice told me there was a chance he might still have some human left in him, but I could still see the look on my own father's face and I knew that if the sheriff hadn't pulled him off of me that night, my own father would have killed me. Jennings would do the same to his son.

I lifted my head from the glass, Wyatt's cries staying with me, and I nodded.

"You better make it convincing, McAllister. I want him believing he was nothing but a hole to you."

That amount of acting wasn't in me. I knew that for sure. But to save Wyatt . . . I could do anything needed for that. All I had to do was muster up that one small part of me that still believed what Lettie had said: "You've got nothing to offer him but dick. Do the right thing and walk away." I'd worked hard at making that believing part of me small. I'd kept it buried deep while I'd let the hope in me grow. But now I needed to change all that. Now I needed to do the right thing for Wyatt.

I looked down at him again. His back was torn and bleeding from the whipping Saunders had given him. His face, pushed upward as he screamed from the raping, was swollen and misshapen. He had blood on his arms and his chest and between his legs. Looking at all those things was going to make the right thing easy. This was what I'd brought to Wyatt. This was what I'd made of his life. If I did what Jennings wanted, Wyatt would go home to California and live his life as a lie. A chunk of his heart would be missing where I'd torn a piece out, and chances were good he'd never know real love again. But he might get married and he might have a child and that was a different kind of love that could make him happy. A child would make Wyatt happy. And if I was selfish and didn't do what Jennings wanted, I would watch Wyatt die a death not even an animal deserved.

Jennings's men untied me and I got to my feet. Nothing seemed real. I couldn't feel my arms or legs or the floor beneath me. I focused hard on that small part I'd been trying to bury. Wyatt would be happier leading the life that was expected of him. Maybe not at first, but in the end, he would be. I believed that. I had to believe that. I watched the next man step up to take a turn at Wyatt and I turned to Jennings.

"Give me the money."

Jennings gave me two stacks of bills. "You look like shit, McAllister. You better be able to make this convincing."

I grabbed the man nearest me, held him tight to my body, and snapped his neck like a chicken bone. His body hit the floor before either Jennings or his other man could react.

"I'll do this because Wyatt's life means more to me than my own. Otherwise I would just kill you, Jennings, and let this other shithead kill me. But it's gotta have an ending." I walked toward the office door. "This has got to finally end."

I went out and around to the opening of the cave. Jennings stayed in the office but his man went with me. As soon as Saunders saw me he pulled his gun, but the man with me nodded up at the picture window. Saunders looked up and Jennings waved him off.

Wyatt's head was down and I thought he might be out cold. I went behind him to the man who'd just pulled his dick from Wyatt's ass and I did the same to him as I'd done to the hired hand in the office. When his body hit the dirt his dick was still hanging from his pants. Saunders jumped up but still Jennings waved him off. Jennings would let me have my little revenges but he wouldn't let me get away with too much. It made me feel better, though, to snap those necks, and it helped to stir up the pure anger that I needed to make my act work.

Puke rose up in my mouth and I swallowed it down. I pictured Wyatt smiling his big old smile and bouncing a baby on his knee. I squatted in front of him and lifted his head so he could see me. My fingers were tangled in his hair and a flash of memories raced at me full speed, about knocking me off my feet. I steadied myself and got the picture of Wyatt and his baby back in my mind, then I took a good look at his face. Both his eyes were swollen close to shut. His lips were split in more than one place, upper and lower. His left cheek had a purple bump on it the size of a walnut and a cut across his forehead dribbled thickening blood down his face. I tried to ignore the golden scent of honey coming from him. I concentrated instead on the wounds left by my love. I thought back to that day, a lifetime ago, when Wyatt first looked at me, and I readied myself to do what I should have done that very first day.

"Hey, Sweetlips. You awake?"

Wyatt moaned and his swollen eyes tried to open.

"Deke?"

Like a knife through the heart.

I steadied myself.

"Yeah, Sweetlips. It's me."

His right eye made it open a ways but his left was too swollen.

"Deke."

There was too much relief in his voice. Too much gratefulness.

I swallowed more puke.

"Sorry it turned out like this, kid. I didn't know they would be so rough on you."

The open eye tried to focus. A blue as bright as the sky peeked out from purple lids. I looked at the cut on his forehead and away from the blue.

"It was a lot of fun, kid, I gotta admit. And I am fond of you, truly I am. That's why I hate to see what they've done to you. Still," I held the stacks of bills up in front of his eye. "The $20,000 in cash is helping ease my pain." Saunders's men laughed. "You're daddy's a generous man, Wyatt. I can't believe you ever walked away from all that money. And just for dick, too." I pulled Wyatt's head up higher and looked straight into that sky blue slit. "I mean, I know I'm a good fuck, but I can't believe I'm that good." I took a deep breath and prayed that I could pull it off. "Because I can tell you for sure that you ain't worth that much. That's why I'm taking the $20,000. Your daddy's making me a free man. No more law after me and no more little man-boy chasing me around."

I let go of his head and stood up. I had to take a step backward to keep from falling, the dizziness was so bad. Pain squeezed my chest, making it hard to breathe, and bile kept coming up into my mouth.

"What do you men think? You've all had a poke at Wyatt. Do you think his ass is worth $20,000?"

Even Saunders was laughing now.

Wyatt held his head up on his own. A tear cut through the blood and ran a streak down his face. His voice was strong; stronger than I'd thought possible for a man in his condition.

"You're a liar, Deke."

I grabbed him by the hair again and forced his head back as far as it would go. He'd said the right words to bring my anger out full bore.

"Take a good look at me, kid. Do I look like I'm lying?" I was so mad spit flew while I talked and hit him in the face. "This is what annoys the shit out of me about you, kid. You can't see the truth when it's slapping you in the face. You and your fucking fairy tales. Did you actually think that I wanted to play house with you for the rest of my life?" I flung his head down in disgust. "And all those times I went into town alone. I bet you really thought it was just supplies I was getting." He was looking up at me but he wasn't seeing any more. "I was getting some real pussy. I could only take so much of your school girl swooning before I needed to get the real thing."

The cave seemed to spin around me. The laughter from Saunders and his men sounded distant and unnatural.

This had to have an end.

I took a bill from one of the stacks and I threw it toward Wyatt. It floated down and landed at his knees. I tried not to look at the tears making streaks through the blood on his face, but they were all I could see.

"Thanks for the holes, Sweetlips. You deserve something for them."

On legs that could barely carry me, I walked out of the cave. I fell to the ground as soon as I was out of sight and all the bile I'd been swallowing came back up. I wanted to stay there in the mud and puke but Jennings's man pulled me to my feet and took me back to the office. After watching me kill two men barehanded he was making sure he kept his gun on me, but there was no need to bother. I had no fight left. My reason was all gone, left hanging between two posts, broken and crying.

Jennings greeted me with applause.

"That was a wonderful performance, McAllister. I must say, I'm impressed. I'm even going to let you keep the money. You earned it."

Without thinking and before Jennings could react, I dropped the money on the floor, pulled my dick out of my pants, and pissed all over the bills. Jennings punched me and I ended up back in the chair, tied up and gagged. Death was what I was hoping for. Death was all I had to look forward to.

They set me up by the window again and Jennings smiled.

"You need to watch what happens next, McAllister. I think you'll really enjoy this part."

Jennings and his hired dog went out the office door. I saw them appear down below in the cave seconds later. Jennings voice, muffled by the glass, floated up to me.

"Saunders, you son of a bitch."

Saunders and his men were still laughing. They looked at Jennings, his gun drawn, and didn't understand. I understood before they did.

"What did you do to my boy?"

Saunders stopped laughing but it was too late. Jennings and his dog opened fire. Saunders was the only armed one and he went first. The other men scattered for their guns but none of them made it.

Jennings went to Wyatt and got down on his knees.

"Oh God, Wyatt. What did they do? I'm so sorry, son. This is all my fault."

He untied Wyatt from the post and Wyatt fell into his arms. Wyatt's sobs reached me and I turned away from the window. I couldn't watch Jennings win.

I heard them loading Wyatt into the buckboard outside the office door and then I heard them ride away.

I sat in the chair, not trying to escape and feeling so many kinds of pain I couldn't even sort them out. But there was one pain that stood out above the rest. Wyatt had believed my act. He couldn't be expected not to and most of me was glad he did, but that pain hurt worst of all. Wyatt had believed me when I told him he meant nothing. What did that say about me?

CHAPTER 15

I MADE NO ATTEMPT at freeing myself. Dying of starvation while tied to a chair and shitting myself was too good a way for me to go, but it was close enough to perfect that I would settle for it.

I watched from the picture window as coyotes cleaned up the mess Jennings left behind. I pretended Saunders was still alive and I cheered the coyotes on. I drifted in and out of sleep, but nightmares about animals eating Wyatt and his babies kept waking me up.

Sunlight started creeping into the cave and across the office floor. I wondered how far the buckboard with Wyatt in it had gotten. I watched the daylight as it changed color and I could see him in the back of the wagon, his hair changing colors in the same way that I was watching, dark gold to reddish to yellow sunlight.

Wyatt was alive. The same day that was breaking in front of me was breaking for him, too. For the rest of his life, whatever patch of land he would be standing on could always be followed back to me. He was alive. As long as that was true, as long as we were sharing the same chunk of land under the same endless sky, I knew I wouldn't be letting myself die. I could pray for lightning strikes or vengeful Indians or anything else that might kill me on its own, but I wouldn't be doing it myself. Not as long as Wyatt drew breath.

It almost made me mad, this revelation. I'd been looking forward to the peace I was hoping death would bring me. But instead of slowly slipping into nothing, I sat up from the chair as best as

I could and swung it, over and over, hitting the legs against the picture window until the glass broke. I leaned my ropes against a jagged piece sticking up from the window frame and I went to work freeing myself.

It took a long time, and my wrists were a bloody mess by the time I was done, but the ropes finally fell away. I couldn't walk too good at first so I spent some time on the floor, numb inside and out, until the feeling came back in my legs. The inside numb was going to be with me a good long time so I didn't wait around for it to clear up. I stood up and walked out the door.

The hazy sun was blinding and I stumbled around looking for horses. Once my eyes adjusted I could see that there were none. Jennings must have spooked them all away before leaving.

"Looks like Wyatt and me'll be walking again."

I said it out loud and my voice startled me. My words, when they struck me, started me to crying. I dropped to my knees and wailed like a widow. Wyatt was gone. Wyatt was gone. The solid truth of that grabbed a hold of me and started tearing. Wyatt was gone.

I don't know how long I wallowed there in the mud and my tears. Time doesn't carry much weight for a man when he's already dead and is just waiting for somebody to make it official. I would've laid there and let the coyotes finish me off if it weren't for the hard nudge I felt to my shoulder.

I was so fucking surprised to feel someone else's touch that I about fell over myself trying to jump away. When I saw the big black gelding standing there, I almost laughed. He must have wandered back to me, not knowing where else to go. I patted him on his nose.

"We make a good pair, huh Black?"

I dried my face and swung onto the saddle. The black took me to the entrance of the camp then we sat there, looking. I patted him on the neck and asked, "Which way do you go when you just don't give a shit?"

The black answered by heading south.

We wandered for days. I let the horse do all the steering. He was only interested in grass and water and, without me caring, we never went faster than a stroll. I had little appetite so my stomach twisted itself in knots trying to fill the empty. I couldn't muster the energy to shoot something and grass just wasn't appealing.

Every night I unsaddled the black and rubbed him down with my hands, remembering the promise I'd made to the bay. I was going to treat this horse like a king.

Being alive but not really living turned my life into a routine of waking up, getting on the black, getting off the black, and sleeping. I thought of Wyatt every second, but not since my mud wallowing before the black found me did I do any more crying.

Of course, thinking about Wyatt wasn't really what I did. It was more like my body had been emptied of everything but him, leaving me filled with nothing but Wyatt. I saw only his face and his near-man body, lanky and smooth and itching to bust loose. I smelled only honey and peppermint and that sagey sweetness that came from him when he sweat. I heard only his voice, his laughter, his cries of pain. I felt the softness of him when I touched anything and, those few times when I ate, I tasted only his sweet lips. But none of those things made me feel anything: no sadness, no happiness, no guilt. The only thing I felt was heavy. The air seemed to crush me, and dragging my body around took every effort I could muster.

One morning after Lord knows how many days of that emptiness, I shoved my hand in my pants pocket looking for a chunk of hard sap I'd saved for the black, and when my hand came out I was holding a piece of the bay's hide in my left hand. It had the D on it with part of the W tangled up in it. One look at that and the fucking dam burst again. I was in the dirt, all those memories of Wyatt coming to life at once, pounding me into the ground.

Life dragged on like that with little change—stretches of emptiness followed by bursts of sorrow so painfully pure that I couldn't do nothing but lie in a ball and wait for it to pass—until the day my horse walked me into a town. I saw the saloon and decided that whiskey might be a good way to wash Wyatt out of me.

The livery hired me as a stable hand and I mucked stalls during the day and drank myself unconscious at night. It did nothing to get rid of Wyatt, but now when I wallowed in the mud and my tears, I was adding vomit to it, too. The livery fired me after a couple of weeks and the sheriff kicked me out of town. So now my life became stretches of emptiness followed by bursts of pure sorrow followed by drunken attempts at keeping a job. About the only good thing I could say for it all was that I didn't hanker for dick any more. I admit to jacking off now and then, but the memory of Wyatt was the only thing that could get me stiff. I saw the look in other men on occasion but I had no desire to do anything about it. 'Course, the way I was looking and smelling, I seriously doubt they had a desire to do anything about it, either.

It wasn't until about mid-March, four months or so after losing Wyatt, that something started feeling different. Every now and then I would remember a happening with Wyatt and I would smile. I wouldn't exactly say I felt happy, but instead of breaking down and sobbing like the pathetic female I'd more or less become, I'd smile. Soon the rememberings were making me laugh and I'd tell the black about them out loud, doubling over at the funnier ones. It was hard for me to know if I was getting better or if I was just getting crazier, but not too long after that started up, I did start to feel something akin to happiness. Only it weren't my happiness. It was more that mixed-in feeling I used to get from Wyatt. And that's when I started believing that what I'd done in that mining camp that day had been the right thing. Wyatt was happy. I was feeling it. And things got a little easier after that. Not a lot easier, I admit, but a little. I still had my periods of rolling into a ball and waiting for the sorrow storm to pass, but in between those times I actually managed to feel good sometimes.

One morning, after pulling myself up out of the leftovers of one of them storms and still clutching my horsehide pieces, I wiped at my face and realized I had to see Lettie. The need to know that Wyatt was more than just a memory suddenly became so powerful that I had to see Lettie and the kids. They knew me when I was a part of Wyatt. They could make it all real again. I'd never have Wyatt back but maybe, with Lettie and her young 'uns, I could feel closer to him.

I got my bearings and headed to Lettie's. It took me about a week, and most of that way I was as bouncy as Wyatt used to be while traveling. I talked to my horse out loud and enjoyed the sights of spring, but once I got close enough that things started looking real familiar, my body started shaking and my stomach started churning. When I hit the pond where Lettie had first found us and where Wyatt and I had fucked more times than I could count, I turned the black around and started to leave. The stubborn mule wanted some water, though, and I couldn't get him to budge. I finally left him where he was and decided I had the guts to at least sneak up and spy on the place.

I hid in some bushes not far from the henhouse. I couldn't hardly squat I was shaking so hard. I kept remembering Wyatt, shirtless and sweaty, working on that henhouse. I wanted to throw up.

No one was in the yard, and once I got my body settled down a might I started realizing that things didn't look right. Lettie's churn, always outside the cabin door, was gone. Washing was laid out on the fence behind the house, instead of on the rope tied from the house to the barn where Lettie always hung it. The place just felt wrong.

I was readying myself to go peek into the room I'd shared with Wyatt, scared shitless that a peek into there might bring up a storm I'd never be able to weather, when I heard a man's voice from inside Lettie's house. The man stepped out the front door followed by a woman toting a baby.

"I'll be back before dinnertime. Keep the rifle nearby."

They kissed then the man went into the barn. Seconds later he came out leading a saddled horse. He mounted and rode toward town.

My head was spinning with questions. Where were Lettie and Toby and Daisy? What happened to them? And the belongings I'd shared with Wyatt . . . Where were they? Our feather bed, the furniture we'd made. The branding iron.

Holding that iron was suddenly the only thing I could think of. I had to get the branding iron I'd given to Wyatt.

The woman went back in the house and I snuck from bush to bush until I reached the barn. I made my way to the back where our room had been built on, and the stink hit me before I even reached it. My mind wouldn't let me accept what it was I was smelling but when I reached what used to be our door, I saw my nose was right. One wall of our room had been torn down, and the home I'd shared with Wyatt was now a sty for hogs. Nothing of ours was there. Nothing that proved we'd existed together was there. Just hogs and muck and slop.

I stumbled back to my horse, my head reeling. I'd come back to Lettie's because I'd needed to make Wyatt more than just a memory. I'd needed to prove to myself that we'd had something together once. Instead I found nothing. Even the memories now seemed wrong, and I felt like I was losing Wyatt all over again.

I reached into my jeans and pulled out the hide pieces. Two scraps of old horseflesh were all I had to show that my life had meant something at some point. I'd lived for over thirty years, and a couple of pissed on clumps of hair were all I had to be proud of. If I hadn't already thought I was less than worthless, that right there was enough to convince me.

I needed to find Lettie. Finding Lettie would prove what I had to know, but how to go about tracking her down? The townsfolk didn't care enough to know anything and even if they did, they wouldn't care enough to help me. I wondered if Jennings had something to do with Lettie's disappearing, and I wondered how long she'd been gone. Did she take the kids and run as soon as Wyatt and I were late back from our hunting trip, or did Jennings and Saunders find out about her place and do something to her? Where would she go if she were trying to hide? We were her only family besides Toby and Daisy.

If I couldn't find Lettie, that left only one other person who could prove my love for Wyatt had been real. And that was Wyatt.

I got on my horse and rode. I had to see him. Even if it was only from behind a bush, I had to see him. I doubted I had the balls any more to actually talk to him, but just knowing he was real would be enough.

I rode hard, an eerie feeling urging me on. I made it to the Crooked J days later without remembering any of the trip. As soon as I got to the outer edge of the ranch where all of it had started, I had that same sense of something being wrong that I had had at Lettie's.

I rode further onto the spread and I came across a flock of sheep, five-hundred head or more. The shaking started in my legs again, and the churning in my gut. Harlan Jennings was a cattleman to the bone. He'd burn every inch of the Crooked J before he'd allow sheep on his land.

I held the hide pieces in my hand and kicked the black toward the ranch house. I was half scared I wouldn't find Wyatt and half scared I would. If there'd never been no Sweetlips, no love, no loss, then I was just plain loco and I was finally free to put a bullet to my head and end the nightmare. If I did find him, what would that do to me?

When I was almost in sight of the entrance to the ranch yard, I tied up my horse and headed in on foot. As soon as I saw the gateway to the ranch, my legs gave out and I ended up on my knees. The sign above the gateway said the Star K Ranch. Not the Crooked J.

I looked at the pieces in my hand again, barely able to focus my eyes. Under the W was the faint mark of another brand but it was too small and too faint to be decipherable. I shook my head. I couldn't have made it all up. I couldn't be that fucking crazy.

I went back to the black and, mustering every ounce of courage I had left in my bones, I rode right up through the Star K gate. A cowboy walking an unsaddled horse stopped me and asked if he could help. My voice was as shaky as my legs.

"Didn't this used to be the Crooked J?"

"Yes, sir. I heard it was."

I felt relief and disappointment and excitement all at once.

"What happened to Jennings, the man who owned it?"

"Don't rightly know. Jeremiah King owns it now. He's up at the house if you want to ask him."

I thanked the hand and steered my horse toward the grand ranch house. My heart was beating so fiercely I had to breathe in gulps. I kept my eyes straight ahead, too afraid to look over at the bunkhouse and the tack room standing to my left.

I reached the house and somehow made it to the front door. An older gent with graying hair and a fine suit answered the door. He told me he was Jeremiah King and I asked him my question.

"Jennings is dead."

The world started spinning. "Dead?"

"Yes. Murdered by a former hand. A mute cowboy who'd been scalped, from what I understand."

His voice came at me from a distance. He was spinning faster than the rest of the world and I had trouble focusing on him.

"I bought this place at auction. Were you a friend of Mr. Jennings?"

I shook my head. "I used to work here." If Jennings was dead, Wyatt was free. Wyatt and I could be free. "His son. What happened to his son?"

My heart was pounding so loud I was afraid I wouldn't be able to hear his answer. I asked him again, raising my voice to make sure he could hear.

"Don't know for sure. He stayed around long enough for the legal matters to be settled, then he and his missus left."

Jeremiah King's lips kept moving but no words came out. At least none that I could hear. "He and his missus" was the only thing in my ears. He and his missus.

I turned and left with King's lips still moving. I tried to get on my horse but my foot missed the stirrup. King walked up to me, still talking. I got my foot where it needed to be and hoisted myself into the saddle. The bunkhouse and the tack room rushed at me, bigger than life. I rode past but I could feel them following me.

I made it to a cliff east of the ranch. I got off the black and took off his tack.

"Do whatever you want, horse. I won't be needing you any more."

He lowered his head and started nibbling at some grass.

I pulled my gun and sat down at the edge of the cliff.

Wyatt had done what was expected of him; he'd done what I'd hoped he would do. The happiness I'd been feeling told me it had all turned out good for him. I'd done the right thing, after all, when I'd walked away from him that day in the cave. Knowing that made me happy. It made everything I'd been through worthwhile. And it also made it official. I'd been a dead man since that day and now it was time to make it final.

I put the gun to my head and pulled at the trigger, but I was looking east and land spread out in front of me like an ocean, endless and uninterrupted, and that fucking thought hit me again. Wyatt was still alive, standing out there somewhere on that chunk of land.

"Shit! Shit, fuck, goddammit, Jesus Christ, son of a bitch!"

I holstered my gun and walked back to the black.

"Shit, Black. I can't do it. I can't fucking do it. I had something for a few months that most folks don't get in a whole lifetime, and as long as that boy is still breathing, I just can't do it."

The black raised his head and looked at me, chewing his grass in that sideways chew that horses have.

"I know, I know. Then I should quit my bitching and just be grateful. He's happy now. I can feel it. And that's all that matters."

I patted the black on his nose and he sneezed horse snot at me.

"Did I ever tell you about the time Wyatt and me tried to catch a wild boar barehanded?"

The black listened to my story and I ended up doubled over, laughing from the memories. I stood straight, still chuckling, and looked east. That endless chunk of land wasn't really so endless. As I recalled, part of it ran out around Rhode Island.

I picked up my saddle and hefted it onto my horse. While cinching it in place I asked the black, "You feel like going for a ride, boy?"

CHAPTER 16

I'M NOT SURE what I was expecting to find in Rhode Island, but there'd been a time when it stood for my future with Wyatt. I guess I thought maybe I could find a future there without Wyatt, too. It seemed worth a try.

It was a long, long trip, and I broke up the days by stopping and working just long enough to earn supplies, or by having my fits of sorrow that still knocked me on my ass for days at a time. Once in a while I'd feel Wyatt's happiness seeping into me and it felt good being on the happy side of the fence for a bit. It weren't my own happiness, of course, because my own moods generally ranged from plain lonely to shit-faced, hands-and-knees pathetic, but happy was happy and I'd take it from anywhere I could get it.

Once I crossed the Texas border into Louisiana I started getting interested. I'd never been so far east before and I was enjoying the newness of it all. Seems the country's entire water supply laid east of the Texas border. I'd never seen so much green before.

When I finally reached Rhode Island I could only sit on the black and stare. I'd landed in a town called Newport, but it couldn't really be called a town. It was a city, as big and busy as some I'd seen out west, only prettier. The buildings were fancier and the streets were cleaner. People were all dressed in what would be Sunday best out west but here just seemed to be the normal wear. Fine carriages pulled by fine horses filled the streets. Even the air was different. It had a salty bite to it that cleared my head and made me feel like something was coming.

Newport sat on the edge of the sea, so I rode down to the shore and took it all in. Even the ocean was different than the one I'd seen off California. It was calmer here, quieter. It was a good place to be for a man who wanted to just sit and wait.

I had enough money left from my last job to treat the black to a night in a livery stable with hay to eat and a good grooming with a brush instead of just a hand. I made sure he was taken care of then I treated myself to a hotel room. I paid the extra nickel for a bath and a razor. I soaked in a hot tub of water and smiled at the memory of Wyatt describing the bath he had in that town that took him in. Then I thought of him married and having babies and being happy without me and I found myself struggling not to cry.

Wyatt was happy without me. I'd known that would be true a long time back. Wyatt could go on without me but I'd be lost without him. I'd known it and accepted it but now it had come true, and it was staring me in the face and seeping into my bones and that, truth be told, was pretty hard to swallow.

I finished my bath and shaved the beard I'd grown. I hadn't seen myself in a mirror in quite some time and I didn't much like looking at me now. My skin had a grayness to it even though I'd spent my life in the sun. My pants were held up by a length of rope 'cause I'd gotten too thin for my belt. The hard muscles I'd once been so fond of were nowhere to be found. There was even some gray hair mixed into my brown. I forced a big smile and my dimples came out. Those dimples, it seemed, were the only thing left of Wyatt's childhood dream hero.

One thing hadn't changed, though. I looked down at my dick and it was hard, still as long and fat and hound-dog mean as it ever had been. The remembering about Wyatt must've gotten it up without me noticing it. I started to stroke it but decided I'd keep it hard while I went downstairs to have a little supper. It'd be nice to wear it in public for a change and to let folks see that I was still a man after all, even if I didn't act like one.

I had some chow and asked around about work to be had, then I went to say goodnight to the black. He was sleeping in a stall with straw on the floor and a blanket on his back, looking like he was where he deserved to be.

I was crossing the street on my way back to the hotel when a man close to my age crossed my path. He looked first in my eyes, saw what he seemed to be looking for there, then looked down at my crotch. I was still hard and my cock bulged out a good distance from behind my jeans, so I'm guessing he saw what he was looking for there, too.

"New in town, mister?"

I nodded.

"How about a drink?"

I gave his offer some serious thought. If I was going to be starting a new life, that new life was eventually going to be needing some dick, but too much of me was still filled with Wyatt and I knew I wasn't ready for anyone else. It felt good to get the offer, though, and I gave him a smile big enough to show my dimples.

"Thanks, but I need to be getting some shut eye. Another time maybe."

That night I stroked to my usual visions of Wyatt and when I came, I came harder than I had in a long time. I fell asleep feeling happy and it seemed to all be coming from me.

The next morning I went to the general store to ask about a job. I was waiting for the clerk to finish up with his customer when I spotted some jars lined up at the far end of the counter. Peppermints and licorice and rock candy filled them and a rush of feelings came at me. There were good memories, gut-stabbing wishing and pure loneliness all piled on top of each other. I felt my eyes burning and I turned to get the hell out of there before making a fool of myself, but I bumped smack into a woman coming in through the door.

"Deke?"

Too many things were swirling in my head and the sound of my name only made things worse.

"Deke? Oh God, Deke."

I looked down into the face of the woman I'd knocked into. My eyes wouldn't believe what they were seeing.

"Lettie?"

She had her arms around my neck before I was really convinced it was her.

"Deke. Oh God, oh God."

I pushed back from her, holding her at arms length. It really was Lettie, looking as fine and more beautiful than any other woman in Newport. I pulled her tight to me and we said each other's names over and over.

"Excuse me, but you're blocking the door."

Another woman was trying to get past us as we hugged. Lettie and I laughed, wiping at our tears, and we stepped outside. We stood and stared at each other, smiling and trying to believe. Then Lettie burst into tears again, but they didn't seem to be happy ones.

"Oh God, Deke. You look so thin. What have you been doing to yourself? You look so awful."

"I was just about to tell you how beautiful you are but I'll be keeping that to myself now."

She laughed and pressed into my body. I held her tight and laid my cheek on her head.

"You know what I mean, Deke. I can't stand the thought of you suffering so."

"It's not that bad. I only suffer when I'm awake." She slapped me on my backside. "I've just been going through a rough time. That's all, Lettie. I'm fine." I kissed the top of her head. "Especially now."

,--"Sit down. Tell me everything. Oh God, Deke. We've missed you so much. After you and Wyatt left . . . "

The look on my face cut her off. Hearing his name spoke out loud by someone other than me felt like a kick to the head. I wasn't ready for this. I wasn't ready for any of this.

"I gotta go."

I tried to leave but she grabbed my hand. Lettie was a small woman but she was strong. I was considerably weaker than I used to be and I couldn't pry free.

"No. You can't leave. You can't."

"I'm sorry, Lettie. I need to get out of here."

Buildings and people were crowding in on me. I couldn't breathe. Tears were coming on and I knew one of them storms was on its way. I couldn't have Lettie seeing me like that. I couldn't have nobody seeing me like that.

"Deke, no. We won't talk about anything you don't want to talk about. I promise." She pulled me back down to the seat next to her. "We won't talk at all if you don't want to."

And that's what we did for a spell. We sat not talking, holding hands and fighting back tears. I felt downright feminine. If I'd had a lace hankie to dab my eyes with, my fall from manhood would have been complete.

"Better?"

I nodded. She looked like she had lots to say but was having trouble deciding what to say first. I saw the change in her eyes once she'd made her decision.

"You've got to come home with me and see Toby and Daisy. They miss you so much."

Hearing their names made me want that lace hankie. Toby and Daisy. I hadn't let myself miss them too much until now. I felt on the verge of bawling again.

"Oh God, Deke. We need to get you out of here. Do you have a horse?"

I nodded and waved toward the livery.

"Let's get your horse and you are coming home with me. I swear, I've seen drowned puppies that didn't look as pathetic as you."

We got the black and Lettie led me to her wagon. It wasn't a fancy rig but it was a fine wagon. A working wagon. It was hitched to a matched pair of pintos, as pretty a pair as I ever saw. We tied the black to the back of the wagon and we were on our way.

We started out trying to talk about old times, but it was near impossible to do without speaking Wyatt's name. Since that set me to tearing up, we decided to just ride in quiet and enjoy the feeling of being together again.

After a bit, I felt ready to try more conversation. Not to mention, I was more than a little curious about how Lettie'd ended up in Rhode Island, living a fine new life.

"You must be doing good, Lettie. You look beautiful and this team of horses . . . You must be doing good."

"We are." She held out her left hand and I was plumb shocked to see the gold band on her ring finger.

"You're married?"

She was all smiles now, proud and clearly happy.

"Yup. Married, and he adopted Toby and Daisy so they'd have his name."

I was surprised at how angry that made me. We'd been a family. Toby and Daisy had been like my own. What right did she have to marry and let him have my kids? I felt cheated on. It was a crazy way to be feeling, I admit, but I was feeling it nonetheless.

Lettie seemed to sense what was going on in me so she started explaining. "When you and . . . When you didn't come back from the hunting trip when you were supposed to, I got worried. I knew something had happened. Everything felt wrong, like nothing could be the same again. I was certain it was only a matter of time before someone came asking questions. I wanted to get the kids out of there but we didn't have a horse. So we walked the cow to the nearest neighbor and traded for a horse. Took us nearly a full day to get there. After we got home, we loaded the important things into the wagon and left. I found work as a seamstress down near Mexico, and that's where he found me. We got married right away."

I flinched at the thought of them having to walk all that way 'cause we'd taken their horse.

"I'm sorry for everything we put you through, Lettie. Truly, I am."

"Don't be silly. We were family. I knew what I was doing when I took you two on. When you didn't come back, I understood it was because you were trying to protect us."

"But you still saw fit to marry the first man who came along?" I stopped myself and tried to sort through the muddle of feelings I was having. "I'm sorry, Lettie. He's made you very happy. I can tell that and I'm sure he's a fine man."

Lettie studied my face for a bit then she laid her hand on mine.

"You'll get to see for yourself soon. That's our ranch up ahead."

I hadn't been paying much attention to what was around me. I'd been listening to Lettie, fighting memories and feeling sorry for myself. I looked up at her words and there at the end of a tree lined road was a beautiful house on the edge of the sea. I'd never seen anything like it outside of my dreams.

"That's home."

I read the sign above the entry gate. The Drunken Whaler Ranch.

"What the hell kind of name is that?"

Lettie laughed. "My husband's idea."

I wanted to like the man, for Lettie's sake, but so far I wasn't doing a good job of it. I was pissed that he'd stolen my family from me and I was thinking he was some kind of idiot for naming his ranch something as all-fired stupid as The Drunken Whaler.

"Toby and Daisy are in school but my husband should be home."

Yippee. I couldn't wait.

Lettie drove the horses around to the back of the barn and we climbed down from the wagon.

"His office is in here. It's where I usually find him."

I followed her into a cozy room attached to the barn. It was small but didn't feel crowded. There were lots of windows and a second door that led into the barn. The furniture was handmade, not store-bought, and there was a large bed against one wall. I shook my head. What kind of a man has a bed in his office in a barn? The main house was close to being a palace. Surely he had room enough for an office up there. And why did he need a bed in his office? All that pencil pushing wear him out too fast? I knew Lettie was happy but I was having trouble understanding why.

"Darn, he's not here. Why don't you make yourself at home and I'll go find him." She took my hand and squeezed it tight. "Don't run out on me, Deke. Please. The children will be so upset if they don't see you. Please."

"I won't leave."

"Promise."

"Lettie." I honestly hadn't yet given up on the idea of hightailing it as soon as she was out of sight. Being with her was making everything feel familiar in an uncomfortable way. Even her husband's strange sleeping office had an unsettling feel about it.

"Promise, Deke."

Shit.

"I promise. But only long enough to see Toby and Daisy. I'm sorry, Lettie, but I'm just not fit to be among people yet."

She looked like she might start crying again but she nodded. "I understand. Believe me, I understand." Then she left.

Alone in the room, my unsettling feelings got stronger. The hairs stood up on the back of my neck and my stomach got a little bit queasy. I looked at the decorations on the walls to take my mind off my uneasiness and something hanging behind the desk caught my eye. The closer I got to it, the angrier I got. By the time I reached it, I was so mad I was ready to spit fire.

I yanked the branding iron I'd given to Wyatt off the wall. Lettie must have taken it with her when she left the farm, hoping we'd all be together again someday. When she met the idiot she married, she gave it to him and his Drunken Whaler Ranch. Wyatt's branding iron, the symbol of our love, now stood for Drunken Whaler. I was madder than mad. I couldn't believe Lettie could have done that. She had no right.

I went to the door that led to the outside, ready to lay into someone with both barrels, but there was no one around. I was squeezing the iron tight in my hand when I suddenly realized my dick was hard. The iron was having its effect on me even as pissed as I was.

I looked up and could see the ocean from where I stood. Even mad I couldn't help but think how this was the kind of ranch I'd wanted for myself. I had a flash then, as if from some far distant dream, and I felt suddenly full and warm. That's when I knew someone was standing behind me.

I turned slowly, afraid of what I might not see, but there stood Wyatt. His face was not quite as I remembered it—scars and bumps where there'd been none before—but he was every bit as beautiful as I remembered. Eyes just as blue, hair just as golden.

Tears filled his eyes and I went to him, almost too weak to take the few steps separating us. I reached for him, afraid that something would happen in those seconds and I'd never feel his touch. I said his name but wasn't finished breathing it when Wyatt hauled off and punched me. I stumbled backward and landed on the bed.

"Shit, Wyatt."

"That's for thinking I'd ever believe that bullshit about you not loving me." He stripped off his shirt.

"I was trying to save your life." I pulled off my jeans.

"You promised me at the jail that whatever happened would happen to both of us. Together." He shucked off his pants.

"That was about the Apache thing. That promise had nothing to do with the cave thing." I tore off my shirt, too riled to bother with the buttons.

Wyatt jumped onto the bed and landed on top of me. He sat on my stomach and pinned my wrists to the mattress.

"Don't ever try lying to me again."

"I wouldn't think of it."

We both looked down at our cocks and they were tangled together. Wyatt looked back up at me and let loose with his happy pup smile.

"Welcome home, Deke," he whispered.

He bent and kissed me and Wyatt was mine. Eyes just as blue, hair just as golden, lips just as sweet.